SHE IS HELPLESS, AT THE TWISTED WHIM OF AN INSANE KILLER'S MERCY...

Kara sat in the chair, immobile, her sleeping child crushed against her breast in arms numbed by his weight. If only she could think. If only she knew what to do.

And then, before she could do anything, any possible choice was removed from her. She instinctively fought to hang on to Ricky. The battle was futile. Startled awake, screaming and sobbing, he was pulled from his mother.

Then Kara felt the pills in her mouth again. Although she tried valiantly to avoid them, they were forced down her throat.

The darkness came quickly; then she didn't have the option to think at all. . . .

Books by B. L. Wilson

Bloody Waters
Thrill Kill

Published by POCKET BOOKS

Most Pocket Books are available at special quantity discounts for bulk purchases for sales promotions, premiums or fund raising. Special books or book excerpts can also be created to fit specific needs.

For details write the office of the Vice President of Special Markets, Pocket Books, 1230 Avenue of the Americas, New York, New York 10020.

BLOODY WATERS

B.L. WILSON

POCKET BOOKS
New York   London   Toronto   Sydney   Tokyo   Singapore

The sale of this book without its cover is unauthorized. If you purchased this book without a cover, you should be aware that it was reported to the publisher as "unsold and destroyed." Neither the author nor the publisher has received payment for the sale of this "stripped book."

This book is a work of fiction. Names, characters, places, and incidents are either the product of the author's imagination or are used fictitiously. Any resemblance to actual events or locales or persons, living or dead, is entirely coincidental.

An *Original* Publication of POCKET BOOKS

POCKET BOOKS, a division of Simon & Schuster Inc.
1230 Avenue of the Americas, New York, NY 10020

Copyright © 1993 by B. L. Wilson

All rights reserved, including the right to reproduce
this book or portions thereof in any form whatsoever.
For information address Pocket Books, 1230 Avenue
of the Americas, New York, NY 10020

ISBN: 0-671-73908-5

First Pocket Books printing April 1993

10 9 8 7 6 5 4 3 2 1

POCKET and colophon are registered trademarks of
Simon & Schuster Inc.

Cover art by Tim O'Brien

Printed in the U.S.A.

For Kathryn Davis and husband, Michael, who help make the twisted delights of writing—and life—more pleasurable; for my editors John Scognamiglio, who refined and defined *BLOODY WATERS* to the proper depths with such skill and patience and Lisa Kazmier, who generously and good humoredly kept the book afloat with sound shoring at a critical time; for Samlee, who gave me much needed grounding; for W.M. who helped with the research, and for my family: Ellen, Carmen and John, and my adopted family, June and Eileen.

Love and Kisses!

Prologue

As the slender killer laboriously struggled through the trees and underbrush, carrying the limp burden to the edge of the river, the sweltering summer night added to the mental and physical distress. Clutching, trembling hands tried to shift the dead weight of the corpse to a more secure position. The teenage boy's body and the cement block were heavy, and the exhilaration of killing mixed with the frantic need for speed sapped the bearer's strength. Incredible concentration was required to accomplish each step.

Pain shot through the murderer's arm and up the length of the strained shoulder; harsh breathing mimicked the sounds of other human life, echoing eerily in the small cleared space.

The killer feverishly scanned the thick vegetation along the riverbank in each direction, then glanced across the way at the island of trees in the middle of the swiftly running water. Every sound was intensified, threatening—the whispered talk of the trembling, overgrown bushes as they touched each other, the leaves murmuring nervously with muted rustling sounds, even the rapid rush of the river.

The act itself was nearly completed. It was too late to stop now. A previously hidden raincoat and boots protected the perpetrator against blood splatters. Standing at a preselected spot, the shadowy figure juggled the slack body, trying to ease it down to the water. There could be no mistake this time, nothing that hadn't been planned.

A huge fallen tree was lying half in the water, still attached to the muddy bank by one major arching root and many smaller roots along the bank and beneath the water. It would protrude out into the dirty, reddish river for a long time, keeping its secret bounty captive until the body was eaten by muskrats, turtles, catfish, and other water inhabitants. The rotting flesh would feed the roots of the tree, making them grow even larger and stronger for future use.

A nocturnal creature suddenly scurried off the death path, startling the murderer. The cement block slipped, almost jerking killer and victim into the water. Only the killer's desperate digging of one boot heel fiercely into the slippery, spongy ground, had kept them both from plunging into the dark depths of the river.

"Help me, God!" Fresh fear elicited an unconscious plea.

Why were things starting to go wrong? There was so little time and still the final deeds to do. Earlier the begging, weeping teenager had been silenced by a deep stab wound to the lower back above the kidney, and a blow to the head, but there was other work to complete.

Nearly palsied hands dragged the young man's body to the river, and managed to position him on his back. When a ghoulish groan seemed to emanate from the dead boy, the murderer recoiled in horror, then panicked, quickly pulling the knife from a coat pocket and desperately slashing the throat from ear to ear.

Strength heightened by adrenaline resulted in too much use of force; the cartilage crunched so loudly that the thin figure tensed, frozen in fear, the snapping sound imitating that of someone stepping on a twig. Wide, dilated eyes glanced all around before another final, fierce slash was made across the throat of the young man.

Then the dripping knife was flung into the water. For a moment the sight of the blood draining from the gaping wound was mesmerizing. Although the evening was young, the moon was already out. It cast a golden glow over the grisly scene on the riverbank; the murderer was briefly hypnotized by the sight.

Finally, with an economy of motion, the raincoat was ripped off and the dead boy's arms were forced into the sleeves. The body was grasped by the legs and placed where it could be maneuvered in between the twisted and tortured roots of the huge tree. The head flopped about, threatening to separate from the body.

Struggling furiously, the slayer managed to get the corpse in position. At last there was the sound of a small splash and the body sank from sight, where it was intended.

Heaving a sigh of relief and thankfulness, the murderer dabbed at beads of sweat that dotted a furrowed brow, then swiftly set about erasing any signs of the act. There must be no evidence left at the disposal site.

1

At the side of her new husband, Kara Noble Worthington was trying to be her usual lively self, circulating among their guests, smiling warmly. She didn't really know the people, even though most had attended her wedding when she came to this small Virginia town on the North Carolina border to marry John Worthington two months ago.

"After being back in California seven weeks, I was almost afraid the town wouldn't be as picturesque as I remembered it during those three incredible days of our wedding," she whispered. "It's even more lovely than I recalled."

He laughed deep and low. "I hope you'll think that when you settle in."

"I know I will," she said brightly, her eyes glowing. "The drive from the airport was so beautiful, the farms, animals, trees, and all that green grass. The chauffeur drove fifty-five miles an hour on nearly empty roads. When I had to travel fifty miles in California, it meant a three-hour drive."

"I'm sorry I wasn't there to meet you," John said. "I was tied up in court and I just couldn't get away. We had the preliminary hearing for Asterson. He still can't make bail."

John met Kara's gaze. The *real* reason he hadn't gone to the airport himself was because Mother had insisted he

5

help with the party which was being held at the most prestigious country club in town. He'd weighed his choices and decided it was easier to placate her than cause more bitterness over Kara.

"Hi," Kara said warmly, when a couple walked up. She extended her hand to the minister who'd performed the marriage ceremony.

"Welcome back, Mrs. Worthington," he said. "I hope we'll see you in church Sunday."

She smiled. "Please call me Kara."

Although he nodded, he didn't invite her to use his first name. "You remember Mrs. Willits." He ushered his overweight wife forward.

"Yes, of course," Kara said, again extending her hand. "I meant to thank you for singing at our wedding. You sang beautifully."

Mrs. Willits had a limp handshake and a wan smile. "I usually sing at all the weddings," she said impersonally.

Kara noted that Mrs. Willits's round face was perspiring, a fine dew lining her brow and upper lip. She was reminded that she'd married in April; if this humidity was typical of summer, it was going to take some getting used to. The thought struck her that a lot of things here might take some getting used to.

"How are you, John?" Minister Willits asked.

"Fine, now that my wife has come home," he replied.

Kara couldn't help beaming as she glanced at Mrs. Willits. She was delighted to hear John confess he'd missed her; she'd missed him terribly.

The empty smile remained on Mrs. Willits's pale mouth. "See ya'll in church Sunday, hear, John?" she said, leading her husband away with a curt nod to Kara.

When they had gone, Kara murmured, "Am I imagining it, or were they a bit cool toward me?" She managed a laugh. "Did I forget my underarm deodorant? Is my slip showing?"

"It's not you," John said with a tight smile. Actually, he knew it *was* her, but wasn't this what he wanted?

"Anyway," he added, "you're not wearing a slip." His pulse instantly raced at the thought.

She agreed. "I'm not. Nor a bra. Is that the problem? Is my dress clinging in this humidity? I asked if it was appropriate, and you said it was fine."

She seemed genuinely upset. John was irked because of it. He'd wanted Kara because she was so independent, so—libertine. It hadn't seemed to him that she was at all concerned with other people's priorities. Her philosophy was so basic: live and let live; and anything that brought pleasure without hurting anyone else was acceptable.

"I want you to be proud of me, John," she said. "You know I rarely wear a bra, but I thought the material and the color concealed nicely."

Running a finger around his suddenly too-tight shirt collar, John looked away. Kara's words made him recall his mother's prophesy: *That woman will ruin you, John. She'll be an embarrassment to all the Worthingtons!*

"I *am* proud of you," he said vehemently. "And, yes, the dress is fine."

He didn't want to discuss her dress; Mother had badgered him all day. Mother with her rules and regulations and hawk eyes, Mother with her harping and droning on about evil and saving souls.

John's eyes held Kara's questioning blue ones. "This isn't California, Kara. Everything happens in its own time," he muttered. "You can't expect the townspeople to take to you right away."

Kara was surprised he sounded annoyed. John wasn't usually irritable with her. What time they'd spent together, they had been like children playing a joyful, uninhibited game; she had intuitively known her sense of fun was one of the characteristics he admired most about her.

Reminding herself that it had been a long, tiring day for them both, she attempted to lighten the tension. She widened her blue eyes playfully and murmured, "I didn't know I was on trial! Are the charges moral or criminal?"

His smile was vague as he tasted the bittersweet triumph in his choice of bride. Though he had deliberately married a woman totally foreign to his mother and her wishes, he was only beginning to learn his defiance had more ramifications than he'd anticipated.

He was extremely disturbed by his mother's fury. The price for his marital victory would be forever walking a thin line between his wife and his mother—not just as long as he lived under Mother's roof, he'd already begun to understand, but as long as Mother lived!

"John?" Kara murmured.

"Moral, if there were charges," he retorted. "We aren't known as the town of churches without justification. People are provincial for the most part in their attitudes, especially Mother's acquaintances," John said. Especially *Mother*, he told himself.

"I didn't notice that when they came to the wedding," Kara said. She sensed something was different between her and John; something had happened in her absence, something vague, but something potentially serious. She wanted to understand what.

Ah, the wedding, John thought, struggling to get in a better frame of mind. After all, he had wanted this woman; he hadn't married her *only* to defy Mother. "You were too ecstatic to notice anything except me. Did you ever see these people?"

Kara smiled. "It's true I only saw you when I walked down that aisle. I didn't look to the right or the left. Of course, I saw Minister Willits because he was in front of us; however, when we stood in line at the reception, I was so eager to escape with you that I didn't *really* notice anyone else."

A vision of Kara in her bridal gown made John glance away, his attempt at levity dampened by the memory. He and Mother had argued heatedly about Kara's choice of white.

Kara hadn't given her selection a second thought. When John had subtly questioned the color, she'd thought he was joking.

"Good grief," she'd insisted with a laugh, "if only virgins wore white, it would vanish as a choice; there aren't many virgin brides. Personally, I don't put stock in fashion rituals, but if you do, modern etiquette suggests white for first-time brides, and off-shades or pale colors for subsequent marriages."

"Then I guess you'd better wear white," he'd intoned solemnly, "because I don't intend to get divorced. No Worthington ever has."

John had been foolish enough to think modern etiquette would appease Mother. Lorraine, however, decreed she wouldn't attend the ceremony if "that woman" who'd had a baby out of wedlock wore white to the church. Under no circumstances would she be shamed in front of the townspeople.

John had salvaged the occasion by convincing Kara that a light beige color would look lovely with her pale blond hair and darkly tanned skin. It had quieted his mother, but only temporarily.

"Have you lapsed into silence because you're gloating over my obsession with you?" Kara murmured, blue eyes twinkling.

He mustered a smile. "I was thinking that the cliché 'it's a small world' is true, in this town anyway. Generations of locals have married into each other's families, until it's standard to hear just about everyone say someone is a cousin by marriage."

"Oh, dear," Kara sighed playfully, "does that mean I won't be accepted until we have children and they have children who have children who marry each other's cousins?"

"You'd be dead and gone by then, so what would it matter?" John asked, smiling a little.

She pretended to pout. "I'm not planning a hasty demise, and I want to think that I'll be accepted at *some* point."

"Yes, of course," he said, for the first time actually considering whether his wife would fit in locally. Maybe Kara couldn't find a niche for herself here. She had been a golden girl in California, surrounded by her friends, by sunshine, by things vibrant and new and ever-changing.

Now she was in the South, an area old, tight, and stingy, clinging to the past, overgrown with decades of decay and tradition and generations of never-changing circumstances, from the cotton-mill working class living on the north side of town to the moneyed elite scattering their mansions and their pastimes along the lushness of the wide, winding river on the south side.

He couldn't shake the thought that Kara somehow seemed tarnished by his mother's view of her. He tried to ignore the descending depression.

"Although the people here are slow to warm to strangers, once they do, they're loyal and friendly," he defended, trying to reassure himself as much as Kara.

She kissed him lightly on the lips, not noticing the way he nervously glanced around to see if anyone was watching the public display of affection.

"The most important thing is how you feel about me," she said cheerfully, trying to hide her disappointment.

She'd never had trouble making friends; she'd anticipated getting to know an entirely different group of people here. Although still determined to do that, she sensed it was going to be a challenge—or worse. Some survival instinct warned her that this really might be a trial, a strange test of some kind to prove herself worthy. Of what, she wasn't exactly sure.

"This isn't Los Angeles," John said, as if to confirm her thoughts. "On the plus side, we don't have congestion and long lines; we don't have significant crime; and we don't have high housing prices. On the negative side, we don't have the Greek Theater, Hollywood Boulevard, fancy restaurants, all-night cafés, or Sunday orgies."

"John, we don't have Sunday orgies in California!" she protested. "Or at least *I* never did!"

He grinned. "Everything is relative, and compared to that party you threw, this one, which is pretty typical of those in our circle, is a Sunday school picnic."

He frowned, as if he still didn't trust his memory. "Were those girls actually swimming naked in the pool, and did champagne really flow from the water fountain out back?" he asked.

"It wasn't that outrageous," Kara murmured low, her

honey-colored skin reddening as she recalled the night she met him.

In truth, the party had been wild, even for her liberated companions. One of her friends had finally hit the big time with a book sale, the advance in the six-figure range.

Kara was one of the few in her struggling singles crowd who owned a house, and that was because she'd inherited it. Her closest friends were would-be actors, actresses, and writers who doubled up in apartments and small houses, none of which were cheap in the overpriced California housing market and uncertain economic times.

John's expression was animated. "Don't get me wrong, honey. I loved every minute of it. It was an eye-opener for a criminal lawyer from a little southern town. We have two speeds here: slow and stop. I don't think my heart—or my hormones—could take that fast life-style."

He studied her a moment, doubt nagging darkly at him again as he wondered if he'd done the right thing. He certainly hadn't wanted to live in California, but he hadn't wanted to leave this exciting piece—he smiled at his definition of Kara—he hadn't wanted to leave his exciting piece of California behind. Kara was a rich treasure he wanted to keep tapping.

Laughing up at him, Kara resisted the urge to tug on his tie. He looked like he was suffering enough in the pinstriped suit, despite it being lightweight. The sweltering June night had caused perspiration to bead up on his full upper lip. Her gaze settled on it briefly before she dabbed at the tiny drops with her index finger.

"Somehow I don't think a lawyer who's representing a murderer is quite as naive as he makes himself out to be," she said. "Nor do I think a town where two bodies washed up in the river can be classified as being without *significant* crime."

Automatically, Kara glanced at the ruddy river visible on the other side of the fence. As muggy as the evening was, she found herself shivering as she remembered John telling her about the grim discovery of two mutilated bodies in the water.

"Huh, compared to your area, we're crime-*free*," John said, drawing her attention back to him. "Anyway, as I pointed out, everything is relative."

"Isn't the man you're representing a serial killer?" Kara asked, troubled by the thought of her husband dealing with someone that deranged.

He shook his head. "I don't believe he's a killer at all, Kara, and he's definitely not a *serial* killer. Only one murder can be circumstantially linked to him with any credibility. He got roped into the other by virtue of both being river murders and the victims being friends."

"Doesn't that still make him a serial killer if he's accused of two murders?" In her mind, one murder was horrible enough, but someone who killed repeatedly had to be depraved.

"I just told you I don't think he killed either man," John said testily, his usually rich voice rough. "So how can he be a serial killer? Serial implies continued killings—a *series*, like your Hillside Strangler and Freeway Killer—not one murder and maybe two, even tandem. Several: one after the other," he emphasized, as if he were lecturing an inferior.

Kara wondered what had happened to the man she talked with hour after hour at her home in California, discussing anything and everything that came up—as equals. She wanted to ask, but instinct warned her away from further comment. Somehow her southern gentleman had been transformed into a stranger.

"Asterson is as much a victim as anyone," John said sharply. "The mayor wants this case wrapped up, and wrapped up fast. Reputations are at stake here. Politics are involved."

Kara felt like she'd been reprimanded for questioning John. She wanted to protest, but she thought it would make her sound petty. Anyway, she didn't know about crime *or* politics, particularly in Virginia.

"Besides," he said, his tone once again civil, "my point is that we have very little crime compared to heavily populated areas. These are the only known cases of murder during the entire year, and they both were committed months ago. The bodies washed up after the hurricane came through."

"Hurricane?" Kara murmured. "You're kidding?"

He chuckled at the anxious way she looked. "They don't happen often," he said. "We're too far from the coast."

Suddenly there was a commotion down the way from them. Kara saw a few people gathering around someone who'd apparently had an accident.

"Who is it?" she asked, peering at the woman on the ground.

John sighed. "A hurricane of a different sort," he muttered. "It's probably Dee Dee."

"Dee Dee—our Dee Dee—our sister-in-law?" Kara questioned, frowning.

"The one and the same," John said dryly. "Wait here. I'll be right back."

"John—"

"Wait here," he reiterated, moving away from her.

Kara didn't realize she was holding her breath until she exhaled raggedly. She didn't recall ever feeling so out of place, or so unwanted, at a party—especially one in her honor.

2

When John returned moments later, Kara asked, "Was it Dee Dee? Is she okay?"

John nodded. "Just a small mishap. She slipped and fell."

"Slipped and fell?" Kara questioned.

"She's okay. Listen," John said, "let's talk about something pleasant. Let's talk about you and me. We're celebrating your return. We're celebrating us!"

Kara smiled, more relieved than John could possibly know.

"I'm definitely all for that," she said "I've missed you so. I couldn't wait to get back. I know I'm going to be happy here."

She gestured toward the lush lawn of the exclusive country club. The night was laden with the thick, sweet scent of humidity-weighted blossoms of honeysuckle and blackberry vines tumbling over the split-rail fence which created a barrier to the outside world.

"I'm looking forward to small-town life with a good ol' southern boy." Her expression softened. "I'm eager to have Ricky grow up in a peaceful and tranquil place. This will be good for a two-year-old. Do you know that he's never seen a horse or a cow except on television and in books?"

BLOODY WATERS

John barely kept his smile intact. Ricky: the primary source of disagreement with his mother. No, not just Ricky, he reminded himself. Kara, too. Mother didn't like the package or the wrappings. Kara with her carefree ways, ebullience, and unrestrained laughter, not to mention her colorful jewelry and makeup.

Impulsively, John hugged his new wife to him: he was a grown man, he didn't need Mother's approval anymore. "I'm glad you're finally here to stay," he said.

"Me, too, John," Kara said earnestly. "I've been away from you too long."

She and John had been separated since they returned from a New Zealand honeymoon, with the exception of a weekend he'd managed to steal from his busy schedule last month.

After her hasty marriage, Kara had, by necessity, gone back to California to tie up the loose ends of the twenty-six years of her life, including selling her house, giving notice at work, and preparing Ricky for a new world.

She still couldn't believe she and Ricky had arrived earlier in the day to find that her mother-in-law, Lorraine, had planned a surprise welcome-home party for her. For *tonight!*

However, she didn't want to start her new life on a sour note. She'd managed a quick nap, pulled herself together, and with two glasses of white wine already relaxing her, she was doing what she felt was expected of her.

Anyway, the anticipation of making love to John in a few hours carried her through the event. If ever there was a dream come true, John Worthington was it. He'd swept her off her feet, showering her with attention and gifts, winning her over in a brief week of continual togetherness. She wasn't about to ruin their reunion by being petulant or ungracious about the unexpected—and she felt untimely—party.

"What are you smiling at?" John asked.

Kara laughed merrily. "Any time I'm smiling, you can naturally assume you're on my mind," she said. "The time apart was horrible! All I thought of was you!"

15

He squeezed her shoulder. Her bright smile, sexy California good looks, sparkling blue eyes, and sun-highlighted, waist-length blond hair had captured him from the moment he wound up at the party in Kara's backyard when he was in Los Angeles for a lawyers' convention.

Although he'd been attracted to her immediately, he hadn't seriously thought about a relationship until he spent the rest of the evening talking with her. He'd been intrigued by her free-thinking views and her outspokenness.

He almost moaned inwardly. Kara had been a new experience in sensual delights, her uninhibitedness carrying over to her sexuality, but he didn't dare start thinking about that now.

He did his best to concentrate on her other admirable traits—traits he'd hoped Mother might approve of. He'd been impressed by her determination to raise her son alone, as well as her vulnerability when she spoke of her parents' death and how much she missed them. By the time the evening was over, he hadn't wanted this unusual, enchanting creature to escape.

He grinned as he thought of the incredible courtship that had ensued. Kara hadn't disappointed him at any turn. She'd been as eager as he had, and, true to her self-confessed romantic side, quite willing to give up everything familiar and move to Virginia to be with him.

Then came the fly in the ointment: Mother—damn her! Mother hadn't approved of *anything!* Mother had been appalled by the entire affair and certain that John's hasty marriage to a total stranger would be a disaster.

John had tried to soothe his mother without his wife knowing she was the object of severe disapproval and harsh speculation.

Mother's position was understandable, John had told himself. She had raised four boys alone after the death of her husband, when John's youngest brother, Bucky, was a few weeks old. John had been eleven, William twelve, and Mel fifteen when their father vanished, apparently caught in an eddy in the river.

Father had been so different from Mother: proud of his

sons, proud that he'd fathered four boys. The three of them had done "male" things: fishing, hunting, boating. Father had had an eye for the women, and he'd taught his sons to appreciate a pretty behind, a fine pair of tits, and long, shapely legs.

John smiled vaguely. Mother exerted a heavy hand in the child-rearing of four rowdy sons. However, with her strict adherence to her religious beliefs, laying down the law, so to speak, came readily to her.

She was a good Christian woman. Although John understood that she had wanted an *appropriate* wife for her lawyer son, he'd grown tired of the prissy little ladies Mother handpicked for him ever since he'd brought Claudia Lindheart home from the University of Virginia the Christmas he was twenty-one.

Claudia had been a passionate package with pretty wrappings—too passionate and too pretty for Mother, who'd dubbed her a cheap, painted, husband-hunting hussy! But Father would have appreciated her.

Father would have appreciated Kara, too, for in many ways she and Claudia were alike. Both were liberated, independent, and extraordinarily sensual. Claudia had been the sexiest, most wanton female John had ever met—until Kara.

Ah, Claudia. How she had flaunted her sensuality! She had been a walking love machine. She had introduced him to exotic lingerie and sex toys, among other things. John smiled.

He would always carry a memory of Claudia the way she looked the very first time he'd seen her in only a black bra, black G-string bikini, black silk stockings, a black garter belt, and stiletto heels.

"And what are you smiling about?" Kara murmured, seeing the curve of John's full mouth and the faraway look in his eyes.

"You," he answered. He was partly truthful, as Kara jarred him from the thoughts of the buxom brunette Mother had shamed him into giving up.

"You're the most unique woman I've ever met," John

added with the familiar seductive charm that had won Kara. "I wanted you from the moment I saw you. I want you now. All I have to do is look at you in that strapless blue concoction and I want to take you here and now. I swear, Kara, I never knew what passion was until we made love."

Smiling, Kara murmured, "You can't want me any more than I want you, John. It's unfortunate your mother planned this party for tonight." She glanced around. "At least she could have hired a band so we could hold each other without being too obvious."

John laughed. "Mother—hire a *band?* Never! Don't you know dancing is a *sin?* I had to plead for wine, and I think that was only allowed because Christ drank it."

He put his arm around Kara's nude shoulders and drew her close. "This is a straitlaced, only-for-show, engineered-by-the Worthington-matriarch get-together, just to reintroduce you. Anyway if, *God forbid,* a band were possible, I'd probably seduce you on the dance floor. I don't need to tell you what happens when I hold you against me. The result would send Mother to her knees in prayer."

Kara laughed. "John, she can't be that bad." It occurred to her that she was asking a question, not making a statement.

"Don't misunderstand me," he said in a tone Kara could imagine him using in a courtroom. "She's not *bad* at all. While she's very religious and strict, the four of us Worthington sons owe all we are to that righteous, upstanding lady."

Seeing the look on his wife's face, John asked himself why he couldn't stand someone else—*anyone else,* including his new wife—criticizing Mother. He knew she had flaws—

Sensitive to his mercurial moods, Kara realized she was stepping on sacred ground. "I didn't mean to insult her, John," she assured him.

"I hope not, Kara," he murmured with conviction, pretending to smile at a family approaching them. "I hope not."

It was difficult enough knowing that his mother disapproved of Kara without having to think she thought the same of Mother. He hated being pulled in two directions.

Besides, he had enough problems with his work. He didn't need family problems to intrude. The Asterson case could make him a big name as a defense attorney—if he could win it. So far he'd been powerless to find a way to circumvent the electric chair.

Looking up at John, Kara felt a slight chill, despite the hot, sticky night. She had an unnerving notion that if it came to a choice between her and John's mother, she would be on the losing end.

It was all she could do to smile when guests came forward to greet them. Standing on the bright green lawn, Kara imagined herself on ground as shaky as that produced by a California earthquake.

The thought frightened her. She wasn't even aware of the contents of the brief greetings she exchanged with a string of strangers who had suddenly become threatening.

"Speaking of Mother," John murmured as a woman departed after perfunctory hellos, "here she comes." He was irritated to realize that the very sight of her made him sweat profusely.

Looking across the lawn, Kara watched the petite, pristine, gray-haired woman, her plain, scrubbed-clean face brightened only the slightest bit by a set smile. Elegant in a white dress, complete with nylons and white high heels which sank into the grass with each step, she appeared stern and unemotional, unaffected by the stifling humidity of the sullen summer night.

John quickly squeezed Kara's hand; he wasn't up to any further confrontations. "I want you to know I'm appreciative of your flexibility," he whispered. "I didn't know Mother had this arranged until it was too late to put a stop to it. I know how tired you must be after the trip."

Before Kara could reply, Lorraine Worthington had reached them. Still, Kara was left standing on a bit firmer ground by John's expressed concern for her position.

Lorraine's shrewd eyes raked over Kara disapprovingly: no bra, no nylons, no heels, almost *no* dress, red lips, red nails, even red *toenails!* The brown eyes swept on briefly to the boy across the lawn, tanned and blond like the woman who had given birth to him. Then the unsmiling gaze returned to John.

"Son, you mustn't confiscate the guest of honor," Lorraine said. "Why don't you show your manners and mingle while I speak to Kara for a moment."

Kara was a bit disappointed by how willingly John acquiesced, yet she supposed she should have expected that. His mother, despite her small size, was a forceful figure who carried considerable weight in the town.

Obviously she wielded more than a little weight in her own family, Kara decided. She'd seen traits in her mother-in-law she hadn't especially cared for during the three days she spent at Homeplace, the family mansion, where the wedding took place. She'd overlooked them, telling herself that Lorraine was naturally a bit possessive of her third son, who'd remained single and mostly at home until he was thirty-three years old.

Not that living at home was unusual in this family, Kara reminded herself. John's older brother Melvin, and his wife Priscilla and daughter Lorrie, lived at Homeplace with Lorraine, along with the second brother, William, and his wife Dee Dee. And then there was Bucky, the youngest son at twenty-two.

Kara glanced at John as he watched his mother lead her away. His smile seemed to say that this was only a temporary delay and Kara should have patience. In truth, he was thinking what a strange pair they made: this loose-limbed California woman who was willing to engage in a new future, and the stiff, self-righteous, narrow-minded southern belle who refused to let the past go.

Kara smiled at John, determined to deal with Lorraine's steel-cold personality. Although exhausted after a flight that included five hours on planes with a three-hour layover in Atlanta, Kara intended to be patient with Lorraine, who'd insisted she *had* to reintroduce Kara promptly upon her return.

After all, some people thought the marriage, highly unprecedented to begin with, was already over because Kara didn't return with John to Homeplace after the wedding. The entire hasty hoopla had been cause for gossip and speculation on the town's part, and Lorraine had resented it deeply. She resented Kara for involving the prominent Worthington family in her shenanigans.

Lorraine had thought she was finished with all that shame and disgrace when she was through with William Buchannan Worthington. She should have known God would test her again. After all, she'd slept with an adulterer—inadvertently, innocently, it was true—but she'd done it all the same, even though she hadn't known her marriage bed was defiled.

Worse, she'd produced four more Worthington males to continue their father's adulterous legacy. It pained her that the sins of the father were passed on to the sons, and she'd tried her best to stop the evil at its source. God as her witness, when the sin had been revealed to her, she'd tried to purify herself of the guilt of laying with an adulterer and producing his offspring. She'd done her best to keep her sons from following in the footsteps of their father, and despite their bad genes, she'd thought she'd succeeded.

Until John was out of her sight. He had gone to California and taken up with *that woman*. Lorraine seethed with such fury that her head began to ache. How she resented John for letting such a sinner seduce him! And to compound the compromising of his Christian upbringing and all his mother's teachings, by marrying the woman and bringing her into their home!

Of course, she hadn't expected Kara to refuse John. It had been John's duty to resist the temptation of a woman with loose morals. Kara appeared to have no shame at all about sleeping with a man and bearing his child without benefit of marriage; in fact, she flaunted her illegitimate son!

"It's an interesting party," Kara said, her impatience getting the best of her.

"The most prominent people in town are here," Lorraine

noted, pressing a hand to her right temple to ease the throbbing. "People of the cloth, people of law and order, people who share common interests. You know that, don't you, Kara?"

Shrugging lightly, Kara stood firm in her determination to try to please her mother-in-law, and yet she had to be true to herself.

"I don't really know them," she said neutrally, "but I'm sure they're fine people."

"I'm glad you realize that," the small woman murmured, her voice remarkably vital, "because I need to ask a favor of you, which I'm sure you'll understand."

Lorraine's penetrating brown eyes roved over Kara, from her long straight hair to her bare legs. She wanted to scream out her frustration. She honestly didn't know how John could have done this to her—married this cheap, classless fornicator.

Her mind wandered for a moment as she stared blindly at another guest who was passing by. Of course, she *did* understand, John being his father's son.

At least William Buchannan Worthington had never *married* any of the trash he took to bed. Lorraine smiled bitterly to herself. He couldn't have, unless he'd wanted to divorce his wife. He never had the chance to commit that particular deed, thereby dragging her further into his sins.

She'd blamed her father for choosing William to be her lifetime mate. Father Stokes had been a greedy man who wanted the alliance of the two most prominent families in town.

He had been, God rest his wicked soul, a mortal man who seduced Lorraine's mother for her family fortune—earned honestly, Lorraine took the time to note. Lorraine had obeyed her father and married William Buchannan Worthington, as her mother had urged her to follow her father's dictates in such matters.

But Lorraine, unlike her dear, departed, emotionally fragile mother, had not blindly obeyed her father when she'd revealed William's newly discovered infidelity.

After she'd stormed into Father's prestigious office,

she'd been outraged to hear him brush aside William's infidelity. "Lorraine, man is weak, and you must remember it was Eve, a woman, who introduced sin into the world. Man has strayed ever since. I, myself, have been known to be tempted by the apple. The Good Book teaches us to forgive."

The hotly contested and unprecedented argument that erupted in the office that burning July day left Father Stokes with no doubt what his headstrong daughter thought about his own confession.

"Don't you dare speak to me of the Good Book," she'd hissed. "Thank God Mother isn't here to witness this. Thank the blessed Lord that He spared her poor mind from the ugliness of life. But you, Father, will *not* be spared!"

"Now, Lorraine, dear," he'd begun, "I know there's nothing like a woman scorned, but—"

"You shock me, Father!" she'd interrupted, barely warming to her topic. "Christ came to teach man not to sin," she raged. "You're a churchgoing man. William is a churchgoing man. You know God's commandments. Infidelity is sin, and the wages of sin is *death!*"

She had never allowed the subject to be mentioned again in her presence, but time had proved her right. God smote the wicked and the righteous prevailed. Hadn't the passage of twenty-two years proven that?

She'd tried to atone her own inadvertent sin by steering William's sons into the ways of the Lord, into a moral life, guiding them in their choice of wives as best she could; and, until Bucky came of age, she'd succeeded in directing the boys into successful careers that would enhance the Worthington name.

Williams's ill-gotten gains had been put to good use by sending the boys to school to become lawyers. William Buchannan Worthington's web of crooked real estate deals and deceptive stock practices had vanished when she'd sold his businesses, properly tithing ten percent, of course.

Just as William had vanished. There was never a trace of him found after he'd drowned in the river early one morning while fishing. The same week, Father Stokes had suffered a fatal stroke when Lorraine told him of William's disappearance.

Kara was sure the look in Lorraine's eyes had been condeming as it lingered on her legs. She quickly suppressed the thought when Lorraine smiled at a passing guest. Surely her mother-in-law hadn't taken her aside to criticize her attire.

Kara suspected she was probably the only woman at the party who wasn't wearing nylons, but it was just too hot for them. She never wore them at home, and she hadn't considered it a breech of etiquette to come to this outdoor party without them. This was the nineties, for heaven's sake!

"What favor did you want?" Kara asked.

Snapped back to the present, Lorraine smiled solicitously. "You surely know, dear, that we're all proud of your little Ricky, as we demonstrated during your previous three days here."

Her eyes held Kara's, and Kara unaccountably felt her pulse race. She was instantly unsettled.

"However," Lorraine continued, "this is a very old, very traditional town, and people of the better classes aren't as liberal as you Californians."

Kara felt the tension building in anticipation of some kind of conflict, and she fought to remain calm. Hadn't she just told herself that she could understand Lorraine's possessiveness of her son John?

But this was Kara's son they were about to discuss; she was admittedly defensive when it came to her own child. She was also uncomfortable with the roundabout way her mother-in-law was broaching the subject.

"Has Ricky done something wrong?" she asked. "Was he not welcome at the party? He's so young that I didn't want to leave him alone with someone he didn't remember."

She automatically glanced across the wide expanse of green lawn, where Ricky was being cared for by the housekeeper, Thelma. He was behaving himself perfectly for a two-year-old child.

BLOODY WATERS

"Really, Kara," Lorraine said, the fixed smile in place, "he's part of the family. Why ever on earth would you think he'd not be welcome?"

Kara could think of a couple of reasons, given what she already knew about her mother-in-law; she waited uncomfortably.

"It's the matter of your being a single parent, dear. Of course, the family doesn't judge you—God says judge not lest ye be judged—but the other town people . . ." Lorraine smiled a little tolerantly. "Well, the family and I just don't see any need for you to bring up the fact that Ricky's father never married you."

Kara could feel the color draining from her tanned skin. "Mrs. Worthington—"

"Lorraine will do nicely. We're family now, aren't we, Kara?" She lowered her voice. "I wanted to speak to you sooner, but I didn't get a chance. Honestly, it's such a small matter that it need not be a molehill turned into a mountain. Since it's for Ricky's good, I'm sure you, as his mother, want what's best for him, don't you?"

Kara felt that Lorraine was twisting words to suit her purpose, not Ricky's. Kara didn't want a confrontation, but *as a mother,* she felt now was the time to make her position clear.

"I'm not ashamed that I was an unmarried mother, Lorraine, and you should know that any stigma has long since vanished in this day and age. I don't feel a need to lie about my son's birth."

"Of course not!" Lorraine said, fairly bristling. "I *abhor* lies. *God* abhors liars! I'm not asking you to lie. I only asked you *not* to broadcast the fact that you're a—*single*—parent!"

"Lorraine—"

Reminding herself that the righteous would triumph, Lorraine continued. "In some places like Hollywood being an unwed mother may be trendy, but as a mother of four sons, I want to impress upon you that is *not* the case here. The family and I discussed this. Ricky carries the name Noble, and there's no reason for anyone to know that he's not legitimate."

The blood rushed back to Kara's face as quickly as it had drained away. Surely the family discussion included John. Kara was hurt because he'd apparently agreed with this.

"Ricky is *legitimate!*" she said vehemently, passionately. How could this supposedly religious, nonjudgmental woman cruelly label a little boy so harshly? "He's as legitimate as anyone here!"

Lorraine closed her eyes briefly, feeling an ache against her temples. The throb-throb-throb of pain seemed to speak to her, to send her secret messages.

Was it possible that this woman didn't know her child was a bastard? That she was a whore? That she had produced the offspring of a fornicator, and his male child would perpetuate sin in a world already filled with sin?

Lorraine Worthington didn't believe it for a moment. When she had faced the Devil, she had ceased to be an innocent. Still, only a fool confronted another fool. And she was not a fool.

Meeting Kara's eyes, Lorraine murmured in a seemingly conciliatory tone, "Of course you must do as you see fit. I'm only thinking of the child and his future."

Kara breathed a sigh of relief, grateful that Lorraine was trying to ameliorate a potentially volatile and damaging situation. God knows she didn't want to do battle with her new mother-in-law. All her life she'd wanted to belong to a large family, and to do that in the Worthington family, she had to be accepted by John's mother.

It was becoming quite plain just how unusual this part of the country was to her. She'd heard that areas of the South took pride in being traditional, in living life at a more leisurely, more gracious pace than the rest of the states, and she supposed that meant different mores. John himself had said the town was provincial, a town noted for its churches.

Kara felt a heaviness settle over her as she reminded herself that there was nothing worse on the face of the earth than misdirected servants of God, whomever He was perceived to be. Maybe Lorraine did think she was looking out for Ricky. Kara reminded herself that her reality wasn't everyone else's.

Drawing in a steadying breath, she forced a smile that touched only her lips, not her heart. "I seriously doubt that the issue will come up," she said evasively.

She'd been raised in an extremely open family. Her father had been a mediocre author of western novels, her mother his typist, and their modest home in the Hollywood Hills had been a haven for every sort of artist from the down-and-out to the rich-and-famous. Unconventional behavior and radical conversation could be found in the cramped living room any time of the day or night.

The house was a revolving door for fascinating, avant-garde people, some who were eccentric, but always tolerant and accepting of others. They were characters in their own way, yet they were nothing like the Worthingtons.

However, she wasn't in Hollywood, and this was John's mother, not hers. Before she could think of anything else to say, Lorraine spied her youngest son, Bucky.

"One moment with you, son," she commanded, seeing that he turned in the opposite direction.

To say that Kara was relieved by the intrusion was an understatement. She watched as the twenty-two-year-old came toward them. He looked trapped, unexpectedly snared, just when he'd thought he'd gotten away. When she met Bucky at her wedding, she'd thought that he was a troubled young man.

Now she believed she could understand why. As the youngest child, deprived of a father, reared by Lorraine, poor Bucky probably hadn't had much of a chance for a normal life.

Kara couldn't help wondering if he dreaded his mother's "one moment" summons as much as she herself would from now on. She shivered as the thought sent a chill over her hot skin.

3

Bucky, the shortest of the Worthington sons at five feet seven inches, Kara's own height, was perhaps the most handsome, after John. He was almost—pretty, Kara supposed was the best description, his features similar to John's, yet more youthful and less rugged, his frame less muscular.

As he wove his way through the crowd, Kara saw that he was ill at ease, staring at the ground as he walked. He was also sweating profusely, though he wore only slacks and a white shirt with a tie, unlike most of the men, who were dressed in suits.

Kara noticed that few people spoke to him; he clearly didn't warrant the same respect the other Worthington brothers received. The group, confirming both John's and Lorraine's point, did appear to be conservative; Bucky clearly went against the southern fabric in the Worthington clan and at this gathering. He probably detested these command performances of his mother's. Possibly people here knew that.

Sighing, Kara watched the young man shove his hands deep into his pockets and shuffle along as though he dreaded each step. She surveyed the crowd he passed through. Feeling protective, she told herself that the others were the ones overdressed and uncomfortable on this sultry night, relentlessly fighting off bugs attracted by the light, the odor of perfume, and overheated bodies.

Parties in California had been a time of fun and freedom, especially outdoor parties. However, as Lorraine had also pointed out, this wasn't California. Perhaps these low-talking, slow-sipping, ham-and-biscuits hors d'oeuvre–nibbling people were typical of traditional southerners, and then again, perhaps they were only typical of the Worthington clique.

Still, people were people, Kara assured herself. She was being overly critical because Lorraine had upset her. She had always enjoyed meeting people; as an editor for a small West Coast publishing house, she knew that everyone had a story to tell, and some proved quite interesting.

"Hello, Mother," Bucky said, forcing a timid smile. He then turned his attention to Kara.

She smiled warmly at him. "Hello, Bucky."

"Hi, Kara. You look beautiful," he said, almost cautiously, as if he didn't want anyone else to hear, or as if he wasn't sure he should be saying it. His eyes darted in her direction, then away.

Kara was pleased all the same. Her own turmoil subsided somewhat as she looked at Bucky. She knew that he was the object of his brothers' teasing. Out of the four sons, he was the only one who had chosen not to become a lawyer. He was set on being an actor.

That in itself made Kara feel closer to him than to the other brothers. With him, she was on familiar ground. He was sensitive and shy, more typical traits of an artist. She suspected his temperament accounted for much of his separateness from the rest of the Worthingtons.

"You look very nice, too, Bucky. That tie's great!" Kara said, noticing that he'd braved stuffy tradition to wear a multicolored tie.

Bucky stared at Kara, immensely pleased by her approval. Most people didn't notice him at parties. They appeared to look right through him, but Kara was looking *at* him, noting the care he'd taken with his clothes for this occasion. In fact, he'd picked his favorite tie because this party was for her.

"Do you really like it?" he asked, tugging at his left ear.

For the first time Kara saw that the ear was pierced, or had been at one time. The hole seemed pretty well healed over.

"Yes," she said, "I do."

"It's in extremely poor taste, Bucky," Lorraine contradicted. "Look at you! You're not even in a proper suit, and you're damp from head to toe!"

When she turned to Kara, Kara unconsciously braced herself for a dressing down of her own. Instead, Lorraine said, "The humidity bothers Bucky terribly. It troubled his father, too. Some men simply sweat like beasts. There is no nice way to say it. Bucky's father, William Buchannan Worthington, was one of those men."

Her voice sounded peculiar at the mention of her dead husband. Kara wondered if Lorraine still felt the loss after all these years. She'd been told that William died in a river accident when Bucky was only a few weeks old.

Bucky brushed at his mother's hand when she smoothed back his wet curls. He seemed to wither at her touch. "Mother, people will see," he mumbled.

Abruptly, a tall woman walked up to the threesome. Without any preliminaries, she asked Bucky, "Have you seen Toby? He said he was going to stop by before he left for California. I can't find him anywhere."

Bucky shook his head. "I haven't heard from him in a couple of days. I drove myself over here, but I came when the rest of the family did," he said, not looking at the woman, staring fixedly off in the distance.

The woman looked disgusted. "Teenagers! I suppose it was another of Toby's lies. He's probably not coming at all. Conceivably he's already driving to California without even telling me good-bye! I swear that boy worries the life out of me!"

Tears welling up in her eyes, she looked embarrassed. "I'm sorry. Excuse my rudeness. Toby's my only child and he's a handful. I think that's what happens when a boy's raised without a father."

She glanced at Kara. "My husband left when Toby was ten." Her voice reeked with bitterness that had survived the intervening years. "I, myself, don't believe in divorce—it's against my religion. I was left to rear the boy virtually by myself. You know how that is yourself, Lorraine," she said, turning to the other woman.

Lorraine smiled placatingly. "There's no reason to apologize, Agnes. Kara and I were just talking about circumstances that force a woman into the position of head of the household, weren't we, dear?"

She gave Kara a disarming smile.

Kara nodded, for indeed they had been discussing the subject, although not quite in that light.

"You do remember Agnes Chaney, don't you, Kara?" Lorraine asked. "She came to the wedding, of course."

"Hello, Agnes," Kara said, smiling, although she didn't remember the woman; she'd met so many strangers, including family members, in the three days she had previously been here.

Suddenly Lorraine glanced away, her expression perturbed, despite her attempts to keep a smile on her thin lips. "Pardon me a moment, won't you?" she said, not really looking at either Agnes or Kara. Grasping Bucky firmly by the arm, she drew him toward a short, buxom redhead.

Kara felt a little surge of anxiety as she recognized Dee Dee, her younger sister-in-law; it didn't take a second look to see that she was already drunk. The wine in the glass she was carelessly holding sloshed out as she determinedly weaved toward a young woman sitting on a bench with twin boys. No doubt she'd fallen earlier because of her inebriated state.

William, her husband, caught up with her just as she reached out for one of the children. He said something, his hand on her shoulder, but Dee Dee shrugged it off and spun around to face him.

The anxious young woman gathered up her children and

disappeared into the crowd. William and Dee Dee began to quarrel, William in a stern, controlled tone, Dee Dee in a rising, shrewish voice.

"Poor Dee Dee," Agnes said, watching the scene without a trace of the sympathy in her eyes. "We all have our crosses to bear. She's not been quite right since the deaths of her babies."

The words caused an ache in Kara's heart. She couldn't comprehend how devastating it would be to lose two children in less than three years to crib death.

"It's sad," Kara murmured, more to herself than to the woman she believed not to be truly sympathetic.

"Does your son sleep in that same nursery?" Agnes asked, bright gray eyes filled with curiosity. "As far as I know, it's the only room in that sprawling house set aside for children. All the Worthington sons slept there."

Kara felt a tightness in her throat. She swallowed and answered as casually as possible. "Yes, he does. The nursery is next to John's room. It's convenient for Ricky to be nearby."

Agnes nodded. "I think I would feel a little—well, you know—uneasy about the room, but then I'm superstitious," she added.

Kara experienced a peculiar fluttering in her heart. Actually, she hadn't realized that Dee Dee's babies had died in that room.

It seemed that she hadn't known much about anything at Homeplace until tonight. She oddly found herself thinking about that old adage of haste making waste. She desperately hoped that wasn't about to come true. Already she was beginning to question the wisdom of falling in love so recklessly, and marrying John Worthington before she had time to truly know him.

No, she corrected. That wasn't what she was doubting at all: what she was doubting was marrying the entire Worthington family.

For that was surely what she'd gone and done. Of that, she was now certain. Somehow she felt betrayed, deceived, as she'd felt when Ricky's father, Richard, had announced he wanted no part of her or the child she carried.

It wasn't the same, she knew, yet somehow it *felt* the same. Intuition warned her that it could hurt just as badly.

If not worse.

"There you are, Kara," John said, stepping up to put his arm around her waist, startling her. "I thought you and Mother had disappeared." He nodded to Agnes Chaney. "Good evening, Agnes."

She returned his nod. "John." She didn't say anything else, even though she didn't leave.

John drew a good-looking, blond-haired man forward. "Kara, I want you to meet Ellis Davidson. We've been friends since childhood."

Ellis took both Kara's hands in his, clasped them warmly and drew her forward. He good-naturedly winked at John. "You don't mind, do you, old friend? Since I wasn't able to come to the wedding, I didn't get to kiss the bride."

Blushing, Kara fully expected the man to touch her mouth with his own. To her surprise, he bowed and let his warm full lips linger on each of her hands in a most courtly manner. Taken aback by the unexpected romantic gesture, Kara giggled merrily.

Ellis grinned as he freed her hands and turned back to John. "She's beautiful, John, more lovely than you described. Are there any more like her at home?"

John laughed. "I'm afraid not. She's an only child."

"Pity," Ellis said, shaking his head as if genuinely disappointed by the news. "I wish I'd seen her first."

Kara laughed, delighted to discover that there was at least one interesting person at the party. She liked Ellis right away; she appreciated his bold charm and sense of humor.

"Thank you kindly, sir," she said, curtsying playfully. "I declare, I've heard about such southern gentlemen, but I never thought to meet one in the flesh—Rhett Butler having passed on some time ago. You, however, seem to fit the bill."

"Now just a minute," John protested in mock anger. "*I'm* your southern gentleman. Besides, you mention bill to this man, and he'll send you one. He's the most expensive psychiatrist in the area."

"Psychiatrist?" Kara asked. After Lorraine's speech about how conservative the area was, Kara thought she must have subconsciously imagined that psychiatrists would be taboo, too.

Ellis laughed. "I have to charge high fees to stay alive. Most people here think someone only goes to a psychiatrist if he or she's crazy," he said in a teasing whisper. "As the local nut-doctor," he continued, making a wild face and crossing his eyes, "I'm viewed as a tad 'off' myself."

Kara smiled. In Hollywood only certifiable crazies living on the streets didn't flaunt their therapists, because they couldn't afford to have them. She knew because she'd made several visits to a psychiatrist herself after she'd had such a difficult time coping when her parents were killed in an auto accident.

Agnes Chaney nodded to confirm Ellis's observation. "Most people who do see a psychiatrist *are* crazy, are they not, Dr. Davidson?" she asked pointedly.

Ellis Davidson's smile was utterly charming. "Now you know better than that, Agnes. An informed lady like you knows that we treat a host of problems."

She smirked. "Yes, and I know that many of your patients wind up at the Virginia Mental Institute."

Wagging a finger at her, he declared, "Not true, Agnes. Hearsay." He turned to John. "Tell her about hearsay, my friend."

John grinned. "You tell her, Ellis. You know as much about the law as anyone, including me."

"Since everybody knows so much about the law," Agnes said testily, "why doesn't someone come up with a way to keep children from running away from home?"

"Who ran away?" Ellis asked interestedly.

"Toby, that's who!" Agnes announced in a quaking voice. "He just graduated high school and now he's off to California to be a movie star! Why can't the law do something about that? You know he has no business out there with those—those freaks and fruitcakes and—"

She seemed to run out of steam as she glanced at Kara; however, Kara suspected she hadn't run out of epithets.

Ellis grinned at Kara before addressing Agnes. "Now, Agnes, you know that Toby is eighteen years old. He's not a child, and the law can't do a thing about him going to California. He has rights, just like any adult. Isn't that so, John?"

"That's what my legal training leads me to believe," John agreed.

"What about a mother's rights?" Agnes snapped. "I spent my best years on that boy, and he ups and takes off when I need him."

Ellis reached over and patted her cheek. "Agnes, you're in the best period of your life! Your child-raising years are over. Meet a man. Fall in love. Get married again!"

"I'd sooner die," she declared acidly, her mouth pursing prunishly, "than marry again." With that pronouncement, she marched away.

Ellis appeared to pull on a nonexistent beard for a moment, then snapped his fingers. "Man-hater," he decreed. "My on-the-spot opinion, of course, but I don't think Freud would say I'm off on this one."

John laughed. "Me, either. And speaking of off, Ellis," he said, leaning near the other man, "I'd really like to leave with my wife. I don't need to tell you that Mother's timing for this party was inopportune. You don't mind if we just drift away, do you?"

Ellis laughed, pretended to look Kara up and down with a lecherous gleam in his green eyes, then declared, "If you want my professional opinion, any sane man would do the same."

Kara knew he was teasing with his leering appraisal, but to her acute discomfort, John suddenly whispered to Ellis, "What do you *really* think of her, Ellis? Isn't she something? Not at all what you expected, is she?" he murmured, as though he were talking about some kind of trophy, or making men's locker-room conquest talk that Kara couldn't hear.

Ellis smiled indulgently. "I think I've made that more than clear. She's gorgeous—and charming."

"Do you remember Claudia Lindheart?" John whispered, his eyes glowing. "Doesn't Kara remind you a little of her? Look at this shapely beauty, Ellis!"

Kara felt her face turning red. She didn't have any idea who Claudia Lindheart was, but she didn't like the way John was behaving. There was something unflattering about the comparison, although Kara didn't know what. Before she could tell John how uncomfortable he was making her, Ellis spoke.

"Really, ol' buddy," Ellis murmured, "I don't need any comparison to anybody to see what a beautiful wife you have."

"Yes," John continued, "but you do remember the girl I'm talking about, don't you, Ellis? That bombshell I—"

"John, you're embarrassing the lady," Ellis said, his tone exaggerated, as if he were exasperated with his friend.

John laughed. "Hey, Ellis, remember that old joke—that's no lady, that's my wife?"

Clearly trying to end an uncomfortable situation, Ellis changed the subject. "Tell me if this lovely woman is going to keep letting you play poker on Friday nights with us boys, and then, John, have the good sense to escape with your bride before more guests come over."

Kara was still smarting from John's first unexpected comment, and feeling the bite of the second, when she felt the third sting.

"Let me play? *Let* me play? Who's asking? She's my wife, not my warden. I don't need Kara's permission to play cards, do I, honey?" he asked, his question almost a dare.

"Of course not," she agreed, for he didn't. He was a fully-functioning individual—or at least she'd thought he was.

Now, uneasy and confused, she wasn't sure what she

thought. Why was he behaving this way? Was he trying to prove a point, and what was it?

"See," John bragged to Ellis, then turned back to Kara. "But mum's the word to Mum. Mother takes a rigid position on poker!"

Kara stared at John. Did he really hide his poker games from his mother, and was that what this macho display was about? Was he establishing that his wife wasn't going to be as domineering as his mother?

When Ellis's eyes met Kara's, she quickly looked away. She'd been so sure she and John had touched in some special way that made a long-term relationship before marriage unnecessary, that they had known each other right away and had known that they were in love.

Maybe she was a fool. She'd been a fool before.

"Go on," Ellis urged John. "Get out of here while you can." He touched John's shoulder. "I think you're a very lucky man, John."

John nodded, then grasped Kara by the hand. Before Kara knew what had happened, he had whisked her away.

"What about Ricky?" she asked breathlessly, hurrying along beside her husband, looking back over her shoulder.

"Trust me," he said. "He's perfectly all right with Thelma. And he'll be in bed before we will. I've got to have you to myself a moment." He groaned as he studied her face, his gaze settling briefly on her mouth.

Kara stopped abruptly. "John, what was that all about?"

"What?" he murmured, trying to urge her along. "Me wanting you to myself?"

Kara didn't budge. "That scene with Ellis. That comparison of me to Claudia Lindheart. Who is she, and why did you need to go on about whether I'd *let* you play poker?"

He looked steadily into her eyes, then grinned. "Don't take offense. Claudia was a very pretty girl I dated once. I was just joshing around with my oldest friend, sweetheart, just paying you a compliment. Ellis thought Claudia was—well—special."

Inhaling deeply, Kara murmured, "I didn't see it as a compliment, John. There was something about your attitude, something almost insulting, as if you'd gotten a trophy instead of a wife. I felt demeaned the way you compared me to another woman, and implied that I wouldn't dare tell you not to play poker."

"I'm really sorry. I didn't mean to insult you. Quite the opposite," he said, so sincerely that Kara had to believe him. Or perhaps she only wanted to, she thought.

"I have been away from you so long that I guess I have loving on the brain," John added. "When Ellis looked at you the way he did, I knew he thought you were as special as I do. That reminded me of Cláudia, who was the fantasy of every man on campus."

He paused ever so briefly. "But she wasn't wife material." Or so Mother had decreed, he reminded himself with no small amount of bitterness.

"That's why I consider myself so lucky with you," he continued. "You're every man's fantasy come true, and you have all the best traits in a wife, too. You're not the type to try to own some man, Kara. That's all the comment about poker amounted to."

When Kara looked deeply into his eyes, still wanting to believe he'd meant to compliment her, he chucked her chin. "Let's not quarrel. We've both had a trying day. I've been dying to get you to myself."

"You do sound desperate," she said, attempting to tease. Maybe she was overreacting again. It *had* been a trying day.

"I am," he said hoarsely, his voice echoing the desire that had begun to replace her doubt.

They smiled as they crossed the lawn, quickly leaving the others behind. The escape was abruptly thwarted when Melvin and Priscilla showed up with Lorrie.

"John! Kara!" Priscilla called in a drawling, sugary voice. "Don't you *dare* try to run off! Lorraine will faint *dead* away."

Melvin laughed loudly, causing the belly that swelled over his belt to heave. "Hell, she'll have you up on criminal charges."

Resigned to staying, Kara greeted the couple, then spoke to Lorrie. "How are you this evening?"

"I wanted to stay home and watch television," the twelve-year-old said peevishly.

Kara smiled. "I know what you mean. I wanted to stay home, too."

"*You* didn't want to watch television," Lorrie said, waspish for one so young. "Grandmother told me so. You wanted to stay in the room with John and not see anyone else."

"Out of the mouth of babes, eh?" Melvin said, leering at John. "Not that I blame ya'll." He winked lewdly. "If I hadn't been with my woman in weeks, I wouldn't have let Mother pull this."

"You know Mother and her social protocol," John said defensively. "I thought I'd get it over with. She would have had this party sooner or later, and since I didn't know about it ahead of time, it was too late to ask for a recess while I got my defense ready."

Both men chuckled, and Priscilla rolled her brown eyes at Kara. "You'll get used to everything being slanted to legalese," she said. "These men were raised on lawyer talk. You know Lorraine's father, Father Stokes, was one of the finest lawyers in town."

"So I've heard," Kara said. "Did you know him, Priscilla?"

"Goodness, no," the small brunette said, straightening up slightly, her regal posture making her appear taller than she was. "I thought you were told I was reared in Richmond, Kara. Why, I met Melvin at a party for an old friend of the family—Judge Chatman—many years ago. We were quite properly introduced, and a quite proper courtship followed," she added, smiling prettily at Melvin.

Quite properly introduced, quite properly courted. Kara found the phrases appropriate for another century. Was it an affectation on Priscilla's part? Were these people actually that far behind the times? Or had Priscilla meant to needle Kara because of her hasty marriage? Kara didn't want to ponder it. God knows she must be blowing everything out of proportion tonight.

"I didn't recall," Kara said truthfully, letting her gaze travel fleetingly over the smaller woman. She did want to like her sister-in-law. Her mother and father had taught her early that all people had worth.

Still, Kara couldn't help but think Priscilla fit perfectly into the Worthington clan. She imagined Lorraine had been pleased when Melvin married a woman so much like his mother. Priscilla, too, was dressed in white, right down to heels and clutch bag. Her small stature, rigid bearing, and short hair reminded Kara of Lorraine.

Lorraine suddenly appeared again, immediately reaching out for Lorrie with open arms. "Look at you!" she exclaimed. "An angel all in white. Why, you're the picture of beauty, so feminine and lovely. Come to Grandmother, darling," she cooed. "I want you to say hello to Senator Wiley. He swears you're the prettiest little girl he's ever seen."

"He says she looks like a baby version of you," Melvin noted wryly.

Lorraine smiled a bit smugly as she led Lorrie by the hand across the thick carpet of green grass to a wicker chair where an elderly white-haired man was sitting.

Agnes Chaney caught up with the two couples. She had another woman with her. "Have you seen Toby?" she asked Melvin.

He shook his head. "Have you gone and lost that boy again, Mrs. Chaney?"

Agnes pursed her lips. "He was supposed to come by the party on his way out of town. He's off on a ridiculous trip to California, you know," she said as if she were spitting out poison. "That silly boy has illusions of becoming a *movie star*."

"It's a long shot, but stranger things have happened," Kara noted.

Agnes gave the tall blonde a cold look. "Ridiculous! Who's going to notice Toby among the thousands of other star-struck boys hanging around that hotbed of sin? God only knows what might become of him. I can't reach him at home. What if something *violent* has happened to him?

BLOODY WATERS

He's told everybody in town that he's leaving with a lot of money and my car!"

"Now, Agnes, don't go getting hysterical on us," Melvin said condescendingly.

"Don't you dare 'Now, Agnes' me! Melvin Worthington. He's not your son, so you don't give a hoot what happens to him. For all any of us know, my boy could be murdered in the river like those other two boys while ya'll enjoy yourselves at this party!"

"Agnes—" Melvin said, his tone solicitous.

"No!" she shot back. "Don't you try to humor me like I'm some witless female! I'll tell you something right now," she said, shaking a trembling finger at him, "I want you to know that I blame all this on your brother Bucky. If he hadn't put that foolishness in Toby's head, Toby would be right at home where he belongs."

With that, she marched off again, evidently to continue the search for her missing son, the other woman trailing in her wake.

John smiled at Kara and whispered, "Crabby old gossip. Toby was a change-of-life baby, and Agnes Chaney's never known what to do with him except smother him. It sounds like he seized his chance to escape and made off in his getaway car while the getting was good!"

"That puts her in the same boat with Mother dealing with Bucky, doesn't it?" Melvin asked, laughing raucously.

John smiled. "I'm afraid it does. She's bent on guiding him her way, but he's resisting."

Melvin brayed with laughter. "It's too late, I fear, my man. She's already turned him into a sniveling mama's boy."

"Oh, he'll be all right," John said. "He's a late bloomer. He just needs to be prodded a bit, pointed in the proper direction. When the right girl gets hold of him, he'll get inspired and straighten up."

Melvin snickered. "Prodded? Pointed? Straightened up, huh? Think the boy's got it in 'im?"

"Of course," John said. "He's a Worthington, isn't he?

He's got an eye for a pretty skirt, just like the rest of us. Don't you worry about our little brother."

John smiled at his oldest brother. After all, he was doing his best. And Bucky sure seemed to get a rise out of sexy lingerie and girly magazines. Any man who could respond like Bucky was in fine shape.

"By the way, where is he?" John asked, glancing around.

Melvin shrugged. "I haven't seen him."

"He was here with your mother and me," Kara volunteered, grateful John hadn't been as harsh as Melvin on Bucky, yet still feeling the need to say something positive about him. "I believe he was helping Lorraine and William with Dee Dee."

"Oh, damn," Priscilla said in a voice full of disdain, "is she inebriated already?"

Melvin guffawed. "Inebriated hell! Honey, she's plain ol' drunk!"

"Melvin," Priscilla chided, "don't tell the whole party."

"Who has to tell 'em?" he roared. "They've got eyes."

Kara looked at John. The uneasiness she'd experienced earlier had returned. She was struck by the reality that she really didn't know these people at all.

Not even her own husband, she admitted, stunning herself with the frightening revelation.

4

"Bucky probably drove William and Dee Dee home," John said.

"Hell, if I was William, I'd drive myself everywhere just so I'd be ready when that woman started hitting the sauce."

John exhaled heavily. "Stop sniping, Mel. William does the best he can. You know if he drives, Dee Dee throws a temper tantrum when he puts a stop to the drinks, then she tries to drive herself home."

"Hell," Melvin snorted, "a *man* wouldn't let her have a set of car keys."

"She doesn't," John said. "But that never stops her from going out to the car and carrying on about driving anyway."

Poor woman, Kara thought, the idea of Dee Dee stuck at Homeplace without transportation making her feel sorry for her sister-in-law.

"Well, would you look over there!" Priscilla said, spying someone. Kara thought the woman had found Toby Chaney until Priscilla announced loudly, "It's Judge Dressel. Ya'll are going to have to pardon us. We simply must go over and pay our respects." She looked at her husband. "Melvin?"

John clasped Kara's hand, startling her. "You're as

jumpy as the proverbial cat on a hot tin roof, tonight," he murmured. "Let's go, too, and get a bite to eat. The moment we see a clear path, we'll leave. I'll take you home so you can rest. Talk to you later, Mel and Pris," he added.

"Yeah, ya'll go on home and—*rest,*" Melvin said, snickering as he waved them off with a beefy hand.

Priscilla pretended to be embarrassed. "Melvin!" she chided, but Kara thought she saw a smile on Priscilla's smug little face. " 'Bye, now, ya'll," she called sweetly, leading Melvin in the judge's direction.

"Good-bye," Kara said, unable to summon a smile. She wanted to leave and she needed to rest.

But she didn't want to go back to Homeplace to do it. In fact, she didn't want to go back there at all. She had an almost overpowering feeling of urgency for a home of her own. She could hardly wait until her and John's house was built.

Bucky got out of the front seat of his car, feeling like a chauffeur as he watched William literally drag Dee Dee from the backseat.

"I've told you a hundred times not to be picking up other people's kids," he said coldly. "What the hell's wrong with you? You know they don't want you touching their children!"

"Shut up!" Dee Dee yelled at him. "What the fuck do you know about anything?"

Bucky looked away, embarrassed, even though the battling couple always acted as if he wasn't there anyway. They fought in front of him constantly, never bothering to acknowledge his presence.

As soon as they were in the house, he parked farther up the driveway and rushed to his own room. Pacing restlessly, he tried to shut out the sounds of William and Dee Dee fighting. He didn't ever want to get married. What he wanted—what he wanted—Jesus Christ in Heaven, he wished he knew what he wanted.

He sat down on the satin spread on his bed and put his hands between his legs, staring at the floor. He wanted to

BLOODY WATERS

be an actor, he'd wanted it *first*. He'd been the one to say he was going to California. He'd said that ever since John first brought Kara to Homeplace.

Only he hadn't said it aloud. He had been afraid somebody would tell Mother. Then Toby had gone and told everyone he was going to California, that *he* was going to be an actor. Everyone started talking like Toby was a big deal.

And the idea had been his—*Bucky's*—not Toby's. Shitty loudmouth Toby Chaney.

Bucky became fascinated with the forbidden words that echoed in his head. "Shitty loudmouth. Fucker," he said aloud.

He loved the sounds of the words. They were so wicked, so forbidden, so sinfully staining the walls of his room.

"Asshole," he said louder, then he quickly shut up, lest William and Dee Dee hear him.

His mind instantly flashed back to when he and Toby were down by the river, acting out the scenes from a play they'd just read. Bucky was a Viking storming a coastal village. Toby was playing the maiden about to be raped.

He shook his head. The Devil had been there that night. Bucky had been powerless. He'd *tried* to tell Toby to quit. Honest, he had, but something happened inside him.

The sound of William and Dee Dee screaming at each other startled Bucky from his thoughts. He sat very still, trying to hear what they were saying.

Dee Dee Worthington staggered as she shoved her husband away from her. "Leave me alone," she screeched at the top of her lungs. God, how she hated him!

William grasped her wrist again and spun her back around to face him. "I won't leave you alone until you promise me that you won't touch anybody else's children," he shot back at her. "When will you ever learn, Dee Dee? The minute you touch a kid, it's like you go crazy and start telling those lies. Why do you do that to yourself? To all of us?"

"I'll never learn!" she spat at him. "Never. I don't have any babies of my own to touch. And you, you bastard, you don't even care! Your own flesh and blood—"

William looked away. "Our babies died, Dee Dee," he said in a gentler voice, repeating it for the countless time. "You know that. They succumbed to crib death."

"They succumbed, all right," she agreed, waving her hands wildly. "To your *mother's* craziness!" she screeched. "And you think I'm crazy. You think I lie! Well, damn you to Hell! Damn all of you to Hell because that's where you'll end up, if there *is* a God!"

William struck her hard across the face, but she didn't shut up. "Hit me all you want, William Worthington," she said in a low, hate-filled voice. "You might as well beat me to death as to force me to stay here."

"You're drunk, Dee Dee," he said, suddenly looking sad and resigned. "Sleep it off."

"Hell, yes, Dee Dee," she mocked, "sleep it off! Doesn't it occur to you that's all I do, you stupid son of a bitch? Don't you know that your mother—"

When William slapped her again, Dee Dee bit her tongue. Blood dribbled down her lip. A pang of sympathy shot through William. If only she didn't keep on day after day, month after month. If only she would acccpt what had happened to their sons.

"All I wanted to do was hold those little babies, William," Dee Dee said, her quiet tone almost making her sound sober and sane, even though William knew it wasn't so. "I wanted to touch them, to feel their little bodies against mine, because I have no babies of my own. Jesus Christ, I'm so empty inside."

Suddenly weary of the battle, she sagged down on the bed. "I have nothing, William," she said so bleakly that her voice didn't even sound slurred. "Nothing. No children. No life. Not even a husband anymore."

"Dee Dee," he murmured bitterly, "you laid down the law of no more coital relations."

"And you know why," Dee Dee whispered. "For pity's sake, how could I live through it again?"

"Maybe another baby would be healthy," he said. "Have you thought of that?"

Had she thought of that? Dee Dee repeated in her mind.

Damn the man to hell! It was all she thought of. When she could think. Which seemed to be less and less often. She existed in a fog, a blurred world in which she was permitted to think only when it was absolutely necessary, like today, when she had to make a personal appearance.

And even then reality was only vague, muted, something she'd known long ago. She knew it. And she knew why. But no one would listen. No one.

Bucky strained harder to hear what his brother was saying, but the conversation had become so low that he could only catch bits and pieces. He thought William had said something about coital relations—sex—although the shorter term wasn't used in Homeplace. Mother said it was vulgar and not representative of spousal love.

Bucky shook his head. He was so confused about sex. John had once said that he didn't know how any man could do it with another man, and that if the man ever slept with the right woman, he *wouldn't* do it.

But Bucky didn't know if that was true. He'd also heard that other people had much more liberal views on what was acceptable between couples—any couples in this day and age.

Of course, that wasn't what Mother said. Mother knew what was proper, and it was confined to the marital bed of a man and a woman.

Frowning, Bucky recalled the one time he'd tried it with a girl. Everything had gone so wrong. He knew now that it was because he had sinned and fallen short of the glory of God by trying to have sexual intercourse without the sanction of matrimony.

But, of course, he hadn't been the one who initiated the wrongdoing. Marsha had been little and cute, and he had thought she liked him. That was the only reason he'd ever had the nerve to ask her out. And all he'd intended was to take her dancing.

Marsha hadn't had a date for the senior prom, and neither had he, but they'd decided not to go after all. Marsha wanted to ride around in his new car. Then she'd wanted to park where a bunch of other kids fooled around on a hill overlooking the town.

Then—then he didn't know what happened. *She* had started kissing him. He recalled how awful he'd felt when she'd told him he didn't know how to kiss, but that hadn't seemed to stop her. Soon they were in the backseat and Marsha had her panties off.

Bucky remembered how strange he'd felt at the sight of her silken underwear, how dizzy with the musky scent, how hard he'd gotten. He hadn't thought about right or wrong. The Devil—and Marsha—had led him. But when he'd tried to put it in her, Marsha had slapped him.

"Idiot!" she'd cried. "Where the hell are you trying to put that thing? You stupid pervert!"

It had been a sizzling summer night in more ways than one. The car windows had been down and Bucky had been afraid other couples had heard Marsha. He was sure people laughed—at *him*.

He sighed. Maybe she'd been right. Nobody had really told him how he was supposed to do it. He'd just thought it would happen naturally when the time came. He guessed he really had been bad at it. At any rate, he couldn't do anything after that. He just took her home.

He just didn't seem to know how to deal with girls, with people. It had happened with boys, too. At first they had been nice to him. Then he'd found out they wanted to sin. They'd gotten hateful with him after he'd told them they were in violation of God's laws. What they did was an *abomination*.

Bucky reached for the bible on the nightstand by his bed. Leviticus 18 was marked with an old church sermon. He read the acts of immorality which were forbidden. He had read them before, but now he needed to read them again.

Those sinners had defiled the land and had to be cut from among their people. The bible said so in black and white. He knew that was why they had been murdered, why they had been taken from the midst of decent people and washed in the river, cleansed of their sin, purified.

Bucky put the bible back down. He realized that William

and Dee Dee had stopped fighting. Their room was downstairs, across the hall from his. He could hear the bed squeaking. He hadn't thought they had carnal knowledge of each other anymore. William was spewing his seed into Dee Dee. And *that* was where a man's seed was supposed to be sown.

The bible said so.

Still, as he listened, Bucky remembered burning with a strange heat. He shoved the thought aside. It was evil. The Devil was still inside him, making him think those things. Wrong things.

He rolled over and clapped his hands against his ears, trying to shut out the rhythmic sound of William and Dee Dee's squeaking bed, but the noise kept growing louder and louder and louder, until it screamed in his mind.

He was aware that his penis was getting hard. He wondered if William and Dee Dee having coitus again after so long, and his own penis growing hard as he listened, were some kind of sign that he should take a woman.

That was bewildering, too, for there was only one who interested him. Just one woman. And what did the bible say about that?

It said thou shalt not uncover the nakedness of thy brother's wife: it is *thy* brother's nakedness.

Bucky tugged hard on his ear. He didn't quite understand that verse. There were so many he'd learned over the years.

He wondered if uncovering Kara's nakedness would be a real sin, a punishable sin. After all, Mother said that Kara was a fornicating whore, bringing sin and shame upon the heads of those at Homeplace. She had slept with a man without benefit of marriage. She had been the vessel for an evil seed. John had been tricked by Satan into laying with her.

Bucky frowned. Of his three brothers, he hated John the least. Melvin was a bully and William was a wimp. Of his three sisters-in-law, Kara was his favorite. Priscilla was a snob and Dee Dee was a sot.

But was Kara *really* his sister-in-law, since she had already lain with a man and had Ricky? If she was a fornicating whore, how could she legally be John's wife? Was a man excused from punishment if he had carnal knowledge of her? Didn't the bible say something about it being better for a man to spew his seed into any woman than on the earth? He couldn't remember.

Bucky began to hum to himself, trying to shut out the troubling thoughts raging in his head. Life was so confusing. Mother was constantly giving him lectures, telling him of her disappointment in him.

Everybody seemed disappointed in him. Except Toby. Toby had said he understood how lonely Bucky was. Toby had acted like he was a real friend. Bucky was beginning to miss him already.

Suddenly he bolted upright in the bed, listening as Dee Dee yelled at William.

"You sorry son of a bitch!" she said, her words slurred but distinguishable. "You said you'd pull it out! You rotten bastard! If I get pregnant, I'll kill you. I swear to your mother's wretched God, I will."

Bucky's heart began to beat fast and his erection shriveled. Beads of sweat formed on his body, even though the air-conditioning made the room cold. Mother would be furious if she heard what Dee Dee said.

He got up and paced his room. Dee Dee shouldn't say those things. He didn't know if he should tell on her or not. If he did, maybe Mother would stop saying mean things about Kara. Bucky really liked Kara. He couldn't help it. He did, no matter what Mother told him.

Her words rang in his head, stirring around with all the other baffling bible verses and conflicting admonishments. Humming didn't stop them, and he was beginning to get a headache. He wished the others would come home so he wouldn't have to feel responsible for reporting the evil things Dee Dee said about God.

That is, he wished all the others except Lorrie would come home. He hated her. Mother used to love him until Lorrie was born. Now it was Lorrie, Lorrie, Lorrie.

His heart began to beat faster as Dee Dee's words echoed

in his head. What exactly had she meant? Had William made her pregnant again? And what if he had?

"Jesus Christ!" he said aloud, knowing he was taking the Lord's name in vain.

Or maybe he wasn't in this case, since he was calling out of need. It really was all so baffling. He wished Mother was here. She could explain it. She always knew the answers. Then he heard the sound of a sharp slap and Dee Dee crying out in pain.

"All right! That's enough! Shut your filthy mouth and keep it shut before Mother comes home!" William ordered. "If she hears such blasphemy in this house, she'll throw us both out!"

Bucky listened, his ragged nerves soothed a bit. He wouldn't have to tell Mother. William was doing his duty, punishing the evildoer himself.

He jerked when Dee Dee responded. "You slimy worm! You creepy leech! I wish the vile bitch would throw us out! Then maybe you'd have to grow up and stop sucking Mummy's titty!"

Aghast, Bucky clasped his hands in a prayerful pose. He couldn't believe that William would do such a thing. He couldn't believe that Mother would allow it. The deafening noises started in his head again, the bible verses crashing with memories from his childhood.

Mother had let him suck on her tit. He remembered. She'd done it when she'd dressed him up in the attic. When it was just the two of them, before Priscilla came. She'd made him stop when he was six years old—before he started to school.

Then he remembered that he was forbidden to mention that. He recalled that Mother had explained over and over that she had been nursing him, as any good mother would. That was why he had been at her breast. He jumped again, his heart hammering when William struck Dee Dee again.

"And where the hell would you go if Mother threw you out?" his brother demanded. "You ungrateful witch. You wanted to marry me badly enough, didn't you? You were eager enough to move to Homeplace, weren't you? You were groveling at Mother's feet then, trying to curry her favor so you could be a Worthington!"

"I didn't know what a sick bunch of sons of a bitch lived here then!" she retorted, her voice full of raw emotion. "You're crazy. All of you!"

When William said something about her needing medication, Dee Dee started screaming so loudly that Bucky couldn't understand anything but the poison profanity spewing from her like vomit. He could imagine it splattering over the walls, spreading out, flowing under the door and down the hall, its stench foul and all-pervading. Maybe it could even reach his room.

Bucky began to shake. Dee Dee mustn't say those things. Someone *would* be punished. He knew it as surely as he lived and breathed.

He dropped to the floor on his knees and began to pray to God, hoping he could shut out the noises inside and outside his head. He wished his mother would come home. He prayed fervently that she would.

Alone at last in John's arms, Kara began to forget the tiring day she'd had and the unplanned party. John possessed that power over her when he made love to her. She could feel the rushes of pleasure as his tongue tasted that exquisite place between her legs, that seat of delicious sensation, that tiny area that could send her entire body into spasms of desire.

Unconsciously she put her fingers in his hair and tugged his face nearer as her passion grew. She could feel her climax building, every nerve ending in her body on fire as she was sent spinning into a vortex of pleasure, until she thought she couldn't stand it any longer.

"Oh, John," she breathed. "John, that feels so incredible. John! Oh! Oh!" She gasped aloud as her body shuddered with release, each spasm of pleasure more intense than the last.

"Tell me how good it feels, Kara. Say it out loud," John murmured.

BLOODY WATERS

For the first time Kara felt uncomfortable with John's request. She knew that he loved for her to talk dirty when they made love. It had started out as a joke when she'd initiated it, because John had so assiduously avoided what he called "obscenities" himself.

She'd playfully tossed out every word she could think of that he might consider "dirty"; she'd been amused when he seemed to be turned on by them. She knew different things sexually excited different people, and to her the vulgarities were innocuous enough, especially "fuck," for which John had such a fascination. She'd asked him if he knew that the word was harmless, an acronym meaning "For Unlawful Carnal Knowledge."

He'd laughed, but as if he hadn't known. She recalled how surprised she'd been to think that a thirty-three-year-old man, a criminal lawyer at that, didn't know the origin of "fuck."

"Tell me, Kara," he urged again. "Tell me how good I am at this."

Kara sighed softly, sorry that she was feeling uncomfortable with John. He was very, very good, his raw passion almost overwhelming when he unleased it. Dazed by the partly sated way her body felt after such a long abstinence, knowing that oral sex was the prelude to more exquisite satisfaction, she thickly told him what he wanted to hear.

"You're the most wonderful lover in the world, John. You know I love what you do to me. Your tongue is a pleasure tool, sending spirals of desire through me. Your lips are hot and tantalizing. You drive me crazy with need. I can't wait to feel you inside me."

"Do me, Kara," he murmured. "Pleasure my privates and tell me how much you love doing it."

Usually Kara was amused by his euphemistic expression for oral sex, but tonight she was tense, recalling how upset she'd gotten when John had talked to Ellis as if she were a trophy *or* his second choice for a wife. Maybe Claudia Lindheart had been his first.

She drew in a steadying breath and told herself that she had to suppress that conversation; John had explained, apologized, and she'd accepted. And, after all, she was the one he'd married.

Moving her long body sinuously, brushing her firm breasts against him, Kara slid along the length of his hairy chest. John began to tremble in anticipation.

"You're the sexiest creature I've ever known," he whispered. "You're utterly unbelievable."

"Do you really think so?" she murmured, wanting to believe that she meant as much to him as he did to her, that their love was indeed rare and right.

"I know so," he breathed, his stomach muscles tensing as she moved lower still. "Oh, mercy, Kara," he murmured, his voice husky, "I start shaking before you even do it. I've never felt anything like it."

She giggled, trying to get in a playfully erotic mood, trying to recapture what had somehow been misplaced in her absence. "I don't believe you," she teased. "You don't act like a virgin."

He smiled in the scant brightness of a three-way lamp he'd left on. He loved to watch her making love to him. It excited him tremendously.

To him, she was a sensual adventure, a totally wanton woman who'd finally made his sexual fantasies come true. Out from under Mother's censorious eye, he'd found the perfect wife: bright, witty, fun, pretty, with an adequate family background, her father having a writer's credentials, but best of all, she virtually abandoned any morals in bed.

Kara willingly—no, eagerly—engaged in all the immoral acts Mother had preached against since he was old enough to know what a man and a woman could do together—besides procreate. The thought of Mother above them, alone in her bed, sleeping while they cavorted so wildly in Homeplace, excited John more.

"I didn't say I was a virgin," he murmured. "At least not in the technical sense. I do swear before God, man, and woman, that I was virginal in that area until your mouth touched my privates."

Kara giggled again, relaxing a little. "Maybe," she agreed, thinking he was probably telling the truth.

She could imagine his mother's views on oral sex. The participants would probably be sentenced to crucifixion, their "privates," as John described them in such old-fashioned terms, pecked off by vultures with cloven hooves for claws and beaks like knives.

She suddenly stiffened, the notion no longer amusing when she thought she heard someone out in the hall. She had a prickly sensation, as if she were being watched, as though another person was in the room with them.

John had assured her that the house was built as solid as a rock, that no one could hear through the walls, but she had doubts. She'd heard William and Dee Dee arguing when she and John came home. Then she supposed everyone in the next county could have heard them.

God, she told herself, she was really getting paranoid. Love and affection had always been a natural thing in the house where she grew up. She'd been aware that some of the guests made love on the couch in the living room; no one had even hinted that it was dirty or vile, but something about Homeplace made Kara feel sullied.

"Honey?" John murmured, Kara's hesitation driving him crazy. "This is no time to tease. I'm a condemned man up here, waiting for salvation."

Kara had to smile. The Worthington sons could be so irreverent when they chose to be. Or maybe it was only their natural choice of words after so many years of Lorraine drilling such terms into their heads.

She supposed that was one of the things that was bothering her: from what she'd seen, John alone was affectionate. The rest of the family rarely touched each other physically. None of them were open, warm people, and yet they were almost incestuous in the way they lived so closely together in this house, consumed with only the family and what pertained to it.

"Kara? Did you fall asleep?"

She smiled again, grateful that John was loving. Then she continued the love play.

"God, how can anything illegal feel so good?" he asked hoarsely.

Kara stopped and looked at him, seeing his eyes half closed. "You're not going to make a citizen's arrest, are you?" she joked.

"Only if you don't continue," he said, his voice passion-thick and urgent. "I've never felt anything so thrilling."

Her fears fading as the John of old savored her touch, Kara stimulated him until he vowed he was about to explode. Then she got on her hands and knees, so that John could penetrate her from behind, his favorite position. Everything was going to be all right, she told herself. The first—and the worst—day of her return was over.

They began to move together, their slow undulations obliterating all else except their act of lovemaking. Both knew this couldn't last. Kara, in the throes of ecstasy, began to moan. She could hear John calling her name, almost strangling on it.

Suddenly she heard Ricky cry out.

She tensed as she strained to hear the sound again.

"Mommy!"

"Kara, just a minute more," John gasped, thrusting faster. "Just a minute. We're almost there."

"Mommy!" It was a shriek this time. Kara couldn't ignore it.

"I'm sorry," she said. "I've got to see what's wrong."

"Thelma will tend to Ricky. That's what she's hired for," John said irritably.

"I've never heard him so frightened," Kara insisted, trying to push free of John. "I have to go to him."

He heaved a sigh of disgust and set her free. "Dammit, Kara, we were almost there," he muttered.

"I hate this as much as you do, John," she said, sliding from the bed. "I'll be right back."

Rolling over, John closed his eyes and muttered, "Damn it to hell. That's why we pay Thelma, Kara. So you don't have to rush off in the middle of doing it."

"I resent that, John," she protested quickly, regret and anger mingling in her voice as she thought how childish her husband sounded. "Ricky's obviously frightened and he's calling *me!*"

BLOODY WATERS

Without looking at her husband again, she pulled on her robe and hurried next door, terribly upset, both from Ricky's cries and John's reaction to her need to go to her son.

She gasped when she stepped into the room. Dee Dee was leaning over the sobbing child's bed. She looked like a crazed woman. Taken aback, Kara stared at her, questioning if, as Agnes Chaney had said, the woman was in her right mind.

Her red hair was in wild disarray. Her expression was tormented. Her nightgown was twisted. She was keening strangely, softly, while she hugged her arms to her body in a rocking motion.

Rushing over to pick up her distraught son, a shiver raced over Kara's damp skin. She wondered if Dee Dee had been wakened by Ricky crying, or if Dee Dee was the cause of the child's fear.

5

Protectively clutching Ricky, Kara fled from the nursery and into the hall. The keening sound Dee Dee was making grew louder. Kara stopped and glanced apprehensively over her shoulder. Her sister-in-law was reaching out with both hands like a spooky apparition, her face drawn, her expression bereaved. The woman actually looked like she wasn't of this world.

"Mommy," Ricky cried. "Mommy." Big tears rolled down his cheeks as he wrapped his little arms tightly around her neck.

Gathering him closer, Kara murmured, "It's all right, sweetheart."

She gasped when someone touched her. Whirling around in the hall, she saw Bucky looking pitiful and embarrassed.

"My room's right above Ricky's," he said. "When I heard him cry, I came to check on him, but Dee Dee wouldn't move so I could pick him up. I knew you and John—I heard—I mean . . ."

His words trailed off and his face turned so red that Kara was sure it would be hot to touch.

She was embarrassed, too. Had she been right? Had Bucky listened to her and John making love? And if he had, who else had?

Thelma appeared abruptly, dressed in a robe, startling

both Kara and Bucky. Without a word she went into the room, grasped Dee Dee's hand and led the moaning woman out and down the hall. Then she returned to where Bucky and Kara stood in stiff silence.

"I'm sorry I didn't hear 'em," she said. "Ain't used to it in the night no more."

"I'll take him to John's room with me," Kara said, aware she hadn't said "our" room.

"Ain't no need in doing that," Thelma insisted. "I'll take care of the child. He knows me now. I'll get him back to sleep." She looked at Bucky as Kara continued to hold her son. "You go on, Bucky. Get on back to bed yourself. You don't know nothing about caring for babies."

Kara caught the resentful look in Bucky's eyes, but she was grateful Thelma was sending him away. She couldn't remember when she'd been so uncomfortable, and yet she knew it wasn't Bucky's fault he'd overheard her passionate lovemaking or her baby crying.

She forced a faint smile. "Thank you for coming to see about Ricky," she told him.

He appeared so pleased by her appreciation that she felt guilty, finding him and herself in this awkward position because of her passion in bed.

"It's okay, Kara. I wasn't asleep." He started away, then looked back at her and smiled sheepishly. "It's okay, really."

When Bucky had gone, Thelma reached out for the child, who had burrowed into Kara's shoulder, sucking his thumb noisily.

"I'll take care of him, Thelma," Kara stressed again.

"All right, but Mrs. Worthington ain't going to be none too happy about me not doing my job."

Kara nodded understandingly. "I'll explain. You won't be blamed."

The old woman shrugged, then went back toward her own room, which was across from Ricky's and down one from John's. Lorraine's bedroom was upstairs along with Bucky's, as was Melvin and Priscilla's, and Lorrie's. Dee Dee and William slept on the same floor as John and Kara.

When Kara glanced down the hall, the door to Dee Dee and William's room was closed.

Her mind filled with the image of the tortured woman, Kara wondered if Dee Dee was drunk, or sleepwalking, or perhaps imagining Ricky was one of her own sons. Maybe she'd awakened from a nightmare made worse by alcohol and couldn't discern what was real.

And maybe, just maybe, the woman really was mentally unbalanced. She certainly wasn't behaving sanely. But then Kara didn't know why she expected sanity from Dee Dee. No one else here did.

Kara was relieved to see that John was asleep when she entered the room. She stared at him. She couldn't have resumed making love if her life depended upon it. Her mood bleak, she settled down in an antique rocking chair, barely moving back and forth, staying there long after she knew Ricky was fast asleep.

The phone rang before seven the next morning. Kara was in a deep sleep when she heard John speak into the receiver.

"It's all right, Mother, I have it."

Kara rolled over on her side and looked at her husband as he murmured, "Uh-huh. Yes. Yes. All right. Just a minute. Hang on."

When he laid down the receiver and eased out of the bed, Kara opened her eyes wide. "What's wrong?" she murmured.

He shook his head and whispered, "Nothing to disturb you, Sleeping Beauty. Go back to sleep." He took a moment to brush her lips with his. "I'm sorry about last night, honey. I was just so damned eager—and then—well, I'm sorry."

Kara recalled how much she'd resented her husband the previous night. For a long time she'd gazed at him while she held her sleeping son. It had been with great hesitancy and reluctance that she'd finally put Ricky back in the nursery. Then she'd lain tensely beside John, the vision of Dee Dee lingering in her mind as she strained to hear any sound from her baby's room. Somehow she'd eventually fallen into an exhausted sleep.

But it wouldn't help to bring her bitterness to the new day. "It's okay," she murmured, needing to forget the incident.

"Agnes Chaney is on the phone," John murmured. "Toby never showed up at the party last night and he still hasn't called. Agnes is frantic. Bucky has his own phone. I'm going to wake him and see if he heard from the kid."

Kara felt a pounding in her heart that was becoming all too familiar as the previous night rushed back to mind. "I'll check on Ricky," she said, sliding out of bed.

John smiled patronizingly at her. "Apparently he was just fine last night, wasn't he?"

Kara didn't want to argue, and she couldn't bring herself to mention what had happened in Ricky's room. But she did want to see about her child.

"He was scared," she said tersely.

John, apparently not wanting more harsh words, handed her a robe. "You're not living alone now," he said with a wink. "Put this on before you open the door and show somebody else all those charms of yours."

Kara hesitated, considering telling him that she knew all too well she wasn't living alone; she decided to go with her first instinct and let the previous night remain in the past.

She gave John a kiss as she pulled on the robe. He was grabbing his own robe as he started toward the door.

When she eased open the door to Ricky's room, Kara was relieved to see that he was still in bed. But as she approached, her heart began to pound. There was a pillow over his head! Rushing across the room, she didn't even remember reaching the bed as she yanked the pillow away. Her son was gone. In his place a girl doll dressed in a frilly pink dress lay still as death, staring at the ceiling with sightless glassy eyes.

"Oh, Lord," she murmured, backing out of the room and stumbling blindly down the hall after John.

"John! John!" she called. "Ricky's not—"

He silenced her with a finger to his lips. "Kara, it's

okay," he murmured, bracing her. "You do need to pull yourself together where that boy's concerned. I made arrangements last evening with Thelma to get Ricky up this morning so you could sleep in. If he's not in his room, then he's in the kitchen with her."

"John," she said frantically, "there's a doll in Ricky's bed. It had a pillow over its face."

Staring at her as if she'd suddenly gone berserk, he shook her. "Kara, are you dreaming?"

"No!" she cried. "Come see for yourself if you don't believe me!"

Disbelieving, John followed her back down the hall. Her pulse racing, her knees weak, Kara plunged into the room. The bed was empty. The doll was gone. The pillow was at the head of the bed, not at the end where Kara had flung it in her panic. The sheet had been pulled back.

"Get a grip on yourself, Kara," John said. "Your mind's working overtime. Go find your child in the kitchen with Thelma."

"There *was* a doll in this bed!" Kara cried, but John had already turned away.

Smoothing back her long blond hair, Kara inhaled deeply. She wasn't overly protective of her son. She knew what that could do to a child. She'd seen it long before she observed the effects of Lorraine's leash on Bucky or heard about Toby's mad rush to freedom.

Still, after she watched John go up the steps, she hurried to the dining room. When she saw Ricky sitting in a high chair at the long oak table, eating cereal, grinning happily, milk dribbling off his chin, it was as if a rock had been lifted off her chest. She hadn't realized how constricted her breathing was until she saw that her child was all right.

"Mommy!" he squealed.

Kara gave him a hug, then turned to Thelma. "You really didn't have to do this. I would have gotten up with him."

"Ain't no sense in the world in that," the other woman insisted. "I told you so last night. I been taking care of babies in this house since I was a girl myself. It's nice to have a little boy around again."

Kara wondered if she dare approach the subject of Dee Dee. She needed to know—she *had* to know if her son was in danger in this house.

"Thelma, why do you think Dee Dee was in Ricky's room last night?" she asked, glancing around nervously to see if anyone else might have come in.

Thelma didn't reply. She didn't even look at Kara. Kara wondered if the other woman had heard her.

"Thelma," she repeated, "do you think Dee Dee would harm Ricky?"

Thelma set a plate down on the table so heavily that Kara feared it might break, but she did not answer.

Anxious because she didn't want to alienate the woman, Kara tried to think of a way to change the subject and get some kind of response from Thelma. She was afraid to let the silence hang between them.

Kara knew that Thelma had a daughter, Tessa, who helped with the cooking and cleaning at Homeplace. She lived in a cottage somewhere on the ten-acre property. Kara hadn't seen her except when she was in the house helping Thelma. She was a tall, light-skinned girl about Bucky's age, and Kara couldn't help being curious about her. Thelma was a light-skinned black herself, but Tessa could almost pass for white.

It seemed that there'd been an epidemic of women having late-life babies here. Lorraine. Agnes. Thelma. While that wasn't rare now, it was twenty or more years ago.

Kara sought the courage to ask another question that might bring stony silence. Hoping that a mother's interest in her child would shatter the chill in the room, she tried again, forcing a smile to her lips.

"Did you want a son when Tessa was born?" she asked brightly, as if Thelma hadn't ignored her last two questions.

"No." Thelma met Kara's eyes only briefly, but it was long enough for Kara to see hatred in her gaze. She didn't know what to make of it, except that she felt terribly uncomfortable.

To her surprise, Thelma added in a low, hard voice,

"Bucky was just a baby when I got pregnant. I didn't want no boy."

Kara nervously tousled Ricky's blond hair, startled by the venom in Thelma's voice. It didn't sound like the woman had wanted a child at all, and yet Kara sensed a special bond between Tessa and Thelma, even though they almost never spoke to each other in the family's presence. Kara had also witnessed how marvelously patient and caring Thelma could be with Ricky.

But was that only when she was around to observe? Kara wondered. And was it because Lorraine ordered Thelma to care for the child?

Or was it something else altogether? Had Thelma's husband, like Agnes's, gone off and left her? Or, perhaps, like Kara, she hadn't had a husband at all. Kara knew how Lorraine felt about babies out of wedlock. Twenty or more years ago her stand on the subject must have been even worse. She could imagine Lorraine berating Thelma. The fact that Tessa was so light-skinned suggested the father had been very fair himself, perhaps Caucasian.

Uneasy, Kara murmured, "I don't want to add to your work. There's nothing I'd rather do than take care of my son. You don't need to spend your time with him."

"I done told you it's nice to have a boy around again," Thelma said, "but 'course you want to take care of him, and you'll be doing the most of it. I'll be fixing breakfast any minute now, and Ricky'll be all yours. Mr. John and me just wanted you to get some rest."

Unexpectedly, the older woman smiled. "You do look some better today. Even with that dark tan of yours, you was looking mighty washed out last evening."

"I was feeling it, Thelma," Kara answered honestly. "I had no idea Lorraine was planning a party for the evening I arrived."

When Thelma failed to reply, Kara had no delusions that the woman may not have heard. She warned herself to be careful about what she said. She'd already made the mistake with John of insinuating that Lorraine was less than perfect. In this household she'd better be wary of such careless comments. Even though she was married to a Worthington, she was more a stranger in Homeplace than anyone else.

She glanced around the room, which, like most of the house, was filled with lovely antiques. Her eye was caught by the picture she'd seen before—one of an angel guiding two children safely across a rickety rope bridge over water rising dangerously high. She stared at the picture for a moment, trying to determine what was peculiar about it. She'd seen it in other places.

Then it struck her. In the other prints of the relatively common picture, the children had been a girl and a boy. In this painting, the children were both little girls. Kara shook her head, wondering why she thought anything odd in this house.

She tried changing the subject again, making her questions sound like casual conversation. "Did you take care of Lorrie, too? Did Priscilla and Melvin live here when she was born?"

Thelma made a wry face. "Yes indeed, they surely did."

Her laughter was an unexpected cackle; she glanced at the door, then leaned closer to Kara. " 'Course, I didn't do too much taking care of her or she wouldn't be such a awful chile. Mrs. Worthington done the caring for that baby. She always wanted herself a girl chile. Mercy, I can't even tell you how much that woman wanted a female chile."

She shook her head and shut up abruptly, as if she'd already said too much.

Wanting to encourage Thelma, Kara agreed, "Lorrie does seem to be the apple of her grandmother's eye."

"Apple, huh!" Thelma grunted. "She's the whole tree, she is. Gracious! That chile knows she can't do no wrong in Homeplace."

"I guess it's not unusual for a grandmother to spoil the only grandchild she has," Kara said. Suddenly she remembered the two other grandchildren Lorraine had had. Dee Dee's tragic figure became full-blown in her mind.

Kara met Thelma's eyes. "How old were Dee Dee's children when they died, Thelma?"

The older woman's face became a closed mask; Kara watched as her full lips compressed into a tight line. She knew Thelma wasn't going to answer questions about Dee Dee, but she couldn't stop now. There were things she had to know for her own peace of mind.

"Did you put a doll in Ricky's bed last night?"

Thelma glared at her. "No!"

"Did you see one there this morning?"

Thelma didn't bother to indulge the second question. "You done eating?" she asked Ricky.

"Thelma . . ." Kara pressed. "As one mother to another, I—"

"I want down," Ricky interrupted, answering Thelma's question.

Kara quickly took the bib from around his neck and lifted him to the floor herself. She was surprised at how badly her hands shook.

"Thelma, talk to me," she coaxed.

Thelma's hard eyes widened briefly as she glanced at the door.

Kara whirled around when she heard her mother-in-law.

"Good morning," Lorraine said crisply, entering with an economy of motion, wearing a blue dress and medium heels of the same color.

"Good morning," the two other women responded.

Ricky looked up at Lorraine. "Good morning," he said boisteriously with a silly giggle.

Ignoring the child, Lorraine addressed Kara. "I see Agnes Chaney woke the whole house. I was always taught it was improper to come or call at anyone's home before nine A.M. or after nine P.M. But then, times change, don't they?"

Kara didn't like the way Lorraine ignored Ricky. If Bucky had heard the child cry out last night, Lorraine probably had, too. Maybe she was annoyed with Ricky because he'd interrupted her sleep; then Agnes, too, had disturbed her this morning.

BLOODY WATERS

"Times do change, thankfully," Kara agreed, trying to make a subtle point, though she couldn't help recalling how people had arrived at her parents' home any hour of the day or night, and were always met with a friendly smile and a cup of coffee.

"I assume you slept well until the phone call," Lorraine said. "After such a grand party, I went to sleep the minute I got in bed."

It occurred to Kara that Lorraine must not have heard Ricky after all. She obviously didn't know about the disturbance. On one hand, Kara was glad the whole house hadn't been awakened, but on the other she was even more irritated because Lorraine hadn't bothered to acknowledge Ricky's presence this morning.

Unconsciously Kara picked him up and held him on her lap, bouncing him on her knees as if she could make up for him being slighted by his new grandmother.

"Of course, the bible teaches us to be kind to those in need, and Agnes is upset about her son," Lorraine continued. She shook her head. "I don't know what that woman would do if she had the responsibility of four sons as I have." She glanced out the window and shook her head again.

"Has Bucky heard anything from Toby?" Kara asked, genuinely concerned. She still held the vision of a tormented Dee Dee in her mind; she could well imagine that Agnes Chaney was frantic about Toby, and probably the boy was deliberately not calling.

Lorraine looked stern as she ignored the question. "I told Bucky to stay away from that boy. He always was—flighty—but Bucky wanted someone who shared an interest in the arts. Toby appeared compatible in that way, at least." Her gaze returned to the window.

"I think it must be worse to have one son than several," she mused. "On the other hand, I don't know whether that's true."

John abruptly stormed into the room, striding angrily, speaking hatefully to Bucky, who was trailing at a discreet distance.

Kara stared at her husband in surprise. She'd never heard him raise his voice, although she was fully aware that as a criminal attorney he certainly had the potential and opportunity to do so.

"Boys, please!" Lorraine said, touching her temples with bony fingers. "What *is* the matter?"

John ran his hands through wavy black hair in frustration. "Bucky wouldn't even talk to Agnes."

"There was no reason to," Bucky said defensively, his lower lip pouting. "I haven't heard from Toby. I told her that yesterday."

"This is *today,* and for all Agnes knew, Toby could have called you by now," John said harshly. "The woman's beside herself with panic. She may be neurotic, but it wouldn't hurt you to have a little compassion. With Asterson's trial coming up, the two murdered teenagers are fresh in everyone's mind. Agnes thinks something's happened to Toby."

"Those murders were five months ago, and you yourself are representing the killer," Bucky said, his voice taut. "Since he's in jail, ready to go on trial, it'd be pretty hard for him to kill Toby, don't you think? If Mrs. Chaney had any brains she'd know that."

"The point here, Bucky, is that other people *do* get killed, as you'd know if you opened your eyes to the real world."

"I have my eyes open!" Bucky declared vehemently, his voice rising.

Kara looked at him. He was dressed in slacks and a shirt. He was sweating profusely; his white shirt was soaked by large wet circles under his armpits.

"And you don't like the real world, do you?" John demanded, sounding like he was interrogating a witness. "Isn't that what this acting business is all about—escapism, pretending that real life doesn't exist, making up things?"

"No!" Bucky yelled.

He glanced at Lorraine, who watched the proceedings interestedly, without commenting. Unconsciously, Kara was sure, Bucky stepped nearer where she was seated with Ricky, as though seeking protection.

Kara stared at the husband she hardly knew. This was a side of John she hadn't encountered, and she was afraid his obvious disdain for Bucky's penchant for acting was only one facet of a deeper dislike for things that were an important part of her own life.

Yet last night he'd told Melvin that Bucky was young and would change. Suddenly she felt sad for the young man facing the older, more formidable one as if he were on trial for some serious crime.

John obviously saw his brother as weak because he wanted to be an actor. Kara had to bite her tongue not to get in the middle of the argument. She was disappointed by John's treatment of his brother. Disappointed and disturbed.

"Why didn't you pick up the phone and talk to Mrs. Chaney?" John demanded, his brows coming together in a frown. "After all, Toby is a *so-called* friend of yours."

"I told you I don't know where Toby is. I told *you* I told *her* that. If he's missing, let her call the police," Bucky said, looking clearly upset at the thought of his missing friend. He seemed to shrink before his older brother, but Kara admired him for not buckling under completely.

She recalled how angry John had gotten with her last night when she left their bed. He hadn't cared about anyone but himself.

"Anyway," Bucky said, "you're the lawyer. Why didn't you tell her what to do if she's so sure Toby's missing and not on his way to California?"

John exhaled as though the fight had abruptly gone out of him. "I did tell her, Bucky, and I still say it was *your* place to talk to her. When are you going to stop hiding behind your acting and poems and songs and walks along the river and participate in life? When are you going to become a *man?* When someone has a problem, a *responsible man* helps when he's asked to. Do I have to explain every little thing to you?"

"Don't start on me again about my life," Bucky said,

moving farther away from John to sit down beside Kara. He looked at his sister-in-law, his big brown eyes beseeching. "Tell him, Kara. You're from California. Tell him I *can* be an actor. People do it every day."

His whole body seemed to plead for her support as he leaned toward her, his pliable features clearly expressing his vulnerability.

Kara felt great empathy for him. She'd seen her father struggle all his life with his books. The arts were a hard road for most, but she honestly did feel that Bucky had a right to choose the career he wanted, whether he failed at it or not.

"Well, people *do* become actors every day," she said.

Lorraine interrupted before Kara could say anything more. "Enough of this family bickering. John, Bucky, you know how I despise that kind of thing. When your father was alive, there was—"

Once more she left a sentence half finished, a trait Kara was seeing more and more in the small, severe woman. Lorraine stared out the window again, mesmerized, her attention caught by a scene only she could see.

Then, abruptly, she faced Bucky as though she had just rejoined the real world. "Bucky, it *was* your responsibility to talk to Agnes, whether you'd heard from Toby or not. It was the only decent thing to do. After all, we are our brothers' keepers. Speaking of which," she said, "go knock on your brothers' doors and tell them breakfast will be served in half an hour."

Instantly dutiful, Bucky rushed from the room, looking small and defeated.

Lorraine turned to Thelma as though nothing was awry this morning. "I think hot cakes and bacon will be fine for breakfast."

"Yes, ma'am." The tall, heavy black woman, who'd remained all but invisible during the altercation, quietly left the room.

"Ricky spilled food on himself," Kara said, wanting to leave, too. "I'll change his clothes."

"And your *own*," Lorraine said, smiling slightly to offset

what amounted to an order. "You, too, John. You know better."

John laughed. "Mother, clothes are clothes. You're so compulsive about what's proper."

"I am not!" she declared. *"Decent* people don't eat in their nightclothes! And need I remind you about what the bible says about family members looking on each other's nakedness?"

"Mother, no one is naked!" John said with a smile. "You're so Victorian."

He was still smiling as he followed his wife out of the room. "She is Victorian, you know," he murmured for Kara's ears only.

"Yes, she is," Kara agreed, too upset to care if she was discreet about John's mother or not. She *had* felt naked when Lorraine's bitter brown eyes raked over her sheer robe and gown.

She'd realized when she was talking with Thelma that it was easy to say things she shouldn't. It bothered her that she didn't feel free to talk to her own husband; once again she was conscious of the fact that they were still getting to know each other, still skirting the edges of each other's personalities. It was an odd sensation, made all the more difficult because they were thrown into the middle of his entire mixed-up family.

"Why so silent this morning?" John asked, wrapping his arms around her waist and drawing her near, catching Ricky between them.

Abruptly, the child reached out and slapped John's face. "No!" he said in a nasty little voice. "Don't!"

"Ricky!" Kara cried, aghast.

She knew it wasn't unusual for a child in his situation to be possessive, yet he couldn't have chosen a worse time. She realized that she was holding her breath, waiting for John's reaction.

John smiled. "It's all right, Kara. He's used to having you all to himself." He grasped Ricky's hand and shook it. "No hitting," he admonished. "That's not nice."

When Ricky turned his blue eyes to his mother, Kara

watched his little lower lip tremble. Clearly he was in a quandary, not knowing where he stood and whom he should obey. Any other time Kara would have kissed his trembling lip to reassure him that, although he'd needed to be corrected, he was still loved.

Now she hesitated, in a dilemma herself, not wanting to undermine John's authority, and feeling guilty about her son's distress in this unfamiliar situation. She watched unhappily as two big tears rolled down his plump baby cheeks.

John was the one to reassure the child, ruffling his hair. "It's okay, son. We'll share her."

Kara suppressed the urge to kiss her child and tell him it really *was* okay. She was beginning to feel more and more hemmed in by her new husband and family.

And she'd only been back in Homeplace *two* days.

Things seemed so different to her. Was it because she'd been an excited new bride that she hadn't noticed the underlying currents of hostility and competitiveness when she was here before, the strange ties that seemed to hold this family while they tore at each other?

She struggled with an overwhelming sinking sensation. She was exhausted, she reminded herself, trying to bolster her spirits. When she was tired, she became depressed; everything seemed more unpleasant than it really was. After she settled in, when a little time passed, everything would be different.

A haunting refrain reverberated in her head: Would it be better or would it be worse?

6

Kara was relieved when breakfast was over. Clearly Lorraine had been no better satisfied with Kara's choice of a full blue jean skirt and white tank top than she'd been with the nightclothes. Kara promised herself then and there, as the older woman boldly assessed her, that she was not going to change her way of dressing to please this impossible person.

The morning was still new; John had gone with his two brothers to the office; Priscilla had gone back to bed; Lorraine was helping Lorrie dress for vacation bible school. Only God knew where Dee Dee was, probably passed out in her room, Kara thought uncomfortably, recalling how demented the woman had looked last night. She hadn't come to breakfast with the others.

Before the stifling heat and humidity of the summer day surfaced, Kara decided to take Ricky for a walk on the riverbank. It would be good for him, and give her time to establish a more positive frame of mind.

She dressed Ricky and herself in jeans, T-shirts, and tennis shoes to protect against the thick brush and vegetation. The child was so excited he could hardly contain himself.

"Let's go, Mommy!" he kept urging, the incident that had left him weeping a short time earlier already suppressed. "Let's go."

"Just a minute," she repeated, laughing each time.

Lifting her son up in her arms, Kara hugged him tightly as she started down the hall toward the sun porch and the long winding steps that led down the high hill from the house to the river below.

Before she reached the back door, she heard the front doorbell. She paused a moment, expecting Thelma to answer it. As she waited, it occurred to her that none of the Worthingtons had had a single guest or a phone call since she'd returned to Homeplace, other than Agnes's frantic call this morning.

The bell rang again. Kara carried Ricky to the front of the house.

"Hello," Ellis said warmly when Kara opened the door. "I didn't think anyone was coming."

Kara smiled. "I thought Thelma or Priscilla would answer. John and his brothers have already gone to work. Lorraine must have left with Lorrie for bible school."

Ellis smiled again. "Well, I'm glad you're home." He looked a little awkward. "I was out of the country when you married John. I wasn't sure what to get for a wedding gift until I saw you last night." He handed her a large present, beautifully wrapped in rainbow-colored paper with silver and gold ribbons. "I'm sorry it's so late."

"Oh, you really shouldn't have bothered," Kara murmured politely, immensely pleased because he had.

Suddenly Lorraine appeared behind her, as silent as a ghost. "What do you want, Ellis Davidson?" the woman asked coldly.

Not the least bit daunted, Ellis smiled. "Not to see you, Lorraine Worthington, so rest easy." A pall seemed to fall over them both with the appearance of Lorraine.

Kara realized she hadn't invited Ellis into the house; angered by Lorraine's rudeness, she pointedly asked, "Please come inside, Ellis."

"He's not welcome at Homeplace," Lorraine said sharply.

Kara bristled. If she was family now, as everyone insisted, then Ellis had a right to visit *her!* "He's bringing a wedding present for John and me," she said.

Ellis touched Kara's hand lightly. "Never mind," he said gently. "I don't want to stay. I hope you'll enjoy the gift. Tell John I stopped by."

"I will," Kara said, watching as he smiled at her once more, turned on his heel and walked away with a self-assured stride.

Suddenly feeling downcast, she looked at the gift he'd handed her. It was a rather flat package about three feet long and two feet wide; she was having difficulty holding it in one hand and a squirming Ricky with her other.

"I want down!" he demanded.

"When we're outside," Kara said, her firm voice shushing him. Brushing past her mother-in-law, she took the present to John's room, placed it on the bed, then went out back through the sun-porch door.

She didn't know what was wrong between Ellis and Lorraine; apparently the feud was a bitter one that left each party with no respect for the other.

"I want down!" Ricky said again, intruding upon Kara's speculation.

When she put him on his feet, she remembered that she'd intended to take time to correct him for his earlier errant behavior.

"Ricky," she said, crouching down so that they were eye to eye, "you behaved like a bad boy when you hit Daddy-John this morning. I don't want you to ever, ever do that again. Do you understand Mommy?"

Predictably, his lower lip began to quiver; Kara made herself be firm, determined not to undermine the lesson by humoring him.

"I want you to tell me you won't do that again."

He glanced at the river, then giggled to distract her. "Look at the water. Look! Let's go, Mommy."

Kara gently held his chin in her hand and made him face her. "When you tell me you'll be a good boy and not hit anybody else, then we'll walk."

"Okay," he said in a tiny little voice, looking down at his blue tennis shoes, kicking at small rocks.

"Promise?" Kara pressed.

Ricky nodded.

Only then did Kara kiss him, take his hand and lead him down by the river.

"Look, Ricky!" she exclaimed when a squirrel raced up a tree.

The boy squealed in delight, and they paused to watch the antics of the furry little animal. Soon sightings of other creatures—a noisy blue jay, a tiny turtle, and a bold green lizard—caught their attention as they made their way slowly along the winding river, which was lined by huge trees on each side.

Kara's thoughts were focused as much on the family she'd married into as on the beautiful morning unfolding around them. While she watched her own happy child, she couldn't help but think of the demons that drove Dee Dee to drink to blot out the world.

Of her two sisters-in-law, she felt more kindly toward Dee Dee; part of it was pity, she knew, but part was because Priscilla was too much of a social climber to suit her. She'd noticed that at the wedding, and at the party last night.

Still, she cautioned herself against making judgments too quickly. All of this was new to her. The people and the place.

She and Ricky both saw Bucky at the same time. He was leaning over a huge root, peering into the murky river water. Kara thought he was talking to himself, or maybe he was singing. As though he sensed them, he looked over his shoulder.

"Hi, Kara," he said breathlessly, hurrying in her direction. "I didn't know you liked the river." He tickled Ricky's tummy. "Hi, little guy. Do you like the river, too?"

"Hi, Bucky. We were just getting some exercise," Kara said, trying to make harmless conversation. "Ricky loves the animals."

"We saw a fuzzy squirrel," Ricky said excitedly.

"What were you watching in the water?" Kara asked Bucky. "Can we see fish?"

"Fish?" Bucky repeated. He glanced back over his shoulder. "There are fish in the river," he said, tugging on his ear, "but I wasn't watching them. I mean they weren't there where I was. There was nothing there—just the water. You can't see anything. Of course, there are twigs and stuff, but you can't see fish or anything."

"Oh," Kara said. Her question was so simple, and yet he seemed to take forever to answer it.

Unexpectedly, Bucky reached out toward Kara's blond hair. He didn't touch it, yet she almost felt like his fingers were in it.

"The sunlight's dancing in your hair," he said. "It looks very pretty."

"Thank you, Bucky," she said, a bit disconcerted by his gesture.

His brown eyes held hers. Something about his expression, or maybe the way he held his hand out toward her, reminded Kara of Dee Dee last night.

"Can I touch your hair?" he asked tentatively, childlike.

For some inexplicable reason, the request made Kara squeamish. She wanted to refuse, yet it seemed childish on her part. Bucky reminded her of a neglected little boy, and she was concerned about him.

She nodded, then found herself bracing for his touch.

He very lightly ran his fingers down the long length of her hair, then quickly jerked his hand back, clasped his fingers into a fist and held them tightly as if he'd captured something.

Trying to joke, Kara asked, "Did my hair fall out in your hand?"

Bucky shook his head. "No. I didn't hurt it," he said quietly. "I touched it gently. It felt silky, like satin."

Kara laughed a little nervously. "It's only hair, Bucky. Dead skin cells, I think is all hair really is."

He looked confused. "How can anything so beautiful be dead?" he asked.

Shrugging, she continued, "It requires an excellent shampoo, a healthy diet to keep the root shafts alive, and plenty of washing to look good."

Bucky stared at her a moment, then gazed reflectively over his shoulder at the tree roots. A healthy diet and plenty of washing worked for them, too.

He quickly turned back to Kara. *That* wasn't what *she* was talking about. It wasn't what *he* was talking about. He'd meant to tell her how much he liked her. Because he really, really did like her.

"You were nice to me this morning," he said solemnly. "I won't forget it."

Kara was embarrassed by his serious tone. She shrugged. "It was nothing. I do think you have a right to be an actor if that's what you want."

"It *was* something!" he said fiercely. "Nobody understands except you. Not even Mother. Certainly not my brothers. You saw how mean John was to me."

Kara felt obligated to speak up on her husband's behalf. "He sincerely felt that you should have spoken to Agnes," Kara murmured.

Bucky didn't seem to hear her. He looked at the river, his brown eyes wearing the same blank expression Kara had seen in Lorraine's when she stared out the window.

"The town people are impressed because Mother's rich *and* religious," he said vaguely. "They don't even know her, but they think they do." Kara had the feeling Bucky wasn't speaking to her as he continued. "They *tolerate* me because of Mother. Melvin said so. He also said they think I'm weird."

He looked at her, then he smiled sweetly, suppliantly. "You don't think I'm weird, do you, Kara?"

Her first impulse was to say he wasn't weird compared to the other members of his family, though, of course, she didn't. She could see how much her approval meant to Bucky and how deeply troubled he was.

"No, I don't," she said gently. "We're all searching for happiness in this life, and we're all seeking it in different ways. Don't let other people's words hurt you."

She found herself thinking that she should take her own advice. Lorraine had upset her with comments about

BLOODY WATERS

Ricky. John had hurt her. She, also, was reacting too sensitively to everyday life at Homeplace.

"I could tell when you stood up to John that you cared about me," Bucky said in a voice that was almost a whisper. "So I want you to know that you don't have to be afraid of anything here. *I'll* take care of you."

Kara didn't know whether to smile or be frightened by the peculiar heroic offer. Bucky's expression was solemn. He seemed so—so dead serious that she decided it would be inappropriate to attempt another joke.

She studied his gentle features, and determined that he was like a fish out of water in the Worthington family. She didn't believe he could take care of himself, much less her, but she was moved by his staunch support.

Perhaps he needed a friend badly. He was a solitary individual, an artistic island lost in a family of blustering, macho lawyers, unfriendly sisters-in-law, and a virulent mother.

And maybe she needed a friend, too, Kara told herself. She hadn't made much headway in that direction. She thought of Ellis and the present waiting in John's bedroom; it had been spoiled by Lorraine's rudeness.

Kara smiled at Bucky. "Thank you for your kind offer."

He stared at her a moment longer, then murmured, "I'm sorry about last night, Kara."

She could feel herself tensing. "About what last night?" she murmured.

"Dee Dee wouldn't let me make Ricky be quiet. I know you and John were trying to sleep. I know how tired you were by the time you got home from the party." He looked at the river, mumbling to himself again. "And I know John is real upset about the Asterson case." He really did hate to see John brooding over it.

When he turned back to Kara, he said, "I heard Ricky, and I didn't want you and John to wake up, so I tried to help, but I couldn't."

"John and I hadn't gone to sleep yet when Ricky cried out, Bucky," Kara said carefully. "We were—talking. Didn't you hear us?"

B. L. Wilson

He looked too innocent to be lying, Kara told herself as he noted, "My room is over Ricky's, not John's."

She nodded. "I know where your room is." She couldn't believe how relieved she felt. Lorraine hadn't heard. Thelma hadn't heard. Bucky hadn't heard her and John.

At least one worry had been removed by her walk along the river. She knew that she had been dreading the thought of making love to John in that house again. It troubled her because she was so bothered about it, but she couldn't seem to help it.

She had one other awful nagging worry. "Bucky, did you put a doll in Ricky's bed?"

"What?" he asked, looking at her oddly.

She sighed. "There was a doll in Ricky's bed when I went to check on him this morning."

Bucky glanced away. "No, I didn't do it," he murmured. "Dee Dee is the only one who has—"

His words wandered off. He remembered he wasn't supposed to say that.

"Dee Dee has what?" Kara pressed.

Bucky seemed totally engrossed in the river.

Kara knew the conversation was over. What was it Dee Dee had? A doll? Did that poor wretched woman have a doll? And had she left it in Ricky's room? And why put a pillow over its head? God, this family was really beginning to frighten her!

"I do like you, Kara," Bucky said openly, like a child warming up to an adult.

"I like you, too, Bucky." She honestly did. She didn't know if it was because she felt so sorry for him or if, oddly, she found him the most sane of the Worthingtons. Certainly he was the most vulnerable.

"I know," he said.

Before she could respond, he motioned enthusiastically. "Come this way. I'll show you some special places on the river. I've played here since I was a boy. Ricky will love them."

He looked down at the two-year-old who was entertaining himself with a stick and pile of leaves.

BLOODY WATERS

"Well, he'll love them when he's older," Bucky said. Not waiting for Kara to agree, Bucky rushed off in the direction of the house. Ricky, eager for motion, hurried after his uncle.

Kara called out, "Bucky, we just came from that way. I want to go in this direction. I've seen that island of trees from the top of the hill. I want to see it closer up."

Bucky tugged on his ear. "You don't want to do that, Kara. The underbrush is too thick." He pointed to the almost junglelike density of vegetation off the beaten path.

"We can stay on the path," she said.

"It's not a good place to walk," Bucky explained. Then, as he got a vacant look in his eyes, he murmured almost imperceptibly, "Besides, the stench lingers there."

"The stench?" she asked, puzzled.

"What?" he asked, looking at her again.

"You said something about a stench," she repeated uncertainly.

He paused for a moment, then plunged on. "Draper Dewberry's body was found in that direction. You know, one of the guys Asterson murdered months ago. His body lay rotting in the shallow ground until the river rose and washed it downstream."

He wrinkled his nose for emphasis. "I can just about smell the stench every time I go by." He waited to see what she would say.

She was pale.

"Anyway," he said more brightly, not wanting her to be too upset, "everything's prettier this way."

Kara looked back over her shoulder. She hadn't known the murdered teenager had been discovered so close to the house. She didn't want to ask, but she couldn't seem to stop herself. "And the other one? Where was he found?"

Bucky pointed in the direction Kara and Ricky had been traveling when they encountered him. "Way down there."

"Why wasn't I told it wasn't safe to walk on the river?" she asked through clenched teeth; she couldn't believe no one had warned her before.

Bucky smiled again. "It *is* safe now, Kara. The only

place not safe is that projection of rocks near the Homeplace steps. There's an eddy in the water there. Anyway, *you* don't have to worry. The evil is over. It's just the smell of wickedness that lingers. We'll go this way instead. That's all.''

He was looking at her, but he seemed to be seeing someone else. "When the rain washes everything clean again, then we can go downriver."

Kara shuddered as if, the old saying went, someone had stepped on her grave. She *didn't* want to go downriver.

"Oh, no. Oh, no, no," Kara moaned. She stepped nearer the edge of the river. The foul smell wrapped around her, enfolding her in its filth. She wanted to pull back, but she couldn't seem to. Her feet were stuck in the muddy bank. She was trapped!

She fought to turn away, but the noise compelled her to look at the water. There was something splashing in the river. Something so horrible that she didn't want to see it, yet she couldn't stop herself from leaning over to look. And then she was falling. Falling. Falling!

Kara gasped aloud as she jerked awake from the nightmare to the relative newness of having a man in bed with her. After a week, she wasn't accustomed to sleeping with John. He wrapped his arms around her and drew her close.

The efficient air-conditioning system in the old mansion was set at sixty-two, the way the family liked it. Despite the unfamiliar summer nights swollen with sweat-inducing humidity which lay over everything like a soggy blanket, the temperature inside was too cold for Kara; she felt a shiver over her skin as John's chilled body molded to hers.

"Having trouble sleeping?" he murmured.

"Oh, John," she said tiredly, "I guess it was only a nightmare, but it seemed so real. I don't know if it was triggered by an actual noise I heard, or if it was all part of the bad dream. I dreamed I was investigating a strange sound somewhere down by the river. I didn't mean to wake you," she whispered, trying to relax in his arms.

"You're just upset over the talk about the murders because Toby Chaney still hasn't called his mother," he said. "He's a thoughtless, selfish little punk. He's probably feeling his oats and purposely hasn't bothered to check in. He was always rebellious, detesting the way Agnes babied him."

Kara sighed wearily, and before she could say anything, John continued. "There's nothing out there to harm you, honey. If you did hear anything, it may have been a deer fleeing from a howling dog, or some other nocturnal creature stirring about. The murders happened months before you considered moving here. Although I don't think Asterson committed them, whoever did probably has long since moved on."

Because Kara knew that he was trying to reassure her, she didn't bother to mention the fact that just last week he'd told Bucky other people *did* get killed. She didn't mention it because it wasn't uppermost in her mind.

She struggled with a way to tell John that the talk of murdered victims washing up from watery graves was gruesome and horrible, especially since the Worthingtons lived on the river and she and John were building a house on it, farther up; but the killings weren't her most compelling problem.

How could she explain that she felt like she was living among strangers whose behavior was bizarre to her? Even he, the man she'd met and fallen in love with in California, sometimes seemed unknown to her. She loved him, but did she know him?

She *couldn't* tell him, because she kept hoping that he and Lorraine were right. After all, a week wasn't long enough to adjust to such foreign surroundings, such unfamiliar behavior, such peculiar personalities, such a restricted way of life.

John was busy all day with his law practice, and often he worked far into the night. Bucky was her only friend, and she was becoming apprehensive about him, afraid that she'd made a mistake encouraging him. Like Lorraine, he seemed, at times, to drift off in the middle of a conversation, to say and do odd things that made her question just how confused he was. And he'd begun to follow her around.

"I'm not afraid of the river, John," Kara told him truthfully. "Ricky and I take walks there each morning. I told you that, and you said it was perfectly safe."

"Yes," he said distractedly, his voice sounding sleepy, "not only safe, but a good idea. I believe you're trying to face the river down. That's why you take the walks; I'm a firm believer in confronting your fears."

An edge crept into her voice. "I take walks on the river because I find it fascinating and mysterious."

She didn't say she never went in the downstream direction, the direction where Dewberry's body had been found, where Bucky said the stench was. That would only add fuel to John's fire.

Or maybe it wouldn't matter at all, she told herself despairingly. John didn't seem to *listen*. He was always one thought ahead of her, one theory up on her, solving whatever situation, as if everything she said was a case to be dispensed with so he could get on to the "real life" problem of saving Asterson from the electric chair.

"Exactly," he said. "*Mysterious:* mystery connotes fear, even if it's subconscious. I believe that's why you dreamed you heard something on the river."

"Lord!" Kara said in exasperation. She was reminded that her mother-in-law considered such idle references blasphemy. But then Lorraine Worthington considered so many things blasphemy. "Must you always analyze everything to death?" she asked, trying to make her voice playful, when she wasn't feeling playful at all. "Do all lawyers do that?"

He grinned, and she felt that he was proud of the way he dealt with every area of life as a lawyer. And he'd accused *Bucky* of not living in the real world!

"Guilty as charged. I'm in the analyzing business, honey. I get paid for it," he gloated.

Kara swallowed hard. "Well, Lawyer Worthington, you'd best go back to sleep. You have a busy day coming up."

"I *am* worried about my client," John said, as if he were offering up new evidence, though she'd heard the same thing every day she'd been here. "Asterson's had the deck stacked against him since the day he was born. The evidence is incriminating, but I'm determined to prove he's innocent."

"You'll get him off, John," she said. No matter how weary she became of hearing law in this house, it did soothe her to think that she wasn't wrong about this man she'd maybe married too hastily.

Underneath the Worthington bravado, and the sometimes arrogant demeanor, John was a good man. She believed that in her heart.

He shook his head, lost once more to his case. "Unfortunately, an indigent's defense attorney's hunch that his client is innocent won't hold up in court. Asterson was caught with Dewberry's wallet on him. He swears he found it near that makeshift shelter he called home along the riverbank. He has no witnesses, a bad reputation, and the need for money as a motive."

She could almost hear the wheels of his mind turning as he went over familiar information.

"Draper Dewberry and Raymond Lewter were friends who often spent time together on the river, supposedly doing harmless activities such as fishing. They weren't killed at the same time, but Asterson was in possession of belongings owned by both of them—Dewberry's wallet and Lewter's class ring. He could have stumbled on the items after the fact, as he claims, but it's hard to prove when everybody wants his blood. They want to solve this case and get back to small-town tranquility."

Kara shivered in the coolness of the room as John continued to talk, more to himself than to her. In fact, she was positive she'd ceased to exist for him. The idea alarmed her.

It was another trait she found peculiar to the family—the way they simply drifted off as their stories developed, twisting and turning away from the real listener until they seemed to discuss the tale only with themselves, asking and receiving answers in their heads.

Bucky certainly did it, as well as Lorraine. Kara hadn't,

thankfully, spent enough time with Melvin and Priscilla or William and Dee Dee to know if they possessed the trait to the degree that Bucky, Lorraine, and John did, though she had seen it in Lorrie. She was convinced Lorrie was a clone of Lorraine.

"There has to be a common denominator here, a clue I've yet to uncover, a tiny something that ties the murders together and frees Asterson," John murmured. "But what it is? What *is* it?"

"I know you're deeply concerned," Kara said.

"What?" John asked, as if he'd just remembered she was there.

"I know you're deeply concerned," she repeated, "and you'll find a way to help him. I believe in you, John."

"Spoken like a true, supportive little wife, honey," he said, in a way she found irritatingly condescending.

"I resent that, John!" she exclaimed, all her patience evaporating in that single moment. "What's gotten into you?"

"Me?" he said sharply. *"Me?* What's with you?"

"I'll tell you what's with me!" she cried. "It's almost as though here in Homeplace I've ceased to be the stimulating, intelligent woman you claimed you were attracted to in California."

John stared at her as if he were evaluating her comment, giving Kara time to squirm under his penetrating eyes, eyes she suddenly found remarkably like Lorraine's.

Was it because they'd married that John saw her in a different light? she asked herself bitterly. The wives in Homeplace seemed almost like chattel, expected to be subservient not only to their husbands, but to their mother-in-law as well.

Kara experienced a terrifying sense of isolation, as if she'd actually been brought to a foreign land. And, at the moment, she didn't believe the man who'd brought her here even wanted her!

7

When John did reply, he continued to speak down to Kara. "You'll learn that practicing real law isn't like the stuff on television," he said.

"I realize I know very little about the law, but I'm not stupid," she retorted.

John shook his head. "No, but you've been exposed to Hollywood too long, and to too much fiction. The good guy doesn't always win. It was just my bad luck to be next on the list for court-appointed attorneys when Asterson needed a lawyer. Still, I certainly don't want to lose."

Kara looked at him, startled. Was it the case or Asterson he was worried about? She wasn't sure.

John's eyes searched her face. "I don't want to lose you either, Kara. You haven't seemed happy since your return. Why don't you have Mother switch our room to the front of the house tomorrow? That way you won't hear the river as well."

Kara exhaled wearily and resisted repeating that the river didn't bother her. John's concern for her seemed genuine, and she couldn't help being relieved. She didn't want her marriage to be over before it had a chance. She was still clinging to the hope that things would be different once she and John left Homeplace.

"You wouldn't sleep as well," she said, letting her anger

ebb. "This has always been your room. You love the river."

"I love you," he said, causing her to catch her breath at the unexpected sentiment. Moments ago she had been ready to believe he regretted his marriage. "I'd sacrifice the room for you."

"It's not necessary," she said, softening toward him. "Whether I dreamed it or imagined it, I *will* get used to the sounds of the water," she added with conviction.

Now it seemed to be her turn to talk to herself. "I've always thought it would be romantic to live on the river," she murmured quietly. "I still do."

This just wasn't the way she'd thought it would be, living here with these people. She snapped out of her reverie. "You'd best go back to sleep, John. I don't want to add to your problems."

He traced her mouth with his thumb. "I waited until I was thirty-three to marry because I was looking for a special woman. You're that woman. We have a whole life ahead of us, and I want it to be a good one. If you're not happy, it *is* my problem."

Kara leaned on her elbow and with her eyes caressed his strong features. She wanted with all her heart to believe him. She wanted to wake up one morning and discover that the fairy tale had come true, that she was John Worthington's bride and her life was magical here in this picturesque town on a winding river.

"I love you, John," she said sincerely. "I'm sure things will be fine when we get a place of our own. I—I'm just not used to living with so many people."

She laughed, trying to lighten the seriousness of her admission. After all, the people she was talking about were her husband's family.

"Now we're getting to the point," John said.

Relieved because he was willing to discuss the situation, Kara told herself she'd been foolish to put it off this long.

"They're strangers to me," she said. "To tell you the truth, they're very different from what I expected."

"Yes, I realize that," he said. "In fact, I suspect in part

that the family atmosphere here has worked against you, instead of for you."

Kara bit her lower lip. The family environment she'd longed for, eagerly looked forward to, *had* been a huge disappointment. The camaraderie, the closeness—the love she'd expected to find among the brothers and their wives wasn't there. There was pettiness and jealousy and competition she'd never imagined.

An only child herself, she had yearned for siblings all her life. She'd been sure she'd been cheated out of some vital experience, even though she'd been adored and loved. Now she wasn't so sure she wasn't the lucky one.

"You have to face anything head-on, Kara," John continued. "That includes the guilt and remorse you've harbored over your parents' death. The incident has to be confronted and put behind you. I think my family has emphasized the void inside you. It's made you feel your loss more acutely—and exaggerated the role you played in that loss."

Kara was stunned. She'd told John that her mother and father had died in a car crash the same week she found out she was pregnant and the father of the baby refused to marry her.

While it was true she had mentioned she was concerned that her father's worry over her may have contributed to his driving carelessly or negligently, she hadn't said she felt guilty or responsible for her parents' deaths. No one could know for sure what had been on her father's mind at the fatal moment.

And she certainly *didn't* believe that coming here, being with John's family, seeing them interact, had stirred her remorse and guilt. He was right about her loss being more acute, but that was because her family had been unusually loving and close-knit, she realized, particularly in comparison to his.

Intuitively she knew it was futile to indulge this discussion. John *didn't* understand! Just because he'd confessed his love didn't mean they were communicating on any other level. Kara knew if they continued along these lines, they would surely get into a full-blown argument.

"Why don't we talk about it when we're both more rested, with less on our minds?" she suggested.

"Okay," he agreed. "You just let me know when you feel you're ready," he added, with what sounded like an incredibly generous gesture on his part. He laughed softly. "In the interim, I know what you need to make you sleep." He put his hands on her breasts and began to fondle them.

Kara wiggled away. The last thing she wanted right now was sex; she was, unhappily, beginning to realize that John felt it was the answer to any problem.

"Hey," he said peevishly, "stop pulling away from me."

Kara wondered if he had heard anything she'd said. His rapidly changing moods left her secure one moment and insecure the next. "I'm sorry. I'm just too wound up to make love."

"Why don't you spit it out?" he demanded angrily. "You're still sulking because Mother opened the wedding present from Ellis, aren't you? Well," he continued before she could answer, "it was to me, too, from *my* friend, and I didn't give a damn that she opened it. What was the big deal? It was only a painting of a California sunset. You hung the damned thing up right over the bed. What else do you want?"

"Yes, I hung it up!" she snapped, recalling how she'd lost her temper when she'd returned from the river and found the present open on the bed. Ellis had included a nail and wire, and Kara had used a high-heel shoe as a hammer that very minute.

"Then you and Mother both should be satisfied," John retorted. "She didn't want the picture in the house and you put it up anyway. Now it's settled, isn't it?"

Kara didn't believe that incident or anything else was settled.

"No, it's not. Your mother had no right to invade our privacy by coming into this room when we weren't here, and she certainly had no right to open a present that wasn't hers. I wanted to share that gift with you. It was a wedding present to *us*, not Lorraine!"

"This just happens to be Mother's house," John noted

in a surly tone, "and she opened the present because she hates Ellis. She's forbidden him in this house."

"Why?" Kara demanded, "and why do you put up with it? Ellis is your friend. Or, at least, he's *supposed* to be," she said with a dig, remembering that he'd used that line with Bucky about Toby.

John gazed pensively at her for a minute, then apparently decided not to take the bait. "Ellis and I have been friends since grade school. We became blood brothers—literally pricking our fingers with a pocketknife and joining them— down on the riverbank one night. He was born on the wrong side of the town, and Mother never approved of him, but I admired his determination and intelligence."

"I'm surprised your mother let you have a friendship with him if he was 'born on the wrong side of town,'" Kara interjected.

"My father liked him," John said, "and Mother was very generous to him, considering," he added sternly. "But Ellis, in his superior mode as a psychiatrist, managed to insult her by implying that one of the family could use a little couch time. She's never forgiven him, but *I'm* man enough to find room for both of them in my life, even if they can't get along with each other."

Kara stared at him, wondering how much of a man he really was. He'd admitted it was all right for his mother to come into their room, their only sanctuary, because the house was hers, and he allowed her to abuse his friend because of a supposed insult.

Instinctively, Kara knew that the disagreement between Lorraine and Ellis was a serious matter, regardless of how John dismissed it.

Kara couldn't help wondering which family member Ellis had meant. She lay tensely beside John, considering if she dare ask. She also pondered what it would take to solve their own problems. Maybe a marriage counselor would help.

She glanced at her husband, and to her surprise—and ire—he was breathing regularly, lost to sleep that eluded her.

In the scant brightness of the crescent-shaped night-light, she stared at John. He was nude, his strong, muscled body barely covered from the waist down by a silk sheet. His wavy black hair and attractive features made him unusually handsome.

Kara recalled how lucky she'd felt when she met him, how wonderful it had been falling in love with him and marrying him. Now she seemed to have doubts about everything. For days she'd given herself first one excuse then another. The town wasn't at all what she'd expected; many of the people she'd met were cliquey, class conscious, and judgmental to the point of bigotry.

But, after all, there were bigots everywhere, just as there were fair and good people. What really troubled Kara was what she believed about the Worthingtons themselves. About a way of life her husband had grown up with.

As she watched John sleep, Kara tried to convince herself that it was *because* she was an only child that she couldn't understand she'd married not just the man, but his mother, three brothers, two wives, and a child, all under the same rambling roof, all going on about something all the time, all—Kara felt—turning up unexpectedly and inopportunely, invading her privacy.

Of course none of that bothered John. These people she found so peculiar were his relatives. He saw nothing odd about they way they all lived in the same house.

And, she admitted, she hadn't thought it odd herself when her mother-in-law offered—no, *insisted*—that Kara and John move into the family mansion until their home could be built.

John's problem wasn't this house or his relatives. His problem was his murder case, defending a suspect who seemed almost certain to be convicted; that, and a wife plagued by sleepless nights and disturbing doubts—doubts which included him.

God, she was beginning to sound like a Worthington, like John, Kara told herself, going over and over the case, looking for clues that might absolve her from guilt for not fitting in, for not understanding, for not accepting the others.

BLOODY WATERS

Pulling on a robe, she walked down the hall and eased into Ricky's room. Gazing at his sweet baby features, she gently touched his blond hair. A rush of fear washed through her as she thought of her only child alone in this room, this pink nursery where not one, but two, baby boys had died.

Down on the riverbank a shadowy figure levered another big rock into the water between the two roots where the body had been left last week. It had to still be there. The boy had a cement block tied to his foot. He wouldn't wash up like the others. He *couldn't.*

This rock, too, seemed to go all the way to the bottom of the river. Wet moss made the rocks slippery, but the murderer picked up another one and carefully edged out on the huge root that stretched into the water.

When the rock was dropped, it seemed to hit something. It didn't sound like a part of the tree had been struck. Sighing, the killer relaxed. The body was where it should be.

Kara shook off her feelings of unease as she stared down at her sleeping son. The deaths of Dee Dee's babies were a terrible tragedy, but crib deaths happened frequently. It had nothing to do with the room.

John himself, and all his brothers, had survived quite safely in the same nursery, as had Lorrie, Melvin and Priscilla's daughter. In fact, the nursery had been painted pink for Lorrie.

Ricky was a vital, healthy, happy child full of fun and mischief. *She* was the one with the problem. Maybe John was right about the river murder being a big fear of hers, too. If someone killed her child—

"Lord, Kara," she said aloud, then caught herself. *"Gracious,"* she amended, testing a new phrase, "try counting your blessings, as Lorraine so constantly points out."

Exasperated, she forced herself to calm down as she studied her sleeping son before leaving the room. She was her own worst enemy. She had to exert more control, to try harder if she had any hope of saving her marriage. Nobody had to tell her that it was going down already, sinking like a stone under the weight of doubts, suspicions, and a sense of something almost sinister that she couldn't begin to comprehend.

As silently as possible, Kara made her way through the shadowy rooms to the screened sun porch that ran the entire length of the back of the hundred-year-old clapboard house.

John *was* wrong about her fears, but tonight, as she gazed out at the dark, brooding waters of the muddy river, she was reminded of what Bucky said about the stench of death downstream. She studied the black snake of water whose sinuous curves were highlighted by the moonlight, making it look menacing.

Had she heard something in the river at the bottom of the hill that dropped down at least twenty feet from the old white mansion? Or had it really been a nightmare?

Nightmares. Daymares. She couldn't distinguish in this house full of constant conflict and convoluted personalities. John's conversation had disturbed more than soothed her. She salved her own psyche by promising herself that she would try to speed up the construction of the new house.

When she went for her morning walk, she wanted to go upriver where their home was being built and see how much progress had been made. She and John had picked out the site, on family land, of course, during the three days she was in town for their marriage.

Her pretty mouth compressing unattractively, she recalled how her mother-in-law had decreed there was no need for her to roam about on her own. Lorraine's explanation had been that the Worthingtons had a place in society, a name, and that they were sought after by the wrong people for the wrong reasons.

Until Kara had been here long enough to know with whom she should associate, she was discouraged from meeting new people. After all, her mother-in-law had pointed out, Kara had her sisters-in-law for companionship, and entry into local society would come at the proper time through social functions.

Kara didn't give a damn about proper local society or proper time. It was all she could do to keep from telling her mother-in-law so; she was trying her best not to lose her temper any more than she already had. She knew John was growing impatient with her, but she was feeling more and more suffocated here.

How had so much changed in the time she'd been away? Or was the better question: How had everything appeared different in the three days she was here? Had the aura of new love and the consuming preparations for the wedding—engineered by none other than Lorraine herself, of course—blinded Kara to reality?

In all the excitement of new husband, new people, a new place, a new future, had she refused to see what she was getting into? She'd noted her mother-in-law's domineering personality. She'd seen one sister-in-law drunk at the wedding, and the other clamoring over the law elite who might enhance Melvin's career. She'd heard the brothers argue among themselves. And she'd suspected right from the start that Bucky had emotional problems.

Kara drew in a steadying breath. She'd been silly to think of her marriage to John as a fairy tale, a dream come true, instant happiness, served up in an old southern mansion isolated from the rest of the world in a backward little town on a twisting river.

She smiled a little, realizing more and more how much she herself had been babied, especially by a father who spun stories for a living. What was it John had told Bucky so harshly? That he had to grow up and live in the real world.

Well, maybe that was what she needed to do, too. Instead of feeling that her dreams hadn't come true, she had to work to build relationships within this new family where she felt like an outcast.

After all, there were seventeen rooms in the sprawling three-story house: space for everyone. Although Kara didn't stray far from her regular route, never venturing upstairs because no one invited her into their private rooms, she was seeing fascinating aspects of the grand old home from outside as she explored the grounds on her morning walk to the river. Still, it felt odd to live in a house where she felt restricted to the first floor, which she and John shared with Dee Dee and William.

The persistent, haunting image of Dee Dee lingered in Kara's mind. She hadn't seen her sister-in-law all day, and she didn't dare ask about her again after she'd failed to learn anything from Thelma the times she'd tried to question the older woman.

"Kara!" someone whispered.

Kara whirled around, jolted out of her reverie by the urgent sound of her name.

"Yes?" she murmured. For a moment she didn't see anyone, yet she was certain she'd heard someone. She scanned the shadows beyond the doorway to the sun porch. "Is anyone there?"

Dee Dee eased forward a little, just enough for Kara to make out who it was. Then, abruptly, she vanished.

Kara spun back around when someone else spoke.

"Hi, Kara."

"Bucky!" she exclaimed. "Where did you come from?" She glanced at the door that led outside to the steps to the river.

"My room," Bucky said.

Kara laughed nervously, thoroughly puzzled as she looked back at the doorway from the main part of the house to the sun porch. "Did you just come in through that doorway?"

"That's how people usually get out onto the sun porch," he said with a grin. "Where did you come from?"

"Well, I came from my room, too," she said, feeling silly. "But—" She looked at the main doorway again. "Did you see Dee Dee when you came in?"

Bucky frowned. "Dee Dee?"

Kara nodded.

"No," Bucky said, his frown deepening.

Kara wondered if she was seeing things. Had Dee Dee

been there? Or had she heard Bucky and been thinking so intensely about Dee Dee that she'd imagined she saw the woman? Lord, now she *was* going crazy!

"Are you all right, Kara?" Bucky asked.

She nodded again. "I'm just a little unsettled."

"Afraid?" Bucky persisted, seeing how wide her eyes were and how breathless she was.

"A little," she confessed. She was. Afraid and confused.

"I told you that you don't have to be afraid here," he said. "Especially not of me."

She smiled. If there was a single person in the family trying hard to be her friend, it certainly was Bucky.

"I know," she said. "I just didn't expect you to turn up here in the middle of the night."

He giggled like a small boy. "I didn't expect you to turn up here, either."

His handsome face was flushed, and Kara thought again how much he favored John. And yet he was so unlike John, so unlike any of his brothers. Strangely, despite his artistic temperament, in contrast to his mother's autocratic demeanor, he was like Lorraine in more ways than he was like his brothers, Kara thought, especially in his obsession with the bible.

Melvin seemed on target in his assessment of Bucky as a mama's boy. He had none of his brothers' aggressiveness, their competitiveness. The older brothers were like Lorraine in that way, Kara mused, while Bucky seemed to possess a vulnerability, a fragility that made him susceptible and weak. She'd seen how Lorraine could send him into a sweat with a single command.

"But then why shouldn't you be here the same as I am?" Bucky asked, drawing Kara's gaze to him. "You live here just like I do."

Kara saw that he was agitated, fidgeting, purposely pacing his conversation. Suddenly she wished she'd stayed in John's room. She hadn't expected to encounter anyone on the sun porch, and she had seen Bucky restless like this before. Inevitably, he rattled on like an old woman, and she wasn't in the mood to listen.

"Kara, do you know that song that says something about a stranger knocking at the door, and in the end the singer reveals that it's Jesus?" Bucky asked. "It was popular when I was young. It baffled me until Mother explained that in being kind to strangers, a person does Jesus' will because any of the strangers could be Jesus."

Kara smiled and shook her head. Yes, Bucky was like his mother with his religious references, right down to her interpretations. Kara wasn't quite sure what he was driving at, but she suspected he'd get around to telling her.

He reminded her of a child in many ways. Little boy lost. She believed that he was almost as alone in this house as she was: not quite the stranger, yet not a true part of the family, either.

"*I* want to be kind to you," he said solemnly. "*I* want you to feel at home here."

His emphasis on himself caught Kara's attention, making her wonder if he knew how lonely she felt in Homeplace— and why. Had Lorraine said something to him about her, or was she reading something into his disjointed chatter?

"Thank you, Bucky. I'm trying to. It looks like it's going to take a little time."

He looked away, staring at the river. "Even though," he said, pacing his words again, "Mother said the song meant we should be kind to strangers, she also explained that some strangers can be Satan instead of Jesus."

Having a hard time following him, or perhaps not wanting to hear his line of reasoning, Kara sighed. "So you're not supposed to be kind to those strangers," she said, almost unconsciously, wanting him to get on with his little sermon.

He widened his big brown eyes. "How did you know that?" he asked, as if she'd been a party to a secret.

Kara stared at him. "It simply sounded logical to me."

"Did you read in the bible that evil people, people of the Devil, are supposed to be cut from among good people, God's people?"

Kara shook her head. "No, Bucky," she said carefully, for she never had. But then, she was no bible scholar by any stretch of the imagination.

"Mother explained," he said patiently, "that the wicked are to be removed from the midst of the good."

She nodded. "I see. And who determines who's good and who's bad, Bucky? Doesn't your mother say judge not, lest ye be judged?"

For a moment Bucky seemed to be caught off guard by the question. He tugged on his ear. He scanned the sun porch as if the answer could be found there. His face became wreathed in frowns.

Although Kara wished she hadn't said something that resulted in Bucky's distress, she supposed in her own way she was trying to make him see that his mother's word wasn't law, nor was it always right.

Finally he relaxed a little; he seemed more at ease as he declared, "It can be confusing, Kara. Very, very confusing. But *we* don't judge: *God* judges. That's why we have the bible. That's why it's down in black and white for us to read and understand. So that we can be servants of God and can do his will, weed out the evil among us—"

Abruptly he tugged at his ear so harshly that he seemed to be causing himself pain. He studied Kara's face until she wanted to shrink inside herself without knowing why. She was trying to come up with some excuse to extricate herself from this awkward situation when Bucky said with vehemence, "Mother confuses me."

Bucky gazed vacantly at the river. *"Some* of the time she confuses me," he added almost beneath his breath. "I know I'm supposed to respect my parent. The bible says that."

He looked at Kara. "But I like you, Kara. I mean I really, really like you. And *I* will be kind to you. The bible also says do unto others as you would have them do unto you, and you've been kind to me."

Kara felt her stomach cramping. She was seriously beginning to wonder if Bucky was emotionally disturbed. His reasoning was off kilter. He was always at odds with himself.

As if to stress her point, he asked, "Do you get confounded by all the different bible verses? Is it only me?"

He pressed his hands to his ears. "Sometimes," he muttered, "they run around and around in my head, crashing into each other, getting jumbled in the accident, making me lose track of which one goes with what."

Poor Bucky, Kara thought sympathetically, her resolve to leave weakening. Lorraine had done this to him. Kara really believed that. And she wished she knew some way to make things easier for him.

"We all get confused, Bucky," she said gently. "The bible contradicts itself. It was set down by man, translated by man, and interpreted by man. It can be very confusing, even to the most learned religious scholar."

He looked both relieved and further perplexed.

Kara smiled, thinking she sounded like a pompous ass. Bucky was already struggling to make the complexities of the bible simple enough to understand.

"I'm sorry, Bucky. That wasn't much help, was it? It's the kind of thing I heard all the time when I was growing up. People of all kinds discussed every topic in the world at our house."

"They did?" he asked, interested.

She nodded. "And I was confused often, but enlightened a lot, in the process. The truth of the matter is that there are vast numbers of people in this world with many different beliefs. What's wrong to one person is right to another and vice versa."

Bucky stared at her in an extremely critical way before he spoke again. "Do you believe in God?" he asked.

The question was charged with emotion. Bucky began to tug on his ear, and Kara knew her answer was very important to him.

And, for some reason, it was very important to her to be able to tell him she did believe. "I think there's a supreme being, God, if you please. Yes."

His entire body seemed to relax. Kara hadn't realized how rigid his posture was, or how closely he was standing to her until he exhaled and smiled.

"I knew it! I told her." He suddenly fell silent.

"Who?" Kara asked gently. She was sure she already knew.

He stared uncertainly. Then he asked, "When you promise someone you won't tell something, do you keep your word, Kara?"

"Yes," she answered truthfully. It was something she'd been taught early on, and she was religious about it. She found herself smiling at her word choice.

Bucky smiled, too, sure that she understood that he couldn't mention who he'd told that Kara believed in God. He also believed he could trust her because she didn't treat him as inferior like other people did.

"I can show you more places on the river," he said, his voice eager, his eyes growing bright, the turbulence of the previous few minutes gone. "In fact, I can show you lots of things—things that no one else knows about—secrets between you and me, but not secrets I promised other people I wouldn't tell."

A warning sounded deep inside Kara, that intuition she'd been tuned in to for so long. She wanted Bucky's friendship; she wanted to be kind to him; she believed that he needed someone with a—she hated to use the term—*normal* outlook on life, yet at the same time she instinctively knew that she shouldn't form too strong a bond with him.

In the week they had been walking on the river together, he'd become too dependent upon her. Throughout the day he sought her out.

She'd assured herself that it wasn't peculiar. She was the youngest of his sisters-in-law, and the newest—a novelty who'd come from California, the land of movies. Bucky didn't seem to know what to do with himself during the days, or the nights, now that college was out for the summer. His acting teacher took the season off to travel to London. Bucky was at loose ends.

Yet as Kara studied his animated face and wondered how to respond to his offer to share his secrets with her, something gut-level told her she didn't want to know anything about those secrets.

In fact, watching his glowing eyes and strange, half grin,

seeing the sweat suddenly forming on his furrowed brow, Kara wanted more than anything at that moment not to be here with her young brother-in-law. In fact, she wanted not to be here in Homeplace at all.

"What *are* you doing up so late, Bucky?" Kara asked, redirecting the conversation to the earlier, safer one.

He grinned mischievously. "What are *you* doing up so late?"

Kara shrugged. "I couldn't sleep."

Bucky imitated her gesture. "Me, either," he said, giving her that sweet smile of his, which he seemed to reserve for only her.

His gaze unintentionally slid over her lovely nightclothes. The azure robe set off her pretty blue eyes and caused her long blond hair to look like gold in the dim light. He could see her matching gown beneath the sheer garment. He could even see her cleavage.

Suddenly the thoughts started to bump together in his head again. *Was* he looking at his brother's wife's nakedness? And *was* Kara legally John's wife in the eyes of God, the only place that counted?

"I didn't expect to find anyone else out here on the sun porch," Kara explained, indicating her thin robe when she saw him staring. "I was in bed for quite some time, but you don't look like you've been to bed at all tonight," she said, noting that he still had on the clothes he'd worn during the day.

He jerked as though he were coming out of a trance. "What?"

She smiled. "I was wondering if you'd been to bed yet tonight. I think you just answered my question. You look like you're falling asleep right here."

Bucky shook his head. "No, I wasn't listening—I mean I was listening, but I was hearing something else in my head."

When Kara frowned, Bucky hastened on. "No, I haven't been to bed yet."

"No?" she asked. "What do you find to do here until the wee hours of the morning?" She really was curious.

BLOODY WATERS

Bucky studied her speculatively. He had a sudden urge to tell Kara about *the* secret that bothered him so badly that he couldn't sleep at nights.

But would she understand? He'd sort of been trying to explain about good and evil for a while now, and she had seemed to know exactly what he was talking about. However, what would he do if she didn't?

He met Kara's eyes. What if Mother was right about this sister of Satan?

"Just things," he said. "Talking to people." That wasn't a lie.

"Friends?" she asked, smiling. Did Bucky have friends after all? She saw it as a good sign, something to be encouraged.

"Yeah," he said slowly. "Kind of."

Kara suddenly remembered Toby. Bucky must have been talking to him on the phone.

"Was it Toby?" she asked.

Bucky tugged on his ear. How had she known? He nodded. "I called him."

Kara couldn't help but think what a relief it would be to Agnes to know that her son was all right. She was about to bring up the subject when someone swept into the room like a whirlwind, startling her so badly she lost her voice.

8

"Buchannan!"

Lorraine Worthington's low, commanding voice caused Kara's heart to beat madly. Bucky didn't seem to fare any better as his eyes grew huge and dark.

"A secret," he hurriedly whispered. "You promised."

Kara tensed as Lorraine strode into the room.

"Buchannan?"

"What Mama?" the dark-haired son asked, instantly obedient, his smile evaporating, the sweat Kara had noticed earlier now beading his brow like drops of blood seeping from a fresh wound.

"What are you doing out here at this hour, son?"

Lorraine's dark eyes raked over Kara as if to ask the same question of her. For a moment Kara felt that she should be as subservient as the son; she desperately fought to dismiss the idea.

She had seen how sons and daughters-in-law alike bent under Lorraine's smile-shrouded commands. She would not let it happen to her. Some survival instinct in the very core of her rebelled against it.

She had already vowed that she wouldn't let Lorraine manipulate her. She'd dealt with difficult people before, temperamental people, but she admitted to herself that Lorraine Worthington was the kind of woman she would have turned her back on forever if she had any choice.

She and her mother-in-law seemed to be engaged in some kind of contest, and for Kara the prize wasn't to win the woman over, but merely to keep her head above water, to remain her own person until she could get out of this house with her personality and perspective reasonably intact.

Kara gave her attention to Bucky when he answered his mother, "I heard someone out here. I came to check."

"And you?" Lorraine demanded.

Kara unconsciously drew her robe around her body. While she enjoyed pleasing John with her lingerie, she was embarrassed by Lorraine's condemning look. She recalled Lorraine ordering John and her to dress for breakfast her second morning here.

Surely she wasn't expected to dress when she got up in the middle of the night. She made herself speak calmly as she met Lorraine's penetrating gaze.

"I couldn't sleep. I thought if I came out here, I wouldn't disturb anyone else." She indicated the lovely screened-in sun porch which featured windows beginning midway up the paneled walls and going to the ceiling, with a panoramic view of the river and grounds.

Then her gaze scanned Lorraine, who, at one A.M., was dressed in day clothes, a fact that intrigued Kara. She hadn't seen the matriarch of the Worthington family in anything except extremely feminine dresses and high-heeled shoes, fashionable, as befitted a wealthy woman who was part of the elite of local society.

However, such attire seemed peculiar for one o'clock in the morning. She wanted to ask the other woman what she was doing up so late, but ruffling Lorraine's feathers further wouldn't help the situation.

"And, pray tell, what woke you this time?" Lorraine asked, her dark eyes riveting. "Was it a howling dog, or was it squirrels on the roof?"

A faint flush crept over the young blonde's ivory skin. "Actually," she said, feeling ridiculous at being reminded of the sleepless nights she'd suffered since her return, "I had a nightmare. I dreamed I heard strange noises, sounds like something splashing in the river."

A tiny film of perspiration was beginning to form on her brow, and though she told herself it was the humid southern night, she had a feeling that she suffered Bucky's malady: Lorraine made her perspire with her very presence.

Kara had wanted to escape the too-cold air-conditioning in John's bedroom, and she'd been comfortable—at least temperaturewise—here on the sun porch talking with Bucky. Now, suddenly she felt overheated; she was in a literal sweat.

She truly felt as if she were being interrogated by Lorraine. She had a sense of kinship with Bucky in more ways than one, having just had a lesson in how quickly this woman could cause the body to react alarmingly. She'd also learned how it felt to be under the gun as Bucky had been when John demanded answers of him.

Unexpectedly, Lorraine laughed quietly, a restrained laughter suitable to a lady from another time. Although Kara was wary, she dared to let her guard down a little.

Stepping nearer her newest daughter-in-law, Lorraine said, "You'll get used to the sounds of the river and small-town southern life, Kara. You're a big-city girl. You haven't adjusted yet. You probably heard an owl searching for his meal along the riverbank. They're nocturnal, carnivorous creatures, you know."

Kara nodded. She couldn't hide her relief; she felt like Lorraine had just taken her down off the rack. "John said it might have been a deer chased into the water by a dog."

"Did he hear it, too?" Bucky asked, eyes suddenly alert.

"No." Kara shook her head. "I'm not even sure *I* did. Perhaps it was only a nightmare. John insists I simply haven't settled into my surroundings yet."

"As I said, dear," Lorraine stressed, her ever-regal bearing appearing a bit less stiff. Her pale, censuring lips curved more fully, though her dark eyes remained cold.

Kara drew in a steadying breath. "I'm sorry I woke you." Thinking the statement inappropriate to a woman who was fully dressed, she amended, "Or disturbed you. I guess you weren't in bed."

The smile vanished from Lorraine's mouth. "What makes you say that, Kara? It's one in the morning. Where else would I have been?"

Faltering, Kara felt the return of unease that had begun to fade in the face of Lorraine's reassurances. "I thought—you—" She indicated her mother-in-law's clothing.

Lorraine stood straighter, her thin, almost girlish figure rigid. "*I* was taught never to appear in front of anyone but my husband in night attire. The *bible* teaches us that."

"I didn't mean to offend you, Lorraine," Kara said evenly.

She reminded herself that she was a guest in someone else's house, no matter how many times she was told she was family now. Lorraine had her own set of rules for people under her roof.

"You didn't offend *me*," Lorraine said, curiously emphasizing herself. "You have learned one way of life and I another."

She smiled faintly, but Kara took no solace in the dry partial curve of the woman's thin lips. "John has brought you into this home—his home as well as mine—and we all want you to adjust. I accept that much of your behavior comes from your ignorance."

Lorraine paused, but Kara was too stunned to think of what to say.

"Ignorance of our family practices," Lorraine continued, as if she weren't insulting Kara in the slightest, simply explaining life in Homeplace. "You will learn," she said, her eyes flashing with determination.

Stung by the biting words, Kara struggled to say how *she* felt about being at Homeplace without making a bad situation worse.

Bucky surprised Kara by casually asking, "Did you know that an owl's call means someone died, Kara?"

She stared at him. He seemed intensely interested in her answer. She found odd bits and pieces of her elusive nightmare floating to the surface of her mind, but she couldn't seem to grasp any concrete images.

"No, I didn't," she said, the words tight, unnatural, forced from her dry mouth.

"Bucky," Lorraine chided, "don't agitate your sister-in-law with superstitions. The poor thing's mind won't let her get any sleep as it is."

Although Kara tensed and clenched her hands into fists of frustration, she couldn't repudiate her mother-in-law's observation. She was under extreme stress; there was no denying that!

"Try to get some sleep," Lorraine said, her voice more even now. "Good night."

She turned away, obviously dismissing Kara. "Bucky," she summoned.

Kara stared after the pair. She'd never been weak or neurotic. She'd grown up a normal, well-adjusted, adored daughter of two very loving parents. Until Richard walked out on her, until her parents died, until she gave up her job, until she came here . . .

She sagged down on the nearest white wicker chair. Maybe she *had* read too much fiction in the past five years. Her grasp on reality was loosening. She had to pull herself together.

As Lorraine and Bucky lingered just beyond the sun porch, Kara couldn't stop herself from listening. Their hushed conversation was punctuated by the sharpness of Lorraine's voice and Bucky's whining responses. Kara strained to hear, even though she disliked eavesdropping.

She eased out of the chair and crept toward the door before she realized what she was doing. Abruptly she stopped in her tracks; now she'd been reduced to spying on people. No, not merely *people:* her husband's mother and brother. Dear Lord in Heaven, what was wrong with her?

She forced herself back to the rows of windows that began at the heavy wooden border in the middle of the wall. Holding on to the ornate wood, she stared down at the water, which seemed even blacker now.

BLOODY WATERS

She couldn't help believing that something besides the river was dark and twisted here. She sensed it; the knowledge was as real to her as the deep, treacherous water that wound its way downstream, carrying only God knew what in its wake.

Kara didn't know how long she stayed there at the window, gazing unseeing at the river that seemed to move faster and faster as her thoughts whirled. The foliage was being tossed about by the wind that preceded a summer storm.

The screens were open and Kara relished the breeze that was blowing. The bushes and trees began to be whipped about furiously; Kara was hypnotized by the sight of maples and oaks and flowering trees trying to hold up against the fury of the elements.

Storms were rare in California, especially storms like this one, which seemed filled with power and violence. Trees dipped and danced and bent under the wind's onslaught, leaves flew through the air, and eerie sounds echoed around the building. Suddenly lightning flashed and thunder boomed, but still there was no rain.

Although Kara was frightened by the angry noises, she remained captivated by the river. The lightning had lit it ever so briefly, and she could see the churning of the agitated water. She couldn't help thinking how the storm paralleled the emotions inside her.

Then, while she gazed at the river below the bending and blowing leaves and bushy limbs, she thought she saw something large bobbing in the water downstream. She peered harder, trying to see in the single pale light that illuminated the outside and filtered inside the sun porch.

With the trees shadowboxing, it was difficult to focus on any single point. There was other debris moving rapidly in the water, but one object seemed caught on something, so that it jerked and bounced madly, unable to dislodge itself.

Kara was concentrating so intently that she didn't hear anyone enter. When a woman spoke, Kara spun around, her heart pounding, her legs weak.

"I didn't mean to scare you," Thelma Cain said.

"Thelma," Kara said with an embarrassed laugh, "it's all right. I've been jumpy since my return."

She almost added that so many people in the house made her feel ill at ease; however, she was learning not to open up to anyone.

"I'm sorry to see that you're troubled," Thelma said.

Kara bit down on her lower lip. Was her discomfort obvious to everyone in the household? But why should she think otherwise? She was getting up during the night, roaming about, then sleeping in the middle of the day because she was tired.

She found a smile. "It's nothing. I just need a little time to get used to a different way of life."

Thelma listened without commenting.

Kara fought the sudden urge to plead with the woman to talk to her about the Worthingtons, about Dee Dee's dead sons, about Bucky, about the odd goings-on at Homeplace. Although Thelma seemed sincerely sympathetic, Kara's previous experience with trying to elicit family facts from her proved futile; she feared alienating Thelma.

Still, the older woman's obstinacy caused Kara to seek some satisfaction by again questioning Thelma about Tessa.

"How long has Tessa lived alone?" she asked. "Isn't she scared because of the river murders?"

For a moment it looked like Kara had pressed her luck too far. Thelma's face was a mask of stone when she looked at the intruder from California.

"Tessa's safe in her little house," she said vehemently. Her gaze was drawn back to the river. "Nobody's going to bother my girl," she said, almost to herself. "Nobody!"

A shiver that had nothing to do with the storm went over Kara's skin. Even Thelma drifted off into herself. The peculiar trait frightened Kara; it was almost like an abnormality inherent in Homeplace—one she didn't want any part of!

"The storm looks like it's going to be a bad one," she said, in an attempt to bring the housekeeper out of herself.

Thelma appeared to welcome the change in subject. "Mmm-hmmm, it sure does."

Kara turned her attention back to the river. "I thought I saw something bobbing about downstream," she murmured, as much to herself as to Thelma.

Thelma half turned to look at Kara, her lined face more severe than usual. "You'll see all kinds of strange things when the river's wild and rising," she said in a tone Kara found ominous. "It's maybe best not to bother yourself about it."

Kara's palms began to perspire. Was Thelma trying to warn her about something, or was her imagination in overdrive again? Thelma, too, had been watching the river.

Suddenly Kara envisioned what she thought the two murdered young men's bodies might have looked like when they washed up; her lack of a frame of reference gave her fertile imagination free reign and the invented sight was a hideous one.

Since Thelma hadn't said anything that even hinted at dead bodies, Kara forced herself not to mention what was on her mind. Still, she searched for the object she'd seen before. It had been quite large as it teasingly rose to the surface of the water, partly submerged, then reemerged—like some ghostly thing ejected from a grave, she told herself, reclaimed, then ejected again.

She sighed. Thelma knew the river, and obviously she wasn't seeing such grim apparitions. Peering harder, Kara realized that she no longer saw it herself. Releasing a ragged breath, she conceded that clearly it had been her overactive imagination. She'd never seen the river in the midst of a storm.

Both women jumped when Lorraine appeared out of nowhere. "What on earth are you two doing standing here with a storm brewing and the windows wide open?"

Thelma's voice and expression lost all emotion. "I heard the storm coming, and came to shut these windows."

"Then why aren't you doing it?" Lorraine questioned, an edge of irritability in her voice.

"I'm getting to it as fast as a sixty-year-old woman can," Thelma replied.

Kara noticed that Thelma's voice carried neither sarcasm nor subservience; she spoke to Lorraine almost as an equal. The two women exchanged a look. Kara moved at the same time Thelma did and started to pull down the tall window directly in front of her. She felt Lorraine's fingers firm on the flesh of her upper arm.

"I thought you went back to bed with your husband."

Kara peered into those piercing dark eyes. "I'll go as soon as I help Thelma."

"Thelma doesn't need your help," Lorraine declared.

Although Kara started to protest, she didn't want to get Thelma in trouble. She had the distinct impression that she was doing that already.

"Good night," she said curtly.

She glanced at Thelma; the other woman was going about the business of closing the numerous windows that surrounded the sun porch. Kara looked once more at the river, then left.

When she reached the lovely French doors that led to the main part of the house, she thought she saw a small, wet clump of mud on the threshold—black mud like that on the riverbank, not the red clay soil that was found around the house. Automatically she looked at the door across the way, the one that opened out onto the stone steps leading down to the river.

Had someone been walking outside tonight? Perhaps Bucky or Lorraine? Or both?

And so what if they had? Although she certainly would hesitate to walk this late, Kara thought, that didn't mean the Worthingtons would. Still, she couldn't imagine Lorraine out on the riverbank in her high heels, and Bucky had said he'd been talking to Toby on the phone.

Kara froze when Lorraine came up behind her, interrupting her musings.

"What *is* wrong with you, Kara?" the older woman asked severely.

Kara felt her own fingers fluttering at her throat. They

seemed as if they didn't belong to her. She could almost imagine that they were caked with the mud she'd seen. She had intended to pick up the clump, for only God knew what reason.

"I'm exhausted from all that's been going on in the last two months," she said frankly. "The wedding happened so quickly that I was left with too many things to do to wrap up life in California and start over here."

"Could you be pregnant?" Lorraine asked unexpectedly.

Kara stared at her mother-in-law. Why hadn't she considered that? It would account for her mood swings, her tension, her topsy-turvy stomach. And her periods had never been regular, so she didn't chart them.

She'd had an awful time carrying Ricky, but she'd attributed it to the circumstances, the unhappiness of Richard not wanting her or the baby, and the death of her parents. She *could* be pregnant.

"That's a possibility, of course," she agreed.

A strange gleam lit Lorraine's eyes; the flame grew as her face became animated.

Kara thought she'd finally done something Lorraine would approve of—*if* she were pregnant.

"We'll have to make an appointment to see the family doctor," her mother-in-law said.

Kara nodded. The *family* doctor. Who else? she asked herself.

Still, Kara felt a small surge of elation. A baby might be the tie that she needed to feel part of the family. And she did want a brother or sister for Ricky.

"We'll go first thing in the morning," Lorraine said. "I'll drive you myself."

"Really, Lorraine," Kara was compelled to say, "I'm quite capable of driving a car." She didn't add that she wanted to go alone, that she wanted to find out if she were pregnant without an audience.

"You wouldn't even be admitted without me," Lorraine said smugly. "The doctor isn't taking new patients."

"Then how can I get an appointment, and so soon?" Kara asked.

Lorraine smiled dryly. "One of the advantages of being a Worthington, dear, is being able to get prompt service when one wants it."

Lorraine's eyes held the younger woman's. "Never forget, Kara, that the Worthingtons—and my family, the Stokeses—are very old names with many friends in, as they say, high places. You do understand, don't you?"

Kara was quite sure she did; she simply didn't care for the message behind the words. "Yes." In fact, she was sure she understood perfectly. "If you'll excuse me, I do think it's time I returned to bed. I'll see you at breakfast."

Lorraine touched her shoulder with what Kara would almost describe as gentleness: unfamiliar gentleness.

"Why don't you sleep in until I can arrange it all? I'll have Tessa bring you a breakfast tray."

"That's not necessary," Kara insisted. "Besides, I like to get up with John."

"Yes, of course," Lorraine agreed.

Kara had forgotten all about the mud until she crossed the threshold into the other part of the house. Now it didn't seem to matter.

She might be pregnant! That would explain so much. Everyone would feel better. She certainly knew she would.

Lorraine Worthington stared after the tall, blond woman in the slinky night wear. She despised vulgar lingerie, but what could she do? Her own son bought it for the woman. She pressed her lips into a tight line. She didn't like John's taste. In women or nightclothes.

Lorraine turned to Thelma. "Did you hear that? Kara might be pregnant."

Thelma nodded, but didn't say anything as she finished closing the windows. Lorraine didn't see the strained look on the black woman's face.

She wouldn't have cared if she did. Her granddaughter, Lorrie, was the light of Lorraine's life. A girl child! Finally, after the four sons she herself had had, there had been a baby girl to dress in pretty clothes, to cuddle and caress, to answer her lifelong prayers, to satisfy her dreams of a girl for herself, to stop William's evil seed.

Each time she'd gotten pregnant, she'd planned for a daughter. Melvin had been a disappointment, though he'd pleased her husband, William, so Lorraine had endured him. Then William had been born. Lorraine had been more disappointed; still, she'd done her duty. John had been nearly too much to bear after pleading with God for nine months for a little girl.

Fortunately, he hadn't been a bad child, and anyway, Thelma did most of the caring for the children. But Buchannan had been the *final* disappointment.

That had been it. No more tries for girls. No more hopes to live on. Another *boy!* All of the beautiful clothes and shoes and ribbons and dolls had had to be packed away again.

Her husband had failed her a final time. After all, it was the male who determined the gender of the child, and William had given her nothing but sons.

It wasn't that Lorraine doubted God's will, and it must have been God's will that she not have a girl. He'd surely heard her prayers. She couldn't understand it; but it wasn't her right to question God.

And then one day, in a blinding light, she was shown the answer to the question that had continued to torment her. Why hadn't God seen fit to give her a girl child? The answer was so simple, so awfully, tormentingly, vilely simple.

William hadn't only given her boy babies, he'd given her sin and shame and heartache: cheating and scheming, with his mistresses, his "office" help, his tawdry indiscretions.

An angry blush stole over her face as she recalled the first time she'd caught William on the couch with his secretary. He couldn't have humiliated her more if he'd hung a banner on Main Street flaunting his whore for the whole town to see.

Something clawed deep inside Lorraine at the degrading memory. She'd been a proper wife, a dutiful wife, accepting William's lust as her lot, having his sons, helping him move up the social and financial ladder, unaware that she was sleeping with an adulterer in a marriage bed that was defiled.

Shocked by his flagrant infidelity, she'd demanded to know why. And William had told her, stabbing her relentlessly with each sharp pointed word: "You're a dried-up, sexless old prude, Lorraine. You'd turn any real man away, and I'm a real man with strong needs. I'd prefer any woman to you in bed."

William Buchannan Worthington, her husband, had said that to *her,* Lorraine Leland Stokes Worthington!

Her family connections had made him successful. Her good name and standing in the community had helped William's businesses thrive. And he'd repaid her with his fornication, making her a party to sin.

Devastated, she'd turned to God for help. Down on her knees, she'd prayed for him to show her the way. Hour after hour she'd asked how she might purify herself. Shut up in her room, refusing to admit anyone, leaving her newborn baby to Thelma's care, she had fasted and prayed.

God had not deserted her. After three days He had spoken to her. He had heard her cry and He had answered.

Lorraine was drawn to one of the windows, oblivious to the summer storm which had become full-blown. Lightning flashed and thunder rolled, but she didn't notice. She was thinking about William. William long dead, rotting away these many years.

How many now? Twenty-two, of course, for it had happened shortly after Bucky had been born, shortly after her last disappointment. That is, the last one until Dee Dee had two boys to perpetuate the Worthington dynasty of liars and fornicators, spewing the seed of the Devil.

"Whoremonger," Lorraine mouthed.

"Mrs. Worthington?"

Lorraine blinked as she looked over her shoulder at Thelma.

"Oughtn't you go to bed yourself?"

For a moment Lorraine seemed unable to grasp what the woman was saying. She was lost in the deadly dark past.

"Mrs. Worthington, it's almost two in the morning. The

storm's real bad. You shouldn't be standing in front of the window."

Of course Thelma was right. Lorraine was putting herself in danger. God only helped those who helped themselves. Not the foolish. Not the reckless. Not the wicked.

"Good night, Thelma," she said. Lorraine knew that Thelma understood her place in the Worthington home; her years there hadn't gone unrewarded. Of course their positions and situations in life had prevented any kind of friendship, despite years of being involved intimately in each other's lives. Years of being allies—and, yes, years of secrets.

"Good night, Mrs. Worthington," Thelma said.

In minutes the woman had vanished.

Lorraine turned back to the window to view the swelling river. Her mind filled with memories of the beautiful, frilly dresses she'd once kept stored in the attic, the ones she'd bought for each of her expected girls. Those were long gone now. But she could buy more.

If Kara was pregnant.

9

The storm made Bucky even more restless than he'd been all night. Although it was after two, he couldn't stop thinking about Kara standing there in the faint light of the sun porch. He went to the ancient trunk with the padlock and opened it with the key he wore around his neck, disguised in the form of a cross, hidden away on a thin chain.

He wished he had a pretty robe like the one Kara had been wearing. Tomorrow he would go shopping. He knew where John brought Kara's lingerie. Bucky could almost imagine how the silky material would feel against his skin. *Almost.* His imagination was never a match for the article itself.

But he did have a wonderful imagination for poetry and music and dance. At first he had hated the thought of the dance lessons Mother had required to improve his social graces.

The music lessons were better, and had led to the discovery that he had a good voice. He loved to sing. He didn't mind the vocal lessons, even though Miss Pritchett didn't let him sing what he wanted.

In fact, now that Kara was here, he was glad Mother had made him take *all* the lessons. He wanted Kara to see what a good actor he would be: he could dance, he could sing, he could deliver lines in a strong voice. He knew that

Kara wouldn't be mean and critical when he sang for her or danced with her.

Bucky frowned. He hadn't actually considered dancing *with* Kara. He was getting confused again. Something disturbing had happened inside him when Kara came to the house. He felt his face turn red and his heart beat fast.

At first the idea almost panicked him. *Almost.* Then the more he thought about it, the more he got used to the notion, the more caught up in it he became. He really did like Kara. She was different from the other women he knew. She was kind. She spoke to him like he was a man. And she was pretty. His excitement was beginning to outweigh his fear.

Anyhow, John had once told him it took a real woman in bed to bring out the best in a real man. Kara was a *real* woman. He could feel himself begin to sweat as he remembered the night he'd listened to John and Kara, the night they'd returned from the party. He was sorry he'd had to lie to Kara about hearing them, but he didn't dare confess how he'd strained to hear each sound.

He'd never heard anybody talk about how wonderful it was like John and Kara had. He had crept downstairs so that he could hear better. He flushed all over as he recalled how both John and Kara had moaned and carried on—the things they *said* and *did!*

The noises had made Bucky start panting himself. And then Ricky woke up! Ricky! Mother was right about boys. They were bad. Ricky had messed up everything. Bucky didn't like Ricky.

He remembered how John had argued with Mother about Kara and Ricky. Bucky believed John didn't like the boy, either.

John didn't say much at all about Ricky, but he'd said plenty about Kara and how different she was from other women, how extraordinary and exciting. That was why John bought the sexy lingerie for her—the lingerie he let Bucky help him pick. He had explained to his brother—for his ears only—that the fancy fabrics on the right woman would excite any man. John had also told the story about a girl in college, and how she'd really turned him on to sex when he was exactly Bucky's age—twenty-two.

John had insisted that it was time Bucky found himself an exciting woman, but the only problem was that *Kara* was the woman who excited him, and he sure couldn't tell that to John! He couldn't even tell John how much he liked Kara, how deep his feelings were for her.

Mother had explained it to him once—the complex thing about feelings and how they couldn't be stopped, but *had* to be controlled, kept within the proper boundaries. It all got so muddled in his mind, what was proper and what wasn't. Of course, Mother had her own idea of proper boundaries, and they didn't coincide with most people's.

But that was a secret between him and her. He couldn't tell *anyone*. If he did, he would be in grave trouble.

The word *grave* made him think of Draper Dewberry and Raymond Lewter, who'd washed up from their watery graves. Bucky remembered how the police kept dragging the river, looking for anything else they might find. Their search had proved futile.

Now John was defending the suspect—Asterson.

Bucky's frown deepened. He didn't want to dwell on it. He wondered why John was so certain that Carl Asterson was innocent.

Anyway, he wanted to think about Kara and how her hair had looked in the golden sunlight. When he went shopping, he was going to buy himself a blond wig like her hair. He would drive across the state line to Greensboro so he could get lost in the crowd.

Right now he had something else on his mind. He opened up the trunk and laid out the prettiest dresses. He wondered which one Kara would prefer. Mother loved the frilly ones; Kara seemed to like simpler styles.

As he considered the selection, he began to make up a song, which he sang in a low monotone voice. "I'm going down to the river, going down to the river. I'm going down, down, down to the river. River. River. Down to the riverside."

Humming the melody to himself, he decided on a long

beige dress with golden threads woven through it. It reminded him of the one Kara had worn when she married John on the sun porch. Bucky had thought she was an angel that day. A real live angel, she'd been so beautiful. He'd never seen anything like her in his life.

That was when he'd started to think the new and confusing things about Kara. Kara and John. Kara and John in bed together. Melvin and Priscilla were disgusting to him. They grunted like pigs when they did it. No wonder they'd produced such a repulsive child. Bucky really did hate Lorrie. Mama had been so preoccupied with that brat since she'd been born.

He knew that Dee Dee and William didn't copulate much anymore. Except for the other night. He didn't want to think about that, either. He hated to think about those things that Mother had warned him against. He didn't want to remember that Dee Dee had blasphemed God. It was for sins like that Dee Dee's babies had died.

He stopped humming, thinking about Ricky again. Mostly he didn't like Ricky because Kara spent so much time with him. She brought him with her every time they walked along the river.

He suspected that Kara thought Mother disliked Ricky. Kara didn't know Mother really didn't like *any* boys. In fact, sometimes he thought Mama hated *him* because he'd been a boy, though it scared him to think so.

When the thought came to him, he tried to hold on to the times when he was little, the best times, the times of faint, pleasurable memories of him and Mother up in the attic. Times when she would help him dress in the beautiful clothes. He'd loved the silk panties best.

Mother got angry when he mentioned it now. She said it was a sin for a man to wear a woman's clothes or a woman to wear men's clothing. He'd tried to reason it out once, why it was all right for Mother to dress him in pretty dresses when he was little and why it was wrong for him to do it now. It seemed that the dividing line lay in the fact that the bible said it was wrong for a *man* to wear a *wom-*

an's clothes. He'd been a *baby* when Mother dressed him in dresses.

He'd been deeply troubled until he'd learned it was all right to wear the female clothes at certain times when he was acting. Actors, by the nature of their work or different status, or something—it was hard to remember what—were exempt from God's law about male/female clothing.

He began to take off his slacks and shirt. He wanted to see how he looked in the white and gold dress. He wanted to think about Kara.

Kara awakened feeling very tired when the alarm went off at seven-thirty. The sun was bright against the windows; she tried to shield her eyes.

"Good morning," John said, leaning over her. Apparently, he'd been watching her sleep.

Opening her eyes fully, she murmured, "Good morning." John's hand trailed down her neck to her breasts, undoing the ties on her gown. "What time did you finally get to sleep?"

"I don't know. Perhaps about two."

She'd been too excited by the possibility of the pregnancy to go back to sleep immediately.

"John," she murmured hesitantly, clasping his hands in hers to get his attention, thinking maybe she should tell him, hoping he would be pleased.

His dark brown eyes were still searching her face. "Yes?" he asked sharply. She realized he was instantly irritated because he thought she didn't want to make love.

She smiled uncertainly. Maybe she shouldn't tell him what she was going to do today. He might be too disappointed if she wasn't pregnant. Anyway, if she was, she wanted it to be a special surprise, something she told him herself, not something she and her mother-in-law announced.

"What is it?" he asked impatiently, freeing her hand. "I've got to get dressed for work."

Kara swallowed, glad she *hadn't* mentioned it. She wondered if John was like this only when he had a troublesome case, or was this short-tempered, self-centered impatient man the real John? Was the one she first met in California only relaxed and caring out of his own environment?

"I love you," she whispered, needing to say it, and needing to hear it. She pulled his head toward hers and opened her mouth to kiss him.

"You, too," he said, returning her passionate kiss. His hands sought her breasts again. Kara was torn between desire and regret as she submitted to John's caresses.

All the others were at the huge dining room table when Kara and John entered. Thelma had already brought Ricky down. He was sitting in a high chair next to Bucky.

"Mommy!" he squealed when he saw Kara.

Kara went over to hug him. "Good morning, sugar," she told the beaming child.

"There you two are," Lorraine said, a trace of scolding in her voice. "We've been waiting breakfast for you."

When her eyes met John's, he offered no apology. "You shouldn't have."

"Oh, Mumsy insisted," Dee Dee announced, attracting the rest of the family's attention.

Kara stared at her sister-in-law, wondering if she could have possibly seen this woman in the middle of the night.

Despite being only thirty, Dee Dee had the bloated appearance of an alcoholic. There were bags under her eyes that no amount of makeup could hide. Her face was puffy under disheveled red hair, and her stomach was distended in the too-tight blue dress she wore.

But it was the pain in her eyes that struck Kara, making her feel sad inside. If there was a family shame, a family secret, a black sheep in the Worthington clan, it was Dee Dee, Kara thought. It wasn't Bucky and his march to a different drummer. When some event or family occasion took place, everyone seemed preoccupied with keeping Dee Dee sober and suitable for the occasion. Nobody worried about Bucky.

Kara glanced at her youngest brother-in-law, who sat on the other side of Ricky. He looked fatigued today; he must not have slept any better than she after their meeting on the sun porch.

"Mumsy says today's a big occasion, and all the rest of the worthy Worthingtons have to wait for John and Kara before Thelma can serve breakfast, so let's get on with it. I'm hungry," Dee Dee continued, talking to no one in particular, her words softly slurred in spite of her sarcasm.

Kara stared at her sister-in-law. She surely had imagined seeing Dee Dee last night. She didn't think the woman would have sought her out on the sun porch and speak so resentfully today. The thought was quickly overtaken by a more urgent one.

Her heart pounding, Kara brushed her fingers across Ricky's hair before taking her place beside John. Surely Lorraine wasn't going to announce to the whole family their suspicions that she might be pregnant. Not now! Then, as if she were watching a movie, she followed Lorraine's progress as the woman, in a pale green summer dress, came to stand behind John.

"Guess what?" she all but crowed to the others.

Kara half turned in her chair. "Lorraine, don't—"

Her words fell on deaf ears. She met John's eyes; he looked at her expectantly, questioningly.

"Kara may be pregnant!" Lorraine announced. "We go to Roy's office today to see!"

Kara closed her eyes and gritted her teeth, wishing she were anywhere except here. She felt John's hand clasp hers, but she couldn't look at him.

"Is it true?" he asked, amid the noise and comments of the others making jokes about how quickly John had ensured himself an heir and offering congratulations.

Kara tried to be civil in spite of her anger. "I don't know, John. That's why I didn't mention it myself. Your mother and I were talking last night when I couldn't sleep. She suggested I might be pregnant. I didn't expect her to say anything this morning."

He squeezed her hand. "It's such exciting news that I'm sure she simply couldn't wait," he said, as though there was nothing wrong at all. Looking self-satisfied, he grinned. "That would explain your moodiness, wouldn't it?"

"Yes, in part," she agreed, a blush on her face.

Only in part, she told herself, thinking this was a prime example of what she considered gross invasion of privacy. She wished more than anything in the world that she and John were alone for this moment—and that she knew whether or not she was pregnant. All of this was so premature—and embarrassing!

Dee Dee clapped loudly, again attracting the attention of the others. "Bravo! Bravo, Kara!" she said tartly. "I just hope for your sake—and the baby's, of course—"

"Dee Dee!" William said sharply. "Shut up!"

"Why?" Dee Dee asked. "Shouldn't *someone* tell our newest family member the facts of life in this frigging white mansion, this mausoleum?"

For just a moment Dee Dee's eyes met Kara's. Kara sucked in her breath. Had Dee Dee been there last night? And was she making a show this morning to warn Kara of something in the only way she could?

"Jealousy isn't becoming, Dee Dee," Lorraine said coolly, scattering Kara's thoughts. "We should all rejoice in the news of a new life, shouldn't we?"

"Well, hell," Dee Dee said, her voice literally sloppy with the effects of too much liquor so early in the morning, "if we're going to rejoice, let's rejoice for two. *I* may be pregnant, also. How about that? Where's my standing ovation?"

Everyone stared at her as though they didn't believe her.

"Well, I may be!" she screeched. She turned to William. "Tell them, you prick. Tell them what you did to me!"

The room filled with tension. Lorraine glared at William, who lowered his gaze to his plate.

"No, *I* don't count, do I?" Dee Dee raged, standing up unsteadily. *"I* might have a baby who *dies!* Isn't that it? Well, goddamn-you-all to Hell!"

"William," Lorraine said coldly. It was only a single word, a name.

William stood up, grasping his wife by the arm, as if he'd been given a command. "Come on, Dee Dee," he said.

"Hell, no!" she roared. "Get your goddamned hands off me."

Kara saw his fingers close more tightly on Dee Dee's arms. She struggled, then began to sob and plead.

"Help me! Help me, oh God, won't someone get me out of this hellhole? Oh God, oh God!" Tears poured from her eyes as she tried to escape William.

Although Kara wanted to go to the woman, she didn't know what she could do. Dee Dee was so out of control that Kara wondered how she'd ever imagined that she read some kind of warning in Dee Dee's eyes. Lorraine, as much as Kara hated to admit it, was probably right. Dee Дее was throwing a tantrum because she was jealous of the possibility of a new baby in Homeplace. Dee Dee probably hated her at the moment. Dee Dee wasn't interested in her welfare at all; she was caught up in her own misery.

As Kara stared at the pathetic woman, she wondered why the family didn't take Dee Dee to a psychiatrist. If they wanted to keep it quiet, they could take her to John's friend, Ellis Davidson. Her desperate cry for help was pitiful and unnerving.

"Bucky!"

Lorraine issued the name exactly as she had William's. Bucky rose from the table and went to his brother's aid. Between them they began to drag Dee Dee from the room.

Dee Dee's shrieks and wailing continued for a few more moments, then stopped abruptly when a door slammed.

"Thelma," Lorraine said calmly, "you and Tessa can start serving breakfast now."

Kara felt her stomach tighten. She didn't know if she could eat. As if making a mockery of the possible pregnancy, or confirming it, her stomach lurched at the smell of bacon and eggs Tessa brought into the room.

"Excuse me," she murmured, then headed toward the nearest bathroom.

"Well," Lorraine said, "if we needed proof . . ." She let the half-finished sentence hang in the air.

Kara could hear Melvin laughing heartily. "You must have driven it home when you were on your honeymoon, little brother," he said crudely. "You trying to get ahead of my record with Pris?"

Kara clutched her stomach and hurried to get away from her brother-in-law and his vulgar comments. She realized that she didn't want to hear her husband's response.

This pregnancy, if that's what it was, was worse than when she carried Ricky. She felt like her stomach was on fire, like something burning and painful had gotten inside her.

Not a little baby. Not a child conceived in what she'd believed was love on their honeymoon in New Zealand, or on the weekend John spent in California. With Dee Dee's words echoing in her head, Kara slammed the bathroom door and immediately started throwing up.

Part of her wanted very much to be pregnant with John's child. But in a deeper, more intuitive part, she prayed that she wasn't pregnant at all. That she would have *no* baby while she was living in Homeplace.

She decided she didn't even want Ricky to be here.

"Stop it," Dee Dee pleaded, ineffectually resisting the rough hands that pulled on her. She winced as she was jerked off the bed. She had prayed for salvation from Homeplace, but as she was being hefted up onto someone's shoulder, she knew that this was another violation—not the escape she had prayed for. Despite her clouded thinking and the distorted reality of the situation, she had a frightening premonition that she was going to die.

But now she knew she didn't want to die, no matter how many times she'd told herself death would be better than the life she was forced to live. She'd only wanted to get away from this horrible place. Among the many thoughts tumbling about in her muddied mind was one that said her attempts to warn Kara had been her undoing.

Ironically, she had survived the deaths of her sons and the beatings and abuse of the Worthingtons while she had fought to come out of the drug-induced fog she lived in, and she was going to die over a stranger. No, that didn't seem quite true; she fought to sort through a mind as jumbled as the heavily wooded path she was being hurried along.

It was a path she knew. A path she'd heard about. A very short path. A path that led to nowhere. Or somewhere, depending on the place someone wanted to go. It wasn't where Dee Dee wanted to go, but that hadn't been what she was trying to think of. She vainly sucked at the still fresh morning air, wanting to clear her head yet knowing it wasn't possible.

Kara. She'd been trying to warn Kara. She'd really wanted the other woman to listen to *her*, to believe *her*—to *help her*.

Her stomach churned and she felt sure she was going to vomit. There was an unfamiliar lump pressed up against her abdomen; she couldn't fathom what the uncomfortable object was or why it had been placed there. Although she tried fervently to protest her fate, she'd been given so much medication this time that the saliva had dried up in her mouth. Speech was more difficult than ever.

"Stop," she mumbled, but the muffled word was absorbed by the back of the person carrying her. Dee Dee knew she wouldn't be taken far. It was early morning. People might be about. She wasn't allowed to be out this time of the morning.

"Hurry!" someone hissed. "Hurry, while there's commotion at the dam. That's the perfect distraction if you'll just get it over with!"

Dee Dee was sure her death was the "it"; she valiantly struggled to raise her head. Maybe she could alert someone to her predicament. Unexpectedly, the contents of her nearly empty stomach heaved out.

She heard an expression of revulsion from the person carrying her, but it didn't matter. Nothing mattered now. It had dawned on her that the path that led to the eddy was too far away from the dam and too overgrown with vegetation for anyone to see.

"God help your servant!" were the last words Dee Dee

ever heard, and the splash of the water was the last sound as the cold river engulfed her.

Kara had taken her time in the bathroom, lingering to splash her face with cold water and hold a wet cloth to her throat as she sat on the side of the tub. She was not eager to return to the breakfast table. She'd vacillated between going to check on Dee Dee and returning to the family. She was afraid she would only upset the household, and her sister-in-law, further. Anyway, what could she do? If there was any hope for Dee Dee, it was in some doctor's hands.

When she entered the dining room, John and Melvin were discussing John's case, with William, Bucky, and Priscilla for an audience. Lorraine was absent. Kara wondered if she'd stayed so long in the bathroom that everyone else had finished eating. Thelma was also gone; she generally remained until everyone was through being served.

Tessa walked into the room with a plate of food that had been warmed in the oven, and a pot of coffee.

"Thank you, Tessa," Kara said, even though she didn't think she could eat. She would try the toast, but she was too nauseous to sample the bacon and eggs.

"You're welcome," the young woman said politely, then left as quickly as she'd come.

Kara watched her, wondering where Thelma was. Kara was jolted back to the present when John began shouting at Melvin.

"Damn it, Mel, Asterson is innocent!" John bellowed angrily.

Although Kara was grateful not to be the focus of attention—John had barely glanced at her when she returned—she was disturbed, as always, to hear the brothers discussing their cases with each other.

She kept telling herself that it was normal, that a family of lawyers would do that, that it was unavoidable; still, it bothered her. Melvin, at thirty-seven, was assistant prosecuting attorney for the Commonwealth of Virginia. That often pitted him against his brothers.

It didn't seem right to Kara that they exposed their hands

so boldly, bragging about who would win, yet perhaps she was naive. She knew so little about it all, but she felt the fate of the defendant was really being decided at the Worthington table, not in the courtroom.

Melvin laughed. "Tell it to God, John, because he's the only one who's going to listen. That murdering bastard is going to die if Julius and I have anything to do with it." He winked confidently. "And you know Julius and I have a *lot* to do with it. Asterson had sex with Dewberry, then whacked off his penis. Lewter didn't fare much better. The jury's going to send Asterson to the electric chair."

"The jury's going to free Asterson," John refuted. "He's innocent!"

Melvin laughed more loudly. "When are you going to give up on that 'inherent good of mankind' theory? Asterson's guilty as charged. Man's an evil creature, born to sin, Johnny-boy. Haven't you learned that yet just by being in our business?"

John's jaw muscle twitched. "What happened to 'a man being innocent until proven guilty,' Melvin?" he demanded.

Melvin chuckled. *"I did!"*

Lorraine came out of the kitchen, crossing the floor to take her place at the table as if nothing had gone awry this morning. She smiled at Kara, but Kara didn't return the smile. When Tessa appeared with the coffeepot, Lorraine shooed her away with a limp-wristed hand. "Get Thelma to bring me fresh coffee," she insisted.

"Mother," Melvin said, "tell John how evil man is."

"Man *is* an evil creature," Lorraine agreed. "That's why God sent His only begotten son to save the world."

Melvin grinned smugly at John. "Mother knows best," he said mockingly. Lorraine didn't seem to notice. "The Good Book says an eye for an eye, a tooth for a tooth," Melvin goaded. "Isn't that right, Mother?"

Lorraine absently agreed, her thoughts obviously on something else. "An eye for an eye, a tooth for a tooth."

"A life for a life, in other words, brother John," Melvin needled. "The wages of sin is death, right, Mother? Asterson is going to fry like an egg on a hot grill."

Lorraine nodded vigorously, speaking more vehemently, as if she were just entering the argument. "The wages of sin *is* death. The bible says that plainly."

Kara looked down at her food, feeling her stomach cramp again. She knew that Melvin was ambitious, that he meant to go far in his career. Although she'd known him only a short time, she believed he would sacrifice anything and anybody to get what he wanted. And she knew he wanted to be a judge.

Kara glanced at Priscilla, who was clearly enjoying the debate between John and Melvin, apparently not bothered at all by the unpleasant scene with Dee Dee that had taken place at the breakfast table earlier. But then, perhaps she was used to it.

"You'd better get out your best arsenal and call in all your troops on this one, John," Priscilla said cheerfully, as though it were all a big game. "You know Melvin's right. You don't have a leg to stand on legally. Admit it." She smiled at her husband. "My Mel's too smart to let that killer go free."

"And John's too smart to let an innocent man die," Kara said, surprised by the ferocity of her defense of her husband.

John smiled at her, as if he'd finally noticed her. "Feeling better, honey?" he murmured.

Kara wasn't sure if he was referring to her physical condition or the fact that she'd just vented some of her own hostility.

She didn't regret the outburst. She considered Priscilla as cold and calculating as Melvin, a perfect match for the oldest son, a woman who'd given Lorraine Worthington the granddaughter she wanted. Melvin and Priscilla seemed to have done everything right.

And Priscilla obviously savored life in Homeplace. She apparently hadn't had any adjustment problems, any qualms about living here with the family.

But why should she? She was born and bred for this life. A successful husband. People to wait on her. A child to please her mother-in-law.

Kara glanced at Lorraine. There was a peculiar look in the older woman's dark eyes. Their gazes locked briefly. Then Lorraine smiled again and looked at her son.

"The moment we know about the baby, John, you'll be notified at the office," Lorraine said.

The brief flash of rebellion Kara had displayed still burned in the glare of Lorraine's bright brown eyes and odd smile when she glanced at Kara again.

"I'd like to tell my husband the news myself," Kara said, unwilling to relinquish more of her independence.

Lorraine nodded. "Of course, dear. I didn't say *I* was going to tell him, did I? I certainly didn't think I said that." She looked at John for confirmation.

Kara sighed. She couldn't seem to win with this woman, and challenging her was useless. Lorraine *hadn't* said she would tell John. It was because she controlled everything else that Kara had naturally assumed Lorraine meant to be the one to call.

Abruptly, Melvin looked over at William and asked in a low, hard voice. "What you going to do about your wife, brother?"

William shrugged, refusing to look at Melvin as he continued to eat, but Kara saw that his hand was shaking.

"I'm talking to you, boy," Melvin said, as if he were chastising a child. "She's getting to be an embarrassment in a big—and I mean big—way. Now what's the story? You going to put her in detox or not? I told you I had a check run on a center in North Carolina. It's private and they'd keep quiet about it or we'd sue their butts off."

Kara was momentarily surprised that Melvin was willing to support Dee Dee's treatment, until she recalled it was to keep the woman from hurting him politically.

William glanced up, then away. "She'd tell those awful tales about the babies, Melvin, and you know it."

"*Tell 'em!*" he bellowed. "Hell, she never shuts up about them. Anyway, so what? People down there are used to dealing with drunks. They know all about alcoholic hallucinators and how to handle them."

Kara stared at William, wondering, like the rest of the

family, what he was going to say, what he was going to do. He and Dee Dee fought like cats and dogs, and God knows the woman needed help.

Abruptly Thelma walked into the room with a fresh pot of coffee, her expression as unreadable as ever. "We just heard on the radio that a headless body washed downriver and hung up on a tree branch at the dam. That storm must have carried it there. They say everybody crossing the bridge this morning can see it. There's a terrible traffic jam."

"Who is it?" Bucky asked, a petrified look in his big brown eyes.

"Well, they ain't identified it yet," Thelma said. "The police's having a time getting out to it with the river so swollen and all, and *it* being right there at the dam on that tree branch."

Kara felt her heart begin to hammer as the woman matter-of-factly related the story.

Melvin jumped up. "I'd better get a move on, see what's happening." Ignoring Lorrie seated beside her grandmother, he gave Priscilla a wink, then he was gone, moving very rapidly for a large man.

John's eyes were bright as he glanced at Kara. "I'd better run, too. I'm not sure what this means, or if it has any bearing on my case."

He shoved back his chair and left without even telling Kara good-bye.

William continued to eat his breakfast. Kara wondered why he didn't leave, too, until she recalled a fight he and Dee Dee had the second morning Kara had been here.

Dee Dee had accused him of being less than his brothers: less bright, less ambitious, less able to stand up to his mother, and less of a lawyer—a ne'er-do-well who primarily handled divorces and petty cases.

He'd retorted by telling her he made enough money to keep her in booze, before Lorraine silenced them both.

Kara drew in a steadying breath as she looked across the table at her small son. Bucky was handing Ricky another biscuit, and the child was shaking his head no. Her own breakfast barely touched, Kara went around the table and lifted Ricky from the high chair.

"Let's walk," he called out excitedly, in anticipation of their established daily routine.

"Not now," Kara said. "I'm going to clean you up."

"No!" he protested, using his favorite word. "Let's walk."

The last thing Kara intended to do was go out on the riverbank this morning. The very idea of seeing the headless body made her want to throw up again.

Kara said "Excuse me" to the others and left.

She had already started down the hall when Bucky caught up with her. "Are you walking down by the river this morning?" he asked.

Kara looked appalled. "No! The thought of such a grisly sight makes me ill!"

Bucky tugged on his ear. Sweat had popped out on his brow. "I'm sorry, Kara," he mumbled.

"There's nothing for you to be sorry about, Bucky. I just can't imagine anyone wanting to see that grim sight, can you?"

His face red, he shook his head, but the moment Kara walked away, he raced through the kitchen and sun porch and down the steps to the river. Hidden from prying eyes, he took a secret trail he'd made long ago through the thickest of the vegetation.

Nobody knew about this tunnel- cut in the junglelike growth; Bucky was sure this time. He'd made the most treacherous trail he could, hacking his way through with a machete. He'd made a mistake when he told Dewberry and Lewter about the other one. And then, of course, Asterson had somehow discovered it and decided to camp out in the hideaway hut Bucky had made for himself.

But none of those people mattered now. Bucky *had* to see who was on the dam.

10

Kara sat down in the rocking chair in John's room, a squirming Ricky in her arms. What was she doing here in this nightmare? What was going on in this town? In this house? Dead bodies in the river, battles in the mansion, peculiar people in the house, strangers everywhere she turned. She felt like she'd lost her way in a maze without end.

She was pondering the question of whether or not to approach Dee Dee and try to talk to the clearly deranged woman when Lorraine abruptly opened her door.

"Do you know where Bucky is?" the older woman demanded.

Kara shook her head.

"Have you seen Dee Dee?"

Again Kara shook her head. "I imagined she would be in her room."

"Well, you imagined wrong, so help Priscilla and me find her!" Lorraine ordered.

"Find her?" Kara repeated. "Do you think she's lost?"

"Would I have asked you to look for her if I didn't?" Lorraine demanded, glowering at Kara as if she were terribly stupid.

Kara supposed it had been a silly question, but then the idea of Dee Dee being lost seemed silly, too. Her first impulse was to deny Lorraine's command; however, the sharp-tongued woman looked so frenzied that Kara relented.

"Leave the boy with Thelma," Lorraine snapped.

Kara did as she was told. There was no point in taking Ricky, but she didn't like being ordered about so coldly by her mother-in-law, no matter what the reason. She almost told Lorraine that Thelma could search while she and Ricky stayed at home, but she knew the woman would only become angrier.

"Are you sure Dee Dee isn't somewhere in the house?" Kara asked as she and Lorraine went toward the kitchen.

Lorraine shook her head. "She's not in the house."

"Did you ask William and Bucky where they left her?" Kara questioned.

"I just told you I don't know where Buchannan is, and if William knew where his wife was, *I* wouldn't be searching for her. Now will you simply do as you're told?"

Bristling with anger, Kara nevertheless went out the sunporch door and down the steps with the mother-in-law she disliked more with each encounter. She could see Priscilla in the distance following the path downriver. Kara physically clutched her stomach.

"You don't need me to go with you to the dam," she said, stopping at the bottom of the steps. "That's clearly where Priscilla's headed."

"Of course it is!" Lorraine declared. "If we need help with Dee Dee, *you'll* have to do it."

Abruptly, the woman launched into a bizarre monologue. "God must be testing me," she said. "God has seen the sin brought into my home, and He's testing me. Evil once removed has returned in another form. Jesus Christ help me be strong. Show me the way."

The look in Lorraine's brown eyes was so wild, so uncontrolled, that Kara decided she'd best go, no matter how she dreaded whatever might confront her downstream. She did know that Dee Dee could be violent, and both Lorraine and Priscilla were small women.

Strangely and shockingly, it occurred to Kara that Lorraine possibly thought Dee Dee was the body in the river. Her stomach lurched. She didn't want to think about it.

"I'll help," she said, causing Lorraine to stare at her. For a moment her mother-in-law didn't seem to know her. Then Lorraine strode off.

Placing one foot in front of the other, Kara hurried along behind the amazingly agile older woman. Her legs felt leaden. She'd never been a queasy, gutless type, but she didn't want to do this. All kinds of appalling thoughts chased each other inside her head. She was reminded of Bucky's confusion over the bible as her head filled with the most wretched possibilities.

She didn't want to speculate on any of this—where Bucky was, where Dee Dee was, or whose body was caught on the tree branch at the dam. But she couldn't help it.

Toby was still missing.

No! She couldn't bear to think about him, either, and she didn't even know him. Besides, Bucky had said he'd talked to Toby last night.

A sudden vision of Bucky leaning over the huge tree root she and Lorraine passed caused Kara to shiver. Somewhere up the way, Draper Dewberry had been buried.

As they hurried along the path, winding through the profusion of summer plant growth, Kara saw that crowds had gathered at different spots along the river, all pointing toward the dam. Several policemen on the bridge kept the traffic moving, though barely at a crawl. Two motorboats were in the water, trying to get close enough to retrieve the body without being swept over the dam. The corpse was caught on the branch of a tree that had been washed downriver during the storm.

Kara glanced at the scene once, grateful she couldn't quite make it register on her brain, then kept her eyes on her mother-in-law. Lorraine moved ahead, pushing through small groups of gaping people, ignoring any comments, obviously singularly focused. Priscilla hadn't slowed down, but Lorraine and Kara, now breathless, caught up with her.

"Have you seen either one of them?" Lorraine demanded of her oldest daughter-in-law.

Priscilla shook her head. "Every fool in town is here, gawking, pointing, making a circus out of this."

Although Priscilla sounded outraged, Kara saw the dilated pupils of her brown eyes; Priscilla was excited by the gory spectacle as much as the others.

Then they heard Agnes Chaney. She was wailing like a banshee, pulling at her hair and tearing at her clothes. Down on her knees on the damp bank, she rocked back and forth, oblivious to those who tried to help her.

Kara's first instinct was to rush up to the woman and tell her that the poor soul in the river couldn't possibly be Toby, that Bucky had talked to Toby last night, yet something told her that not only had she promised to keep Bucky's secret, she couldn't promise that the body wasn't Agnes's son.

Lorraine began to ask people if they'd seen Dee Dee, creating more speculation about the body in the river, but rumor had already spread that the corpse was that of a young man. Kara was surprised Lorraine was openly seeking her drunken daughter-in-law, and she wasn't sure if she found the action commendable or not. She wondered if Lorraine was looking out for Dee Dee or herself.

As Kara scanned the crowd, she suddenly saw tall, blond-haired Ellis Davidson coming in her direction. He nodded to her and said her name as he passed.

"Kara."

She returned his nod, unaccountably relieved to see him. Inanely, she found herself thinking that she and John had never thanked him for the wedding present. Lorraine had ruined it for her, and she'd tried to forget about it, even though the sunset hung over John's bed.

"Ellis . . ."

He turned around. They were about two feet apart. He quickly closed the gap.

"I wanted to thank you for the wedding present," she murmured. "I know the timing's absurd—"

"That's okay," he said. "I thought the sunset over the

water might be soothing to you." His perceptive green eyes searched her face. "Are you all right, Kara?"

She shrugged. "This"—she indicated the scene of teeming, ogling people all around her—"this is all so horrid. I am having some problems."

"I don't mean just now," he murmured. "I mean are *you* all right?"

She nodded, immediately sensing that Ellis was talking about her life, the Worthingtons, her marriage. She recalled that he, a psychiatrist with firsthand information of the family, had insulted Lorraine by suggesting one of the family members needed help.

"I want to see you again, Kara—to talk," he added. "Think about it."

Then he went to Agnes Chaney's side. Kara couldn't look away from Ellis. She recalled the strange feeling she'd had when she met him, how she'd liked him immediately. She watched as he firmly grasped Agnes's shoulders and spoke to her.

Feeling someone's gaze upon her, Kara glanced around at the madhouse scene. Lorraine was still hunting for Dee Dee, but she'd paused long enough to let Kara know that she'd seen the exchange between her and Ellis. Lorraine glowered at Kara, then continued to press through the throngs of people, Priscilla at her side.

Finally the cadaver was snared and pulled into the boat. Her heart tight, her throat dry, Kara stood stock-still, watching as the vessel headed to shore not far from where she stood.

She forgot all about Lorraine and Priscilla as the boat docked, men jumping out to secure it. Agnes Chaney, tearing away from Ellis's arms, ran toward the craft, stumbling and screaming. People tried to restrain her, but she seemed to have superhuman strength as she reached the boat and peered inside.

"Oh, Lord God!" she screamed in such agony that the whole world seemed to grow silent. People hushed as if they all were holding their breath. The birds quit singing, the insects stopped buzzing. Even the river seemed to be calm once it had relinquished its gross cargo.

Then Agnes's shrill voice rent the air again. "Jesus! Jesus, it's my Toby! It's my Toby! I've never seen that raincoat, but I bought those clothes myself for him to wear to California." She clutched at the body, lost her balance, sank to the muddy earth and, mercifully, fainted.

Lorraine shoved through the crowds that had raced like wild animals toward the docked vessel. Ellis and two other men were carrying Agnes away from the boat. Lorraine charged through the people and stared down at the corpse. The expression on her face didn't change. Turning away, she continued her search for Dee Dee and Bucky, Priscilla following in her wake.

Kara couldn't take any more. Her stomach heaving, she headed toward the path, back toward Homeplace, having no idea that Bucky had already gone there, weaving his way in and out of the undergrowth, making sure that no one saw him.

Up in his room, Bucky was rolling on the floor, sobbing. What did it all mean? Where was Toby's head? Was it God's will? Because Toby had done evil with his mouth, had God cursed him forever to burn in Hell headless?

Bucky didn't know. "Jesus, Jesus," he moaned, curling up in the fetal position. The babbling voices and bible verses jammed against each other in his head until he thought there was no more room and surely his mind would explode.

His brain became so crowded that his thoughts began to drift back past today, past yesterday, past last year, to the times when Mother would dress him in silk panties and fancy dresses. He remembered those times because they were the most wonderful times in his life. The times he'd felt loved and adored.

In spite of Mother not wanting him to remember, he could never forget. Mother *had* loved him then. She hadn't cared that he was a boy, even though she'd really wanted a baby girl. It was their secret, she'd said. Their secret, because he was so pretty in the dresses and ribbons and shoes.

He clung desperately to the memory, tears still streaming from his eyes. He couldn't remember when Mother started dressing him like that; he only remembered when she stopped. It was when Melvin started dating Priscilla. Bucky was six years old.

Mother told him that he'd be starting school in the fall and that never again could they come to the attic where she would dress and cuddle him, that he was a big boy. They didn't even need to visit the river in the middle of the night anymore.

Fresh tears flooded down Bucky's face. He knew that Mother didn't lie; she'd taught him well that she didn't lie.

But it *seemed* like she'd lied to him. Maybe he was wrong. He got so confused; still, it *seemed* like that to him. Mother got very excited when Melvin married Priscilla a couple of years later. Then Priscilla got pregnant and Mother unpacked all the girl's dresses. Bucky *remembered* that.

Mother said he was confused. Mother said it didn't happen that way. Mother said she'd dressed him in dresses only as long as it was proper.

Bewildered, Bucky started sucking his thumb, jerking convulsively as he lay on the floor. He thought he would die when Mother quit taking him up to the attic in the middle of the night after his brothers were asleep. He'd been bereft, heartbroken, shattered.

Every night he waited in his room, next to Mother's, listening for the furtive sound of her footsteps, hoping his door would open. He'd wanted Mother to tell him how pretty he was, how special, how sweet. He'd wanted her to hold him on her lap and touch him.

But she never came. He waited and waited, until he finally cried himself to sleep, sucking his thumb, pretending it was Mother's titty. Whenever he tried to talk to her about it, she lectured him so strictly about mentioning the dresses that he became frightened.

Unconsciously, Bucky began to sing softly, "Pretty

baby, pretty little baby," over and over, as his thoughts tumbled about.

He hadn't understood why Mother had quit singing that to him. But he did understand when Lorrie was born that Mother didn't love him the way she used to, that Mother didn't tell him secrets, that Mother watched him all the time, as though he might do or say something bad.

He knew it was wrong to hate Lorrie. But, Jesus, he'd wanted to kill her. Maybe he would have, too, if he hadn't been afraid of Mother. Mother loved Lorrie. Bucky knew she did because she dressed Lorrie in the pretty clothes, some of the same ones she'd once dressed him in.

And maybe Mother *didn't* love him anymore. Mother could do awful things to people she didn't love. He knew she did it in the service of God, but he didn't always understand what constituted the service of God, so he tried not to antagonize her. Just in case she *had* stopped loving him.

When he became very afraid, he had to ask her or go crazy in his head, and whenever he asked her, she vowed that she loved him. She explained that he was still mixed-up, that the Devil made him think he recalled things that hadn't actually happened. Sometimes she was patient when she explained, and sometimes she was very angry; Bucky risked her wrath, asking anyway because he *had* to know.

And maybe it was true. Mother said he may have *dreamed* that she dressed him as a girl until he was six, but that he must never tell people—*never*—because they would think he was odd.

They thought that anyway, even though he hadn't told anyone about the dresses. God as his witness, he'd never told a soul. So why did people think he was weird?

Bucky was terrified that he would burn in Hell. Mother had held his hand over the open flame of the gas stove once to show him how Hell could feel. He had never forgotten the heat or the terror it created inside him.

Now he didn't know what to do. He wanted to talk to Mother, but he was scared. He wanted to talk to someone about Toby. But who?

He gasped, moving spastically when he heard the door

to his room open. His eyes wild, his pulse racing, he trembled before the intruder.

It wasn't Mother. It was Thelma.

The heavy woman stood staring at him for a moment, shaking her head, muttering something to herself, then she quietly closed the door.

"Go away," Bucky moaned. "Go away, Thelma."

She kept coming. Bucky tried to shrivel up within himself, but he was too big. He tried to pretend that he was a little boy again. He frantically attempted to slide under the bed, but he couldn't escape before Thelma grasped his arm.

"Get up, Bucky," she said in a tired, resigned voice. "Get up and go wash your face before the others come. Hurry up now, chile."

Bucky shook his head. "Go away," he mumbled, still sucking on his thumb, lying on his stomach where he'd tried to scuttle under his bed.

Unbidden, the thought came to him about how he'd prayed that he wouldn't grow too big, so that Mother would continue to see him as her little baby. God had proven that He was real, and that He answered prayers. Bucky hadn't grown as tall or as big as his brothers, but maybe he'd grown too big for Mother to keep loving him.

Thelma easily dragged him to his feet and yanked his thumb from his mouth in one quick motion. Lightning fast, she slapped him across the face. Once. Twice. Three times.

Bucky was stunned. He blinked repeatedly; the tears stopped. He went somewhere in his head where he didn't feel the pain from Thelma's blows or the ache in his heart. He didn't have to deal with his thoughts tormentingly banging together. For a moment his mind went blank.

"Get yourself together, chile, 'fore your mama comes back and something awful happens. Go on. Do like you been told."

Bucky stared at the old woman, gave one last convulsive sob, wiped at his tearstained face like a small boy, then slowly made his way from the room. Thelma followed him into the bathroom down the hall.

She stood behind him while he splashed his face with

cold water, then she sat him down on the closed lid of the toilet and held cold washcloths to his face.

"Now," she said, her voice softening into a crooning sound, "take these and go lay down on your bed."

She handed him two small pills and a glass of water. Bucky took them without comment. Then, trancelike, he obeyed Thelma's orders and left the bathroom as he had entered it, as if he were an automaton.

Thelma watched until Bucky lay down, then she shut the door and hurried downstairs just in time to hear someone enter the house through the sun-porch door.

She met Kara in the kitchen. The younger woman looked dazed.

"Are you all right?" Thelma asked.

Kara shook her head. "It was Toby," she said listlessly, her mouth dry, her head whirling with the memory of the gross scene at the dam. "It was poor Toby Chaney, and Agnes was there to witness it when they brought him to the shore."

"Lord above," Thelma said, looking heavenward, her aged eyes pained. "That poor, poor woman."

"Did Bucky come back?" Kara asked. "Is Dee Dee here? I left Priscilla and Lorraine looking for them." She shook her head. "I couldn't take it. I just couldn't."

"Bucky's in bed," Thelma said. "He ain't gone nowhere, and I don't know where Dee Dee is."

"Bucky's in bed?" Kara asked. "What do you mean, he hasn't gone anywhere? Didn't he go down by the river? Lorraine said she couldn't find him or Dee Dee in the house."

Thelma shrugged. "I guess she didn't go upstairs. Bucky was so afraid it was going be Toby that he went to pieces. I gave him something to settle him down." Thelma met Kara's eyes. "He's always been a delicate chile."

"Where's Ricky?" Kara asked, every other thought vanishing as she remembered her own son, a feeling of thick terror tightening her throat.

"He's playing in the den," Thelma said calmly. Her eyes held Kara's. "You better settle yourself down," she said.

BLOODY WATERS

"We can't do nothing about this terrible thing. The more upset we get, the more awful it'll be. Try to get ahold of yourself. If you're pregnant, this ain't going to do you one bit of good."

Kara drew in a steadying breath. She felt drained. She was nauseated. She prayed to God she wasn't pregnant. In the pandemonium, she'd forgotten all about that possibility.

She kept recalling Bucky saying he'd talked to Toby. Toby hadn't gone to California at all. When had he been murdered? And what did Bucky know about it?

Kara was sick in a way she couldn't begin to explain. She had a driving compulsion to confront Bucky, yet she had a deep fear about it, too. She felt, she realized, threatened.

"Didn't Bucky go down to the river?" Kara asked again.

"Like I told you before, Bucky's in his room."

"Lorraine couldn't find him," Kara repeated.

Thelma shrugged and turned back to a sink full of dirty dishes. "Maybe she figured he'd be down by the river like everybody else."

Kara stood still for a moment. When she'd asked Bucky how anyone could want to see such a grim sight, he'd appeared as repelled by the thought as she had. She wouldn't have gone to the river if Lorraine hadn't demanded it of her.

Deeply shaken, she went down the hall to the den. She opened the door to see Ricky happily playing with building blocks. Kara felt an overwhelming rush of relief to find her child safe and sound. Agnes Chaney had lost her son. Dee Dee had lost both of hers. Kara stared lovingly at Ricky for a few minutes, then closed the door.

Compelled to talk to Bucky, Kara made her way quietly up the steps to the second floor. When she knocked on his door, she didn't get an answer. For a while she waited, then knocked again. After receiving no answer a second time, she decided to look inside. Maybe Thelma was lying. Kara realized that she didn't trust anyone anymore.

The sight that greeted her paralyzed her briefly. Bucky was on the bed, stretched out like a dead person, his rigid face pale, though sweaty, his body immobile, the bible clutched to his chest.

Kara stared at him, terror tearing at her insides. Then she saw that tears were slowly trickling from Bucky's eyes. Her terror changed to pity. Maybe he didn't know that Toby was dead. Perhaps he was hiding here, fearing the worst, dreading the news of his friend's death.

"Bucky," she murmured softly. "It's Kara."

The young man appeared unable to move. Opening his eyes, he stared at the ceiling as tears continued coursing down his cheeks.

Her knees trembling, Kara went over to sit on the side of Bucky's bed. He still didn't move.

"Oh, Bucky," Kara whispered, "I'm so sorry."

He looked at her then, slowly, as if he were trying to recognize her, to remember what part she played in his reality. "It was Toby in the river, wasn't it?" he asked in a voice strangled by his tears.

Kara nodded. "Yes, it was. I thought you went to the river. Your mother's looking for you."

Bucky closed his eyes again. "I hurt so bad, Kara," he whispered. "I hurt so bad. I feel empty inside. Toby was my friend."

Without thinking, Kara lay her head on his chest and embraced Bucky. She knew the kind of pain he was talking about. She'd hurt like that when her parents died. Sometimes the pain came back to her in a rush that almost devastated her. Maybe that was why John had seemed like such a miracle. At last she thought that she'd really found love, a new life.

She became aware that Bucky was rigid in her arms. His heart was beating so erratically that she was frightened for him. She held him closer, as if she could force his heart to slow down, but it seemed to race faster.

Kara sat up; she had to talk to him. "Bucky, you said last night that you spoke to Toby," she murmured, her voice catching.

He didn't open his eyes. Kara saw that he was trembling harder.

"Bucky, look at me, please," she whispered. "Did you tell me you talked to Toby on the phone last night?"

His liquid brown eyes met her pained blue ones. "No," he said haltingly. "I couldn't sleep. I was worried about Toby. I called his house, but Mrs. Chaney answered and I hung up. I didn't want Mother to know what I'd done."

He stared back at the ceiling. He wasn't lying. He had called Toby's number; one of the bible verses inside his head had prompted it, although he couldn't remember which one.

"But you *told* me you talked to him," Kara stressed, trying to sort it out in her mind. What she was thinking was too horrible to contemplate.

Bucky's voice was ragged. "No. I said I *called* him. Toby was my friend. He was my only friend in this world." Tears trickling from his eyes, his nose running, he looked at Kara again. "He was my only friend until you came here, Kara."

Kara's mind was turbulent as she tried to remember exactly what Bucky had said. He'd said he *called* Toby, not that he *talked* to him.

God, she was going completely insane here! What was real and what wasn't? She recalled the mud on the threshold leading from the sun porch. It was black river mud. She knew it well now, after walking along the riverbank frequently.

Who had left the house in the middle of the night? And why? Had it been Lorraine? Or Bucky? Or was it someone else? Thelma?

Suddenly the door swung open and an enraged Lorraine stormed into the room. "Buchannan! I've been looking everywhere for you!"

Marching across the room, she said tightly, "Get out of that bed and help me look for your sister-in-law!"

"He just found out about Toby," Kara objected.

"Toby's dead and gone. Only God knows where Dee Dee is," Lorraine snapped. "We've got to find her."

Kara watched in amazement as Bucky rose from the bed, his tears drying instantly, his step amazingly steady as he wiped his runny nose on his arm. Without a backward glance, he followed Lorraine Worthington.

Kara's gaze fell on the bible that had tumbled off his chest when he got up. It had fallen open to a much-used section; the acts of immorality in Leviticus 18 had been underlined with a red pencil.

She stared at it uncomprehendingly. She felt like she'd wandered into an insane asylum and somehow become infected with the madness that lurked in the shadows, not quite hidden, but not out in the open, either. She felt contaminated. She didn't know if she would ever feel clean again.

11

The dreadful day continued minute by agonizing minute. Toby's body was taken away. Agnes was hospitalized for observation. Dee Dee couldn't be found. In a town already frenzied by the grisly discovery, the news that Dee Dee was missing spread like wildfire.

Rescue teams came out to drag the river with grappling hooks, looking for Toby's head. Scuba divers searched each backwash, feeling their way along the muddy bottom. Kara kept Ricky close by her side and waited for the nightmare to end. The radio and television screamed the ghastly news of the river murder. The evening paper was full of it.

No one thought again about the possibility that Kara might be pregnant. The doctor's visit was forgotten. Groups of people gathered to help hunt for Dee Dee. William stoically went about the business of searching for his missing wife. John and Melvin commanded teams of men, women, and youths.

Kara rocked in the big chair in John's room and waited; for what, she wasn't quite sure. People began to bring food to the house, and, oddly, it occurred to her once more that these generous, kind people weren't the Worthingtons' friends. To the best of Kara's knowledge, none of the Worthingtons had friends, except John, and the only friend she knew of was Ellis. They had plenty of acquaintances, but no one came to call regularly, and the phone almost never rang.

As if to mock her, the instrument beside the bed let out one shrill ring, shattering her reverie.

"It's for you," Thelma said, knocking on the door, jarring Kara further.

Kara couldn't imagine who it might be, then thought of Ellis, his smiling, handsome face filling her mind.

"Kara?" the voice on the phone asked. "It's Chelsea. Lanie's on the extension. Are you all right? We haven't heard a word from you, and now your new town is all over the media."

To both Kara's surprise and chagrin, it was a couple of her female friends from California. The gruesome event that had taken place in the small southern town had made national news.

Ironically, Kara had been away from California less than two weeks, and yet it seemed a lifetime, a million miles away. She was shocked that Toby's death was already known in her hometown.

She clutched the phone as if it were a lifeline to sanity. God, she didn't realize how much she'd missed the two women who had lived next door.

Both struggling romance writers, for years they had been renting the house beside her parents' home. They had seen her through the most tumultuous times of her life: when Richard deserted her, when her parents died, when Ricky was born—and when she'd had to decide whether or not to move to Virginia.

Chelsea and Lanie had been at the party where she'd met John, and they had been impressed by the suave southern gentleman, too. Kara wondered what they would think if she told them how troubled she was, how frightened—

"Kara," Chelsea repeated, "is that you?"

"Yes," Kara said quickly. "I'm so glad to hear from you! And so surprised! This has been—such a nightmare."

"Is the river where the body was found the one you live on?" Lanie asked, assuming that the nightmare Kara referred to was only the murder, not her life in Virginia.

"Yes," Kara said. "It's really, really awful."

"I'm sure it is," Chelsea empathized. "Are you all right?"

Kara sighed. She wasn't all right, but she couldn't tell them, she realized. She wasn't a quitter; she didn't intend to give up on her marriage yet, though she was deeply disturbed by all that was happening.

"I'm okay," she answered. "I'm sorry I haven't contacted you. Everything—Everything is so different from what I imagined."

There was a brief pause, then Chelsea said. "Kara, you sound awfully strung out."

Kara struggled to make some sense of what she'd lived through recently without being too revealing or melodramatic. "You'd be strung out, too, if a body had turned up close to your house."

Lanie said consolingly, "I know it must be shocking, but then, Kara, this is the world we live in. Murders are becoming routine, aren't they?"

"Not to me," Kara said. "I've met the boy's mother. I saw her watch her dead son being brought in from the river. It—It was more traumatic than you can possibly imagine."

Recalling what John had said earlier about murder being so common in Los Angeles, Kara realized that she'd never been personally affected by one. Toby Chaney was real, not some character on a television soap opera, or an unknown name on the late night news.

"That must have been horrible," Chelsea agreed. "I don't think I could have stood it. I had no idea that you knew so much about the murder. Lanie and I decided it made the news all over the country because of the gruesomeness of a body without a head."

"Yes," Kara said simply, not wanting to discuss the death any further, no matter how curious her friends were or how much it helped just hearing familiar voices.

"And here we were thinking that you were getting away from the ugliness of big-city crime," Lanie said. "Isn't it bizarre that such a thing happened in that little town?"

Kara drew in a steadying breath. There was no end to

the list of things she found bizarre in this town, but she wanted to forget them.

"So how are you two?" she asked, needing desperately to change the subject.

Fortunately, her friends took the hint and began to fill her in on what was happening in her old neighborhood. After they'd talked a few minutes and Kara had promised to stay in touch and invite them out when the new house was completed, she hung up the phone and sat staring at it. God, how she missed California. It seemed tame, somehow, no matter how much crime; it seemed—normal.

Sensing the presence of someone else in the room, Kara looked up to see Lorraine standing in the doorway, staring at her. She wanted to demand to know long her mother-in-law had been there, listening.

Instead, she asked, "Has Dee Dee been found?"

Lorraine shook her head. "Come to dinner. Everyone else is at the table."

"Thanks," Kara said, "but I don't think I can eat."

Anger flashed in Lorraine's eyes. "I don't have the time or the inclination to placate you under the circumstances, Kara," she said tartly. "If you can chat happily with your West Coast friends, you can come to dinner with the rest of the family. We're trying to carry on here, whether you care to or not."

She glared at Ricky, who was napping on John's bed. "And bring that child with you. *He* might want to eat. And another thing!" Lorraine shook her finger at Kara. "Stop binding that boy to you, as if you need to guard him. It's extremely peculiar."

Taken aback once more because Lorraine had the sheer gall to consider something so maternal odd, Kara responded without thought.

"I don't know your definition of peculiar, but it surely doesn't fit mine. Ricky is my child, and I will do as I see fit with him."

"Not in my house, you won't!" Lorraine hissed. "And don't you ever forget that this *is* my house."

She slammed the door before Kara could counter. Adrenaline surging, Kara thought of a dozen things she wanted to say to the raging shrew who'd just departed. She inhaled deeply. For her sanity as well as whatever was left of anyone else's in Homeplace, she had to get better control.

She told herself that Lorraine, apparently never far from the edge, was nearly over it at this point. She had to stay on an even keel, Kara told herself, until this crisis, at least, was past.

Ricky was sitting up, rubbing his eyes, the confrontation between his mother and Lorraine having awakened him.

"Are you hungry, sweetie?" Kara asked, trying to suppress the lingering fury that caused her voice to quiver. Her hands were trembling as she helped Ricky off the bed, and clasping his little hand, she walked with him to the dining room.

Of course the Worthingtons would be carrying on as usual. Why would she expect anything else? She saw that, if anything, William's appetite seemed to have been increased by the hunt for his missing wife. To be fair, maybe he was consuming food so rapidly because he was distraught or nervous. However, it didn't seem that way. She also noticed that tonight the family hadn't bothered to wait for her before saying grace.

John and Melvin were already arguing about Toby's murder. "It means Asterson's innocent," John said fervently.

"Bull!" Melvin bellowed. "This could be a copycat killer. Nothing will be known for sure until the body's autopsied in Roanoke. It looks like Agnes was right. Toby was probably in the water for a couple of weeks. The body gases brought him to the surface with the help of the storm." He laughed. "A floater. Did the murderer really think that cement block would keep a bloated body down?"

"That's another point," John said. "One of the detectives said the throat slashing looked like a hack job, an amateur. The head didn't appear to have been deliberately severed. The throat was probably slashed so deeply that the decaying flesh holding the head on broke loose."

"So what?" Melvin asked. "What's the point?"

"Well, the same thing was said about Asterson's supposed victims—that the killings were amateurish. This looks like the same killer to me, and it can't be Asterson since he's never made bail."

"Oh, bull!" Melvin said again. "How many killers do you know running around town who are professional? We're not talking about hit men here, Johnny-boy. We're talking about plain old murder, and you know the summer heat always brings them out of the woodwork. This humidity must be rotting their brains, driving 'em crazy. Speaking of which, I got a look at Toby before he was sent off. The river life really did a job on his hands. There wasn't much left but bone. Makes it bad for fingerprint matches, and we don't have teeth. Thank God his mother was there to say it was him."

Kara turned white before she could pull her chair up to the table. She'd just placed Ricky in the high chair. She was sure she was going to be sick again.

"Excuse me," she said, nearly dry-heaving as she rushed from the room.

In the bathroom, she drew in several deep breaths. How could they sit there at the dinner table and discuss that poor boy like that? She was appalled by their lack of sensitivity, by their crudeness, by their disregard for human life.

And William? With Dee Dee missing, how could John and Melvin talk about a dead boy?

She didn't linger in the bathroom this time. Only God knew what might happen in this—this mausoleum, as Dee Dee had called it—in her absence. Reinforcing her vow to see this nightmare to the end, she returned to the table.

"You're going to have to make that appointment to see the doctor tomorrow, Kara," John said. "In all the hullabaloo, I forgot you might be pregnant."

"Really, John," she said, "I'd rather not talk about it now, and I don't think there's any hurry."

"You're joking!" he said. "I want to know if I'm going to be a father or not."

Lowering her eyes, Kara repeated, "I don't want to discuss it. In view of all that's going on, I don't think it's the most compelling issue."

John laughed. "Well, *I* do. It's not every day that I become a father."

Kara met his eyes. "And it's not every day that someone's murdered and your sister-in-law vanishes, for God's sake! What's the matter with you people? Don't you have any concern for anybody? Any compassion?"

Ricky began crying when Kara raised her voice. She started to get up, but John grasped her hand and jerked her back into the chair.

"Thelma!" he yelled, immediately bringing the old woman from the kitchen. "See to Ricky."

Then John faced Kara. "Let's clear this up right now. I'm sick to death of you judging my family—and me! If I'd wanted that kind of woman . . ." He glanced at his mother. His words trailed off.

Thoroughly angered and humiliated, Kara looked at Lorraine, too. There was a smirk on her face. Kara scanned the rest of the family. Melvin was grinning like a Cheshire cat, clearly enjoying the fight. Lorrie was such an imitation of her grandmother that it was disturbing. William was still eating. Priscilla was watching, her lips pursed. Bucky's head was down as he stared at his plate.

John cleared his throat and started in again. "The fact of the matter is that Dee Dee has run off more than once, even though we're doing all we can to find her. If anybody cries wolf often enough, people cease to take it seriously. Now, you've read enough to know that, haven't you?"

When Kara clenched her teeth tightly together, John grasped both shoulders and shook her. "Haven't you?" he demanded. "Answer me!"

"I think we need to have this conversation in private," she said, seething, as she knocked his hands away.

"And *I*," he said, grasping her shoulder again, "think that since your problem involves all of us here, we'll talk right out in the open. You're the one who insisted that you were a woman who could take what was dished out, who could roll with the punches, who could accept life for what it is. Well, this is life! Do you hear me?"

"How can I not?" she said, blue eyes flashing. "You're yelling loudly enough to wake the dead!"

Her unfortunate choice of words seemed to stun John for just a moment. Frustrated, he ran a hand through his dark hair.

"Murder does happen. You knew that I would be involved in it when you married me, but life goes on, too. When you see the doctor, tell him what a hell of a time you're having adjusting to being a criminal attorney's wife. Get some tranquilizers or something until you get used to this!"

Kara deeply resented his fighting with her in front of the family. "I'll never get used to this!" she retorted. "Don't think a few pills will fix it." She looked around the table at the others.

To her amazement, William continued eating. But then, he was used to husbands and wives fighting, wasn't he? Even if his mate was missing at the moment.

In fact, Kara had already been told that a search wouldn't have been launched for Dee Dee so soon if she hadn't been a Worthington, and a murder victim hadn't turned up on the same day. It seemed that runaway wives were all too common. Kara could understand why.

Unexpectedly, Priscilla left her chair and came over to Kara. "You really will get used to it, Kara. You've had a rough initiation, but someone has to deal with criminals and the less savory aspects of life. John's right. You knew you were marrying an attorney, a different way of life, an uglier way than you obviously anticipated."

Disconcerted by this unexpected source of support, Kara gazed at her sister-in-law. She might dislike Priscilla; still, what she'd said made sense. It was just that this all seemed so horrible, so cruel, such a base reduction of life to the lowest and harshest elements.

"You may not know anything about drunks," Priscilla continued, "but John's right about Dee Dee, too. She's unpredictable. We've gotten used to it. You will, too. You'll see."

Although Kara seriously doubted it, she appreciated Priscilla helping her save face. She hoped that she never became as insensitive as this family.

"Thank you, Priscilla," she said softly. She didn't know if Priscilla was sincere or just feeling superior; regardless, Kara did appreciate her rational input and the calm way she'd spoken.

"Now," Lorraine said, "can we complete the meal?"

Kara glanced at the woman and saw the triumphant gleam in those brown eyes. She chose to ignore it. Picking up her fork, she went through the motions of eating.

Incredibly, Bucky turned the conversation toward a trip to Greensboro he was planning. Kara remembered how such a short time earlier he'd been nearly prostrate with grief. She had to hand it to these people: they were resilient—if that was the best word.

A weary breath escaped her lips. Maybe she was too judgmental; perhaps they did have to live this way. Melvin was in law enforcement because he had high ambitions to be a judge or go far in politics. Even though John and William were defense attorneys, surely they would rather handle big-paying corporate accounts, but when death and despair and man's cruelty became routine, some segment of the population had to confront it and carry on. Kara recalled a time when she'd believed John was a noble man. Maybe she'd just lost sight of that notion.

"Would you like to ride with me to Greensboro, Kara?" Bucky asked. "It only takes about an hour, if you remember. The malls are in the general direction of the airport."

"I think that's a great idea," John said before Kara could speak. "The trip will do you good. Leave Ricky here with Thelma, and you and Bucky make a day of shopping." He pulled several credit cards from his wallet. "Buy anything you want," he said magnanimously, his fury apparently spent.

Kara's hand was unsteady when she took the cards. She didn't want to leave the house; she didn't want to leave her child; she wanted to be here if news of Dee Dee came. Still, perhaps the family was right. This day had been so—

so shocking, so stunning to her, that she had to do something.

Somehow she got through dinner, and surprisingly, she did feel better once she'd eaten. She hadn't had lunch, although Thelma had prepared something for Ricky.

After dinner everyone adjourned to the sun porch. Even though Kara went with them, she was still having difficulty accepting the way they forged on with their lives in face of the horrid day they'd all experienced. Thelma served iced tea, and they sat overlooking the very river where Toby had been found.

It almost seemed like a dream to Kara. No, she amended, not a dream. A nightmare. A real life nightmare.

Thankfully, all of the family retired early. Kara was so depleted, so defeated, she could hardly hold her eyes open. When John pulled her into his arms, she tensed.

"Don't do that, Kara," he said, his voice unexpectedly coaxing. "What happened to the spirited, sensual creature I married such a short time ago? Where's that joy of life? That passionate person who tempted me so shamelessly?"

Kara forced herself to smile. She wondered herself where that woman had gone. She was lost somewhere in Homeplace, overrun by hostility, constant wars, madness and murder!

"That's my girl," John said, as though he hadn't wounded her at the dinner table, as though he hadn't humiliated her in front of the entire family.

He chucked her under the chin, then kissed her. When he drew her against him, Kara found her mind drifting. She was disturbed to easily envision Ellis Davidson as clearly as if he were here instead of John.

The next morning life went on as usual. The Worthingtons talked about the possibility of hiring a private investigator to help locate Dee Dee, and discussed cases on the court calendar.

Kara had the disillusioning feeling that if William was grieving for his wife, he kept it well hidden. She realized that she was getting paranoid about everyone. Dee Dee and William had argued yesterday; Dee Dee had been physically removed from the dining room, and breakfast had continued. Both William and Bucky had been missing a short time. Had Dee Dee vanished then?

She struggled to suppress the nagging possibilities the question posed. She found it odd that none of the family had been questioned about Dee Dee's disappearance. The police investigators had sought all the pertinent information to help in the search, yet none of the family was under suspicion. But then, Kara didn't know why she would think they should be.

Perhaps John was right. She read too much fiction; however, the truth of the matter was that she knew many murders were committed by family members, and in a family always in an uproar like this one, she thought the police would certainly consider such a possibility.

"What time do you want to go, Kara?" Bucky asked, bringing her out of her troubling reverie.

"I'll leave that up to you," she answered evasively.

"Most of the mall stores open by nine," he said. "Why don't we leave at eight-thirty?"

"Eight-thirty," she repeated, grateful to focus on something concrete. "Fine." She realized that she was looking forward to the trip more than she had imagined. She'd been shut up in this house, except for her own excursions on the river, for days.

When she glanced at John, he smiled. "Try to enjoy yourself, Kara." Leaning over, he murmured, "And buy a black garter belt while you're out. There's a specialty shop in one of the malls. Bucky knows which one."

Kara's face filled with color. John's penchant for kinky sex was a contrast to the properly attired, seemingly straitlaced, churchgoing, criminal underdog defender who sat beside her.

"It's rude to whisper at the table, John," Lorraine remarked. "If you have something to discuss with your wife in private, do it in private; otherwise, let us all participate."

John looked his mother right in the eye. "I told her to

shop for maternity clothes," he said calmly. "I want everyone to know I'm going to have a son."

Lorraine's eyes glittered. "You may have a daughter, just in case that hasn't occurred to you. Regardless, I will make the appointment so that we'll all know whether or not there's any need for maternity clothes."

"Thank you, Mother," John said. Then he winked at Kara. "Don't forget to buy black."

For the first time in a while, Kara genuinely smiled. Occasionally, John did seem to take delight in provoking his mother. Not only did Kara see it as a healthy sign, she believed Lorraine deserved it.

"Well, it's off to the office," John noted, looking at his two brothers. "Ready?"

"I'm not going in today," William said quietly.

Kara glanced at him, not wanting to feel pity, yet doing so in spite of herself. Maybe he cared about Dee Dee after all.

"It won't do you any good to sit around here and mope and wait," Melvin said. "Keeping busy and passing time is what you need. No matter where that lunatic wife of yours is, you can't change it by wasting time."

William glanced at him sharply, and Kara braced herself for a round of tart words. She didn't think she would ever get used to the bickering between the brothers.

"My wife is no more a lunatic than yours," William said. "How the hell would you feel if Priscilla was off only God-knows-where?"

Melvin glanced at his smiling wife. "My wife," he said smugly, "wouldn't be off God-knows-where. That's the point. Now act like a man and go on to work. You have people who want to get divorced—a matter that I'm sure has entered your own mind on more than one occasion."

"Worthingtons don't get divorces!" Lorraine said emphatically. "I told all you boys when you married to select with care. Worthingtons *don't* get divorces. Ever! Do you understand me?"

Melvin stood up and made a courtly bow, his bulk almost touching his breakfast plate. "Everyone always understands you, Mother. William hasn't gotten a divorce, has he?" They glared at each other for a few minutes, then Melvin smiled. "Has he, Mother?" he repeated in a manner Kara found distasteful.

She looked at John; he was watching the exchange with an expressionless face.

"No," Lorraine conceded grudgingly. "He *has* not. And he *will* not."

Melvin's smile was sly. "No, indeed. He may be a widower, but he will not be a divorced man."

It was all Kara could do to keep silent. Biting down on her tongue, she glared at her oldest brother-in-law. She was sure he would be a formidable opponent in court, for she was convinced he had neither conscience nor scruples. He certainly had no compassion.

She wasn't surprised when William abruptly placed his napkin on the table and pushed back his chair. She wanted to plead with him to stand up for himself, to stay home and wait for some word of Dee Dee, but this family had survived without her input for a long, long time. She supposed it would continue to do so. She certainly hadn't made much impact last evening.

However, she wasn't at all sure there would never be a divorce in the Worthington family. She thought she might pursue one if she and John didn't leave Homeplace soon.

Bucky owned a flashy red convertible, bought from part of his share of his father's estate. Kara had never thought about how wealthy each of the sons was until Bucky started talking about his car as they approached it.

"Do you like to ride with the top down?" he asked, opening the door for Kara.

She smiled. "I think that would be splendid."

He nodded soberly. "Okay, but we have to wait until we're down the road. Mother thinks it's dangerous to ride without overhead protection."

Kara didn't want to say anything that would cause Bucky more anxiety. She knew that his life was already miserable enough, that he was very unhappy, that he was dominated by his mother and seen as a useless nonentity by his brothers. She wanted more than anything in the world to boost his ego, but she wasn't sure how to go about it.

"What would happen, Bucky?" she asked, the surge of defiance that wouldn't lie dormant surfacing, "if you put the top down like you want to right here in the driveway and we went on off?"

He looked at her as if she'd gone mad. "Mother would come out ranting," he said. "Sometimes I think she watches everything I do."

"You're a grown man," Kara said softly. "You have a right to live your own life, Bucky. Don't you know that?"

His eyes were suddenly large and frightened. "Kara, you push Mother too far. You know how much I like you, and I'm telling you that you mustn't push Mother."

"What is that supposed to mean?" she asked seriously.

Bucky tugged on his ear. "You're my friend, Kara, and I said I'd protect you, so I'm telling you it's not good to anger Mother."

Kara stared at him. Was Bucky giving her a warning, or was she overreacting again? Knowing that she was making him terribly ill at ease, and wanting the outing to be pleasant for them both, she capitulated.

"All right, we'll put the top down after we leave Homeplace, Bucky." She patted his hand reassuringly.

He stumbled back as if she'd burned him. Kara didn't know what to think. She peered at Homeplace, wondering if Bucky had seen Lorraine spying on them, wondering why her young brother-in-law couldn't get away from her fast enough.

Kara watched Bucky stop on the driver's side of the convertible. He seemed to be trying to get through some ordeal before he got in the car. She waited, tense and disappointed. The kinder she tried to be to him, the more distant he seemed.

Bucky was in turmoil from Kara's touch when he opened the car door. A rush of heat warming him, he recalled how she'd lain her head on his chest yesterday, her body against his, her arms around him. He'd thought he might die. He had felt her breasts. He shuddered as he made himself get in the car.

"Is the shopping really great in Greensboro?" Kara asked, to lighten the pall that had suddenly fallen over the trip.

"Yes." Bucky's voice shook.

He seemed so discomforted that Kara didn't dare look at him. "Do you mind if we play the radio?" she asked.

He shook his head.

When she reached out to push the button for the music, Bucky watched her hand. It was the one she'd touched him with. For a brief moment he considered clasping it and drawing it to his lips to feel the soft skin. Then, abruptly, he fiercely grasped the steering wheel, started the car and drove off.

When they reached the bottom of the hill, he stopped, pushed the button to lower the convertible top, and got out to help secure it.

In moments they were en route again, speeding down the highway, the wind blowing their hair.

"This is terrific," Kara said, laughing. Despite the already warm day, the fresh air and beautiful scenery were invigorating. She was beginning to feel like her old self, in spite of her misgivings. Maybe this was what she needed—some distance from Homeplace.

Bucky smiled. "I'm glad you like it. I want you to like to do things with me, Kara."

She smiled at him. "You're a very nice person, Bucky, and don't you ever forget it. Thank you for inviting me."

He gave his attention to the road, too afraid he would say something silly if he kept staring at her. "Thanks for coming."

"Oh, we're going to have a nice time," Kara vowed. "You wait and see. I'm not a bad shopper. I don't dilly-dally all day the way some women do, driving men crazy."

Bucky was pleased to hear her refer to him as a man. He looked over at her. "I want you to do whatever makes you happy," he said. "We have all day long."

She nodded, then thought of poor Dee Dee. What was

Dee Dee doing at this moment? Where was she? What was she thinking?

Knowing it was futile to go on the outing with such unpleasant thoughts in mind, Kara focused on John's request.

"John asked me to get some lingerie. You don't have to go into the shop with me, but he says you know which one."

Bucky's face turned red, and Kara quickly patted his hand. "I didn't mean to embarrass you."

"You aren't embarrassing me," he insisted with false bravado. "I was with John when he shopped for you. I'll go into the store with you."

"You don't have to do that," Kara said quickly, suddenly embarrassed herself. She was surprised that John had taken Bucky to buy sexy lingerie for her.

"But I want to go with you," Bucky insisted, a shiver racing up his spine at the thought.

"I beg your pardon," Kara said, unsettled by a picture of John and Bucky examining intimate items for her.

"I want to go with you," Bucky repeated.

After all, he was planning to get a few things for himself. The store sold wigs. With Kara close by, he could probably get a good match of her blond hair.

He'd like that. He'd like it a lot.

12

As the miles flew by, and Bucky got farther and farther away from home, he began to open up a little, humming along with the radio, then singing.

Kara smiled. "You have a very nice voice, Bucky."

When he glanced at her, his dark eyes were the brightest she'd ever seen them. She realized that he'd been anxiously awaiting her approval of his ability to sing.

"Do you really think so, Kara? I mean *really?*"

She laughed. "I mean really, I do really think so."

His smile was sweet and ingratiating. Kara was moved by his hunger for attention.

"Thank you, Kara."

His sincerity, his gratitude, was such that she wanted to reach over and hug him and tell him that he was a valuable, bright, appealing person who had every right to find happiness.

Instead, she only smiled. Bucky's perceptions of himself and what he could be and what he deserved to be had been distorted over a long period of time. Anger rose in Kara when she thought of the Worthington family, and what she knew of Lorraine, in particular. She'd noticed that even Thelma spoke to Bucky as if he were extraneous.

She wished she knew some way to make life easier for him, to help him understand that he could be whatever he wanted to be, or at least that he should try. Still, she knew a few compliments and kind words weren't going to make up for years of low self-esteem; they weren't going to give him the confidence he needed, the confidence that should have been instilled in him all along. The thought made her sad, for Bucky was truly talented and innocently charming.

"What are you going to do about your acting, Bucky?" she asked. "Is there anywhere nearby you can do summer stock? Perhaps you could get some bit parts in New York. Have you given it any thought?"

His face turned red as he grinned. "It's all I think about, Kara. Well, not all," he amended truthfully, glancing at her, his fingers tightening on the steering wheel. "I mean I think about other things."

He spent lots of time thinking about lots of other things, and Kara was at the top of his list these days. He wished he could convey how important she was to him, what a change there had been in his life since he'd met her.

There was a place inside him now—a very tiny place, granted, but a place all the same—where he could go and feel a kind of peace he'd never known, when he became confused and agitated and the ugliness overtook him.

If Kara never gave him any more than this, he considered it an amazing gift, even though he knew deep inside that he wanted more. He also knew thinking about it started the turmoil and the questions that made his thoughts tumble about and trample each other, leaving bits and parts broken and disjointed so that they didn't fit right. He'd decided it was best to let one day follow another and see how things went.

Like this trip, for example. Never in a million years had he imagined that Kara would be next to him in his car, talking with him, interested in *him!*

"Bucky," Kara said with a laugh, "you must be thinking about those other things now. Do you want to share any?"

She was leaning forward a little, peering at his face, her blond hair falling over one shoulder, covering her breast and the seat belt that locked her at Bucky's side.

She was in his car, sitting right beside him. The idea sent a momentary surge of panic through him. For some reason it made him recall Dee Dee and how he and William had had to drag her away from the table. She had fought at first, and then she'd sort of just given up and gone along with them. She'd kind of leaned on him, her revolting body touching his. Bucky hadn't liked it when Dee Dee's breast had pressed against his arm. He glanced at the blonde again.

This wasn't Dee Dee at his side. This was *Kara*. She had nothing to do with Dee Dee. He was getting confused. He *liked* this woman. He liked her a whole lot. Maybe too much. He looked back at the road, wondering if he should share even a little of what was on his mind.

No, he decided firmly, relieved to have made the decision so quickly. What was it Mother once said? There was a time, a season for everything? Or had the bible said that?

When he looked back at Kara, she was a blond angel again, her bright hair blowing in the wind, the sun captured in it. The sight of her made him start to get hard, and that scared him.

Suddenly he looked up at the heavens and began to pray fervently: *Please, God, don't let me be sinning because I covet Kara. Please, God!*

Seeing that he was driving erratically, his expression desperate, his eyes upward, his lips moving, although he wasn't saying anything audible, Kara didn't know what to think. Was he playing a game, or was he experiencing some kind of emotional distress?

She caressed his hand comfortingly again. "Bucky, you don't *have* to share anything with me," she murmured earnestly. "We're just talking. All right? You don't need to tell me anything you don't want to."

It was all she could do not to mention his driving, yet she couldn't bear to add to his unease. Fortunately, he seemed to snap out of his stupor.

He glanced at her briefly, then concentrated on the road as he spoke. "I do *want* to tell you. I want to tell you so many things, Kara, that sometimes it troubles me. I don't know where to start."

He decided to get on safe ground before it was too late, before he said something he shouldn't, something Mother would be angry with him for. Acting was a safe subject, at least with Kara.

"About my acting," he said, "I want to complete my work with my instructor before I try to get out on my own. You know?" he said, half asking for her approval.

"Have you been studying for a long time?" she asked.

He shrugged. "Not so long. When I started college, my brothers—you know how they are—well, they, or at least John and Melvin—William didn't seem interested enough to bother—laughed at me."

When he looked at Kara expectantly, she wasn't sure how she should respond. She always felt guilty about not defending her husband, and yet she'd seen how harsh he could be, not only with Bucky, but with her also.

There was a pause that seemed to last forever, then Bucky started rambling nervously.

"I didn't decide all on my own or anything. It's not like I made a half-cooked decision based on a whim. Mother wasn't fond of the idea, either, but after I talked to a counselor on campus, he said it seemed I'd been headed in the direction of performing all along, what with Mother having me take dance lessons and singing lessons."

He met her eyes. "Those lessons were all her idea, Kara, even though my brothers ragged me about it. Mother said—well, what she said was that I was socially unacceptable. I know John can dance—Melvin and William, too—and I guess they just sort of learned naturally. I was taught professionally because that was what Mother wanted. My brothers say she turned me into a sissy. But I'm not!"

He seemed to be talking to himself again, and Kara lightly squeezed his shoulder to bring him back to her. When he flinched as if she'd struck him, she murmured, "It's okay, Bucky. I know you're not."

She wanted him to slow down and talk calmly to her, to accept her. It bothered her that he reacted so neurotically whenever she touched him, even though she'd already told herself that the family wasn't affectionate, except for John.

Still, she told herself not to put her hands on Bucky until he was more relaxed with her. Despite her belief that people needed physical contact and caring, that wasn't the Worthington way; she realized she had to proceed slowly with Bucky.

"I think you're a sensitive person, Bucky. That's the artist in you. There's no reason to apologize for those traits, especially to me. I want to be your friend as much as you seem to want to be mine, and that means we need to be comfortable with each other, to feel that we can talk. You understand that, don't you?"

Bucky nodded. He thought he understood what she meant. He believed she was telling him he could trust her. Even with the secret. *Secrets*. Even the ones that confounded him, making him wonder if he'd been right or wrong. He struggled to shove aside the persistent, plaguing thoughts always hovering at the edge of his mind, before they upset him, before they overran him and ruined his day with Kara.

Kara gazed at him pensively, thinking that perhaps he didn't accept her sincerity, that he couldn't believe she wouldn't laugh at him if he exposed his inner self.

Speaking in a kind tone, she said, "What I mean is that you can say anything to me without me thinking badly of you, without me judging you at all, and I'd like to be able to talk with you the same way, Bucky. That's what friends do, you know."

"I do know," he said quickly, not wanting her to think him stupid or insincere. "And I do like you, Kara, for being the way you are. I can't tell you how awful it's been for me to attempt to become an actor. I'm still scared," he murmured hesitantly, awaiting her reaction to his confession.

She smiled. "We're all scared in this life, at one time or another, about something. I worked as an editor after I graduated from college, and despite my having been around writers and artists all my life—or perhaps because of it—I was terrified the first time I had to make a decision on whether to buy a particular book for the company."

Bucky looked at her. "I'm sorry, Kara. It's terrible to be terrified. Was the book that bad?"

"Oh, that's just it," she exclaimed. "I liked the material,

but that didn't mean the book-buying public would. If they didn't, that would be bad for the writer, the publisher—who had a strict budget—and for me!"

She laughed. "How I agonized over it! Years later, it seems such a waste of energy and anguish. But back then it preyed on my mind for days—and nights!"

Bucky nodded sympathetically. "I know how awful that can be. Some days—and plenty of nights, too—I have things on my mind. These thoughts . . . ideas . . . just seem to take over. I can't get them out of my head. I start to go over and over them, and they grow worse and worse. I don't know what to think, what to do."

She smiled. "Think that you and I both are only human, just like the rest of the world. At some point decisions are hard for all of us."

"Yes," he said contemplatively, "but they seem harder for me than most people."

"I'm sure a lot of other people think that, and don't admit it," Kara said, trying to be supportive.

Bucky sighed. "Well, anyway, what I did was work out a plan with the counselor whereby I took all my requirements first—you know, the ones that would be good for any major. Even though we agreed I was going to study drama, I told the family I was leaving my major open."

He stared at the road. "Then I got so excited about the classes and the costumes and stuff that I started talking about it at home. Mel and John mocked me so much that I dropped out for a while."

Kara stared at the passing scenery. She didn't want to think that John, especially, taunted his younger brother. It was cruel, and spoke badly for him.

"Did you like the sexy stuff John bought for you, Kara?" Bucky asked unexpectedly. "I saw it all."

Kara was now the uncomfortable one. She didn't think it was prudent or flattering for John to have taken Bucky with him to buy lingerie for her. Trying not to be too critical of the man she had married, she was still finding more and more reasons to be dissatisfied with him. Then she told herself that maybe John thought he was doing Bucky a favor. After all, she recalled John telling Melvin at the party that he felt the right girl could straighten Bucky out, that Bucky needed to be pointed in the proper direction.

"It's all very lovely," she said, as though she didn't resent Bucky knowing about the erotic garments.

Bucky giggled a little boy giggle full of merriment and mischief. "And sexy, huh, Kara? Wow, I didn't know they made stuff like that! That black bikini and bra look like frilly pieces of elastic. John said men like to see women dress like that, but we don't say so in front of Mother."

Kara supposed it had been educational for Bucky to see the lingerie; still, she felt as if her privacy had been invaded. John could have shown Bucky a store full of sexy items without indicating exactly what he was purchasing for his wife. She was reminded of how John had talked to Ellis at the party, as if she were some kind of trophy he'd won.

However, she made herself smile and agree with Bucky. "Yes, it's definitely sexy."

"Do you get turned on when you wear it?" Bucky asked, his voice vibrant.

Kara felt her mouth compress into a thin line, then abruptly reevaluated the situation. She was, as her mother-in-law had phrased it at the party, making a mountain out of a molehill. She had never been one to be tight-lipped about anything, and she was sure Bucky really was curious. It was the Worthingtons themselves who had her curtailing her conversation.

"Well, John seems to get turned on," she said. "Or at least I hope he does, since that's the idea."

Bucky smiled and settled back against the seat again. He'd seen Kara and *he'd* been turned on. That was for sure!

"I'm sure John does. You're so beautiful," he murmured, the memory of her filling his mind.

Although Kara didn't comment, preferring not to encourage more of that particular conversation, she was glad to see Bucky relax, and glad she hadn't reacted prudishly to his questions.

She couldn't know that Bucky was at that moment imagining how she looked in the black bikini outfit and other undergarments. He'd seen how wonderful she looked that night on the sun porch, but it was the times when he'd been able to peep through the ancient keyhole of the original Homeplace door to John's room to see Kara and John actually doing it that had made him grow fully erect.

"What do you think of Thelma?" Kara asked, causing Bucky to start from his introspection.

"Thelma?" he murmured.

He knew a secret about Thelma, although he'd promised Mother he wouldn't tell. It was a scary secret, too, so he tried not to upset Thelma lest she turn on him. She scared him, although she also took care of him when he was feeling strange. He supposed it balanced out; still, he was careful all the same.

He shrugged. "I don't think a whole lot about her one way or the other. She's kind of like a member of the family, you know."

"I've wondered about that," Kara said honestly. "I like her, but she doesn't say a whole lot. Did her husband work at Homeplace? Did Tessa grow up in the house?"

Kara was surprised to see Bucky squirm uncomfortably in the seat. What was it about these people that made every question seem threatening?

He was considering the question so intensely that Kara felt sorry for him. "It doesn't matter, Bucky," she said. "I was just curious."

He looked at her and laughed nervously. "Did you ever hear that curiosity killed the cat, Kara?"

Despite feeling chilled all of a sudden, Kara made herself smile. "Yes, and I also heard that satisfaction brought him back again."

Bucky glanced away. "I never heard that one. Anyway, I'm not supposed to talk about the family." He looked at her worriedly. "Since friends do talk, I will tell you Tessa's daddy was never around, and that girl was one female child Mother had no use for."

Kara was more curious than ever. Was that why Tessa moved so silently in and out of the dining room at mealtimes? Was that why Lorraine had insisted that Thelma,

BLOODY WATERS

not Tessa, bring her coffee the morning Dee Dee disappeared? Kara felt that she had to get some answers.

"What do you mean, Bucky? Was Tessa 'illegitimate,' as your mother prefers to say?"

"*Ricky* is illegitimate, isn't he?" Bucky retorted in answer to her questions.

Kara wondered if he deliberately meant to sting her with the response. "The term means nothing to me, actually, Bucky; however, I suppose it meant something to a lot of people when Tessa was born."

Bucky seemed lost in thought, then abruptly asked, "You're worried about Ricky, aren't you?"

Kara nodded. "He's my baby. I don't think I could stand it if anything happened to him." She became pensive. "I wonder if that's what drove poor Dee Dee to drink. I don't know how she could endure the deaths of two children."

Bucky grew very quiet. Kara saw him grip the steering wheel until his knuckles turned white. She knew the topic was an unpleasant one, yet as her thoughts turned to Ricky, she couldn't help thinking about Dee Dee, no matter how much Bucky wanted her to enjoy the outing. She tried to force her fears aside. She and Bucky were on a shopping trip to enjoy themselves, not rattle family skeletons.

Kara did have fun with Bucky once they got to the mall. The outing was good for them both. She found the black garter belt John wanted for her, and even Bucky made some purchases in the store—presents, he said, for the women of Homeplace, which he wouldn't allow Kara to see, no matter how much she coaxed. She suspected he'd purchased perfume or sachet from the store's abundant selection; she was only teasing about really wanting to see.

Mid-afternoon, after a lovely lunch, she asked Bucky if they could return to Homeplace, using the excuse that she'd spent more than enough of John's money. In truth, she simply couldn't forget the trouble at the mansion, no matter how much she was distracted by the shopping.

She and Bucky were giggling about their hopelessly mussed hair after they put the convertible top back up at the bottom of the hill and started up the driveway to Homeplace. An icy chill raced up Kara's spine like the touch of a cold wind, in spite of the hot southern summer afternoon when she saw all the Worthington vehicles, the brothers', and Priscilla's, lined up in front of the house. The part-time chauffeur hadn't put Lorraine's car in the garage.

"Oh, Bucky," Kara whispered, hurrying to open her own door the moment he parked the car, "I have an awful feeling about this. It's too early for your brothers to be home from work."

Bucky had a wild look in his eyes, but he didn't say anything as he and Kara left all their new purchases in the car and hurried into the house. They heard a man sobbing harshly the minute they opened the door, and Kara knew the worst had happened before anybody said anything.

Her heart pounding, she glanced around the living room where Lorraine, Priscilla, and the brothers were quietly watching William, his face buried in his hands as he wept.

"Dee Dee?" Kara whispered, her words cracking.

John nodded.

"What happened?" she murmured, going to his side, bending down by his chair.

He shrugged and shook his head. "Apparently it was suicide. Of course the body will have to be autopsied, but it seems like she just walked out into the river and drowned herself while we finished breakfast. She washed up downriver. She had a doll tied to her breast by a rope she'd wrapped around her."

Kara blanched at the memory of that poor woman begging someone to get her out of the hellhole, as she'd called Homeplace. Guilt tugged at her; she'd wanted to go to Dee Dee, or to at least try to talk to that pitiful creature later, but she hadn't risked it. Maybe she could have done something if she'd only extended herself a little. It was too late now.

"Oh, John, how horrible," she murmured. "Poor William." She glanced at her brother-in-law and had no doubt that the man was grieving for real now.

Although she felt terribly awkward, she went over and

placed her arm around his shoulders. "I'm so very sorry, William."

He didn't respond. He just sat there, his tears running down his face between his fingers, dripping on the Persian rug that mocked the somber scene with its swirling colors.

Kara had the most absurd notion that at any minute now Lorraine would tell William to straighten up and, at the least, not to weep on the expensive rug; of course, her mind was operating in overdrive again. She was in shock at learning Dee Dee's life had come to such a tragic end, no matter how much she'd expected the worst.

She would always hold the picture in her mind of that awful night when her sister-in-law had been in Ricky's room. It had been terrifying to see someone so tortured, so frightening.

And the doll. So it *had* been Dee Dee's doll. Why had she put a pillow over its face? Kara had an uncontrollable urge to know that her son was all right. She was almost to Ricky's room when she ran into Bucky. She'd thought he was in the living room.

His arms were loaded with packages. Kara stared at him. Didn't Bucky care enough to at least sit with his brothers at this awful time? Though she knew there was a dearth of family support, Bucky had been the one she expected to be affected almost as much as William, and here he was bringing in his gifts.

"Didn't you hear about Dee Dee?" she rasped.

When he saw that she was staring at the bags he clutched to his chest, he said thickly, "I had to get out of the house. I couldn't stay in there with William and the others. I just can't take any more."

Kara sighed as she met his tear-filled eyes. She'd jumped to conclusions again. She recalled saying the same thing when she'd seen Toby's body in the boat.

Nodding, she brushed past Bucky and went in search of Ricky. She found him in his room asleep, the room where Dee Dee had leaned over his bed and perhaps had frightened him so badly, the room where the doll had been found. Abruptly, she sank down on her knees by the baby bed and began to sob softly.

She was still there when John found her. She gasped in surprise when he reached down for her.

"Shh, shh, it's all right," he whispered, drawing her up against his body. "I know Dee Dee's death is a shock, Kara, but it was inevitable. Eventually, she would have been institutionalized or drank herself to death, or met an untimely end one way or another."

Kara stared at him through her tears. "I don't believe it, John. Why didn't someone get her some help before it was too late? I don't understand."

Despite seeing the anger building in John, Kara couldn't stop. "If no one was willing to send her away to get help, why didn't someone privately arrange for her to see Ellis?"

"She was under a doctor's care," John said sharply. "The *family* doctor."

"But apparently that wasn't enough, was it?" Kara murmured. She recalled the rift between Ellis and Lorraine over a family member. "Was Dee Dee the one Ellis said needed help when Lorraine turned on him?" she asked.

John shook Kara, unnerving her. "You don't have any idea what you're talking about! The woman had emotional problems, but there was nothing Ellis could do. He couldn't bring back her babies, could he?"

"Let me go!" Kara commanded, prying his fingers off her shoulders. "Of course Ellis couldn't bring back the children, but he could have helped Dee Dee with her emotional problems. That's what a psychiatrist does, you know!"

Watching John's jaw muscle working, Kara knew he was furious. She was furious herself—and distraught. What was wrong with these people? She couldn't believe what was going on in Homeplace!

"Dee Dee was not the cause of Mother and Ellis's disagreement, and I don't want to hear that repeated ever again!" John commanded. "Mother would be very angry. You don't know my family, so stop harping on what would have helped in the past. You don't know the past! Priscilla tried to explain the situation to you yesterday, remember? Dee Dee was destined for destruction, and it happened."

"Just like that?" Kara said, snapping her fingers. "Your brother's wife is dead under the most tragic circumstances, and you simply say *it happened*. It's over."

For a moment Kara thought John might shake her again, and she wasn't at all sure what she would do if he did. Instead, he said as calmly as she suspected he could under the circumstances, "We have enough problems with Toby's and Dee Dee's deaths, Kara. I advise you not to look for more trouble."

"You *advise* me?" she repeated.

"You heard me."

"Is that more legalese, or is that some kind of warning?" she asked angrily.

John exhaled wearily. "No, it's not a warning," he said. Unexpectedly, he pulled her to him, catching his hands in her long hair as he pressed her head against his shoulder. "I know how hard all this is for you, Kara. Mother's taking you to the doctor's office tomorrow to see if you're pregnant. Remember to get something for your nerves."

He freed her and started away. Kara tugged on his arm; she wasn't through talking to him. "John!"

The commotion woke Ricky and he began whimpering. "Tend to your son, Kara," John said, then he shut the door.

As Kara reached for Ricky, she shivered. She felt cold all of a sudden, as cold as death.

Kara couldn't deny that she was relieved to find out that she wasn't pregnant, and the doctor—the *family doctor*—did indeed suggest that she needed tranquilizers. Kara wondered if the man had prescribed the same thing for Dee Dee. Was she on tranquilizers, too, right along with the liquor she drank?

Kara sighed. She had never been one for taking pills, relying instead on her own immune system and inner strength to pull her through illness or emotional upsets.

Still, as she'd learned after her parents' death, there were times when she needed additional help. She accepted the prescription as a safeguard for the future, as well as to appease John. She believed that he was going to be quite upset to learn he wasn't going to be a father after all.

Unfortunately, Kara didn't know how he felt until dinnertime. She'd been unable to reach him at the office. By the time John arrived late for the evening meal, after everyone else was seated, the news was old. Lorraine had already told him. *And* the rest of the family.

But Kara didn't know that until Priscilla spoke up. Looking from Kara to John, she said, "I'm sorry about the baby, or lack of one."

"How did you know?" Kara asked, staring at her sister-in-law. "I haven't even told my husband yet."

Priscilla widened her brown eyes. "I didn't know I was letting the cat out of the bag. I only wanted to express my sympathy. Things have just gone so badly recently, and I was hoping, like Lorraine, that there would be a new life in Homeplace."

John shrugged. "You didn't let anything out of the bag, Pris. Mother already told me."

Although Kara fought not to show her temper, she was too upset. "Why did you do that?" she demanded, glaring across the table at her mother-in-law. "I thought we agreed that I would tell my husband *myself!*"

"Yes, if you were pregnant," Lorraine said nonchalantly. "But you aren't, are you, and when you couldn't reach him, I knew I could. I didn't see any reason to keep him in the dark any longer. Now, can we get on with dinner civilly, please? I think this week has already been devastating enough without you spoiling mealtimes."

Kara was stunned. She turned to John, who gave her no support at all. In fact, he began eating as if the conversation wasn't taking place. Kara slammed her napkin down, shoved back her chair and rushed from the room.

God knows she was glad she wasn't pregnant. She didn't want John Worthington's child. In fact, she didn't even think she wanted *him!*

13

Kara automatically started down the hill to the river. She was so angry that she had to do something physical or explode. She began walking rapidly, not caring where she was going, not worrying about dead bodies or unborn babies. Her future with John was on the line, and she had to make up her mind what to do. She couldn't go on like this. She *wouldn't* go on this way!

Unaware that the brambles and bushes tore at her nylons, that her blue high heels sank into the muddy bank of the river, or that the full-skirted blue dress she'd worn to the doctor was being snagged by branches, Kara walked faster and faster, her pulse racing, her heart pounding.

She didn't know how long she'd been walking when she suddenly found herself at the dam. She glanced at the water; the memory of Toby's body in the boat caused her to stumble. Sucking in her breath, she spun around and headed in the other direction as if she could outrun her unhappiness if she just kept moving.

She realized she'd gone all the way back to Homeplace when she heard voices coming from the sun porch. Bitterly, she told herself that she'd obviously been placed in the category of another runaway wife, who may or may not return, and who cared anyway? Instead of making her feel sorry for herself, the idea only fueled her anger. She was not ready to return to the house; if she did, in the mood she was in, she was sure it would be for the last time.

She had to be positive that was what she wanted before she told John they were finished. She didn't want this traumatic week to be the only reason for ending her marriage. She needed to think things out thoroughly.

The voices of the Worthingtons sobered her as she continued away from Homeplace, going upriver. Thoughts of the home she and John were having built filled her mind and she headed toward it.

When she finally reached the site, she was taken aback. Nothing had been done except the pouring of the foundation. She didn't understand. She'd thought the construction had been ongoing. The sight of the cement slab and concrete stones lying around haphazardly seemed unreal to her.

She'd truly anticipated the skeleton of the house by now. Unhappy, she sat down on the slab and stared out at the river. Maybe the storm had caused the workmen to stop work, but surely more than the ground floor should have been completed before the storm.

Lost in her misery, Kara didn't pay attention to time. When she realized it was getting dark, she decided to attempt a shortcut back to Homeplace. She didn't know what she was going to say to John; however, she did know she wanted to try to salvage her marriage in spite of what was going on. The house site reminded her of all the plans she and John had made for a lifetime together. She still wanted to believe that they had a future if they could just get out of Homeplace. She wasn't ready to abandon her dreams yet.

But was John?

After she had struggled up a part of the hillside that seemed the least steep, she headed across Homeplace land, through the trees, sure she saw the lights of the old white mansion in the distance.

Instead, when she drew nearer she found a small log cabin. All the curtains were closed, but the dwelling looked cozy and inviting, with lights showing behind the lacy fabric at the windows.

Kara's burst of temper subsided. She was beginning to become frightened as night closed in around her; she was lost. She should have followed the river back downstream, but it was too late for that now. Trying to soothe her fears, she told herself that this was no doubt Thelma's daughter Tessa's cabin.

The Worthington property was extensive, but Kara suspected that only Tessa was tolerated on the Homeplace grounds. She would ask the girl to show her the fastest way back to the house, if Tessa was home. She had been curious about the young woman since she'd met her, anyway. This might be a blessing in disguise, a chance to get to talk to Tessa.

Kara's optimism abruptly came crashing down around her, quickly replaced by stark terror. She'd barely stepped out of the woods when someone grabbed her from behind! She was so preoccupied, and the assault was so totally unexpected, that she automatically screamed for dear life. The assailant clamped a hand over her mouth and pulled her back into the trees before she could flee.

Panic engulfing her, every fear she'd had at Homeplace coming back to haunt her in a moment that seemed an eternity, Kara kicked and flailed, frantically fighting to survive. The attacker's hand was over her mouth in such a manner that even breathing through her nose was difficult. As Kara tried to open her mouth wider, she managed to bite down hard on the breath-stifling hand.

The attacker grunted with pain and momentarily relaxed the hold. Suddenly she was free! Again she screamed with every ounce of hysterical strength she had, scrambling wildly away from the menace behind her. Her anxiety and tension had been building since she returned to Homeplace, and the terrified cry that filled the air was no less piercing than the one Agnes Chaney had emitted at the sight of the Toby in the boat.

Tessa opened the door of the cabin and called out loudly,

"Who's there? What's going on? I've got a gun, and I've called the police!"

Kara fled toward the safety of the cabin, one of her muddy, misshapen shoes falling off in the flight. She quickly glanced back, expecting her attacker to be in pursuit, but to her relief she saw the dark form running in the other direction.

"Tessa!" Kara cried. "Oh, thank God, Tessa. It's me, Kara. Someone—there was—" She looked back over her shoulder. In the darkness there was no movement at all. The sound of the river rushing on downstream was all that could be heard now.

"Come in," Tessa said. "Hurry!"

Kara didn't need to be urged. She was hurrying with the last bit of strength she had.

"Lord God, Mrs. Worthington," Tessa said, "what on earth are you doing out here in these woods at night? You're scratched and bleeding."

Kara stared down at herself. She was scratched and bleeding, it was true, but most of that had happened during her angry, heedless walk along the riverbank. She felt herself blush, wondering how to explain that her disarray was not from the attack. However, that didn't alter the fact that she'd been assaulted.

"I was walking along the riverbank and lost track of time," she hurriedly explained. "I went to the site where our house is being built, and when I realized it was growing dark, I decided to try a shortcut to Homeplace. I had just stumbled on your cabin when somebody attacked me."

Tessa's curious gaze caused an inexplicable sinking feeling inside Kara. She realized that Tessa doubted her story. "Did you see him?" Kara asked hopefully.

Ever cautious, Tessa shook her head. She felt sorry for this woman. She'd seen how the newest Mrs. Worthington was struggling to fit in with the others at the big house. Yes, she felt sorry for her, but Mama had taught her that her own future depended upon staying apart from the people living in Homeplace. Tessa had learned the lesson well.

"I heard you screaming, but I couldn't see who was in

the woods. Are you sure it was a man?" Tessa asked, studying the disheveled woman.

"A man? Of course." Kara suddenly hesitated, licking her lips. She'd thought it was a man. No—she'd assumed it was. She couldn't be sure. The encounter had been so brief and she'd been totally disoriented and overpowered by her fear and panic. But, yes, she believed it was a man. Didn't she? Why would a woman attack her?

"I didn't see him, but I'm reasonably sure it was a man. He grabbed me from behind just as I started toward your cabin," Kara said, her words tumbling over each other. "When I screamed, he clamped his hand over my mouth and started dragging me back into the trees. He—I—I bit him. He let me go then, and I screamed again and started running. I didn't really see him, but I'm positive it was a man."

Tessa nodded. She didn't know this woman. While she'd served meals at the main house, she'd discreetly studied the newest member of the household and the little boy. But she didn't know Kara Worthington at all.

No matter how sympathetic she felt, she couldn't afford to become involved. Mama would be angry and disappointed. And Mama had suffered enough because of her daughter. Tessa would not add to her mother's misery, no matter how concerned she was for this shaken stranger.

Kara had that awful feeling inside again. She told herself that the girl was used to odd happenings with the Worthingtons, and maybe thought this was just another one.

"You did call the police, didn't you?" Kara asked frantically. "Are they coming?"

Tessa shook her head. She *never* made an unauthorized move concerning Homeplace. She didn't dare. When she had the misfortune to become involved in the Worthington lives, she had been trained to consult one of them, no matter how trivial the incident, from the rare trespasser on Homeplace land to anything that might call attention to herself or any of the Worthingtons.

Even at school she kept a low profile, and she never brought anyone to the cabin. She'd endured the lonely, isolated life stoically, because she knew she had to. And because she had hope for the future. The minute she got her degree, she was leaving, and she was taking Mama with her. Someplace far away. Someplace out of the dangerous clutches of the Worthingtons. Maybe even California. Where Kara had come from.

"I didn't call the police. I wasn't sure what was going on when I heard the commotion outside. The river killer hasn't attacked anywhere except down on the river, and I know Mrs. Worthington doesn't want *anybody* on her property without her knowing about it first."

"The river killer," Kara breathed, only realizing at that moment that she had been afraid she'd been grabbed by the savage serial murderer.

"But I was attacked!" she cried, trying to make sense of what the girl was saying. "Please call the police!"

"I'm going to get you some help," Tessa said soothingly, her training in nursing automatically causing her to offer aid. "And I truly do have a gun. We'll be okay if the person comes back. I'll call the Worthingtons first and let Mr. John call the police."

"We need the police *now!* Why don't you call the police first, then call John?" Kara asked incredulously, running shaking hands through her hair. There were tangles and pieces of leaves and weeds in it. She kept combing her fingers through it, nervously tearing at the twisted strands.

Tessa drew in a steadying breath. She didn't want to be unkind, and she didn't want to play down this woman's obvious terror. But she had to think of her mother.

"Mrs. Worthington—Kara—I've lived in this cabin since I was sixteen. Mrs. Worthington had it built to get me out of the main house, but I knew long before that not to take *any* action, no matter how bad the situation, until I called one of the Worthingtons. Now you try to pull yourself together while I do that."

"I don't believe this!" Kara cried as Tessa picked up the phone and dialed Homeplace. Kara listened in disbelief as Tessa cryptically explained that Kara was at the cabin and *thought* someone had tried to harm her outside, then hung up.

"Don't you understand that the man's getting away?" Kara demanded. "For God's sake, call the police before someone else is hurt."

When Tessa, looking worried, didn't act, Kara went to the phone herself and called the police. She watched as Tessa bit down on her lip and shook her head.

After Kara hung up, thinking that the Worthington name did indeed mean something, for the police dispatcher said someone would be there in minutes, Kara apologized to Tessa.

"I am sorry. I don't want to get you in any trouble, but John isn't the one who'll pursue the attacker, and the sooner the police arrive, the better chance the man will be caught."

Tessa went to the kitchen and got a glass of water. "Here," she said, "please drink this and sit down. You're hurt and you're very agitated."

Kara stared at her.

"Please," Tessa repeated. "I'm a nursing student. The best thing to do is try to calm down until help comes so you can answer questions rationally."

Kara sighed and slumped down in the nearest chair, although she didn't accept the water. She didn't think she could hold the glass with her quivering hands.

"Tessa," she said plaintively, brushing aside the offered glass, "strange things are happening at Homeplace. Help me understand why. Please."

Her eyes flooded with tears as she tried to continue. She was feeling more desperate than ever. She realized that she had envisioned some sort of help from this girl who lived here in the cabin. She'd almost thought fate had sent her here tonight. It was becoming more and more apparent that she'd been wrong. Tessa didn't believe her, much less offer any real source of support. She had to do her best to get the young woman to understand that the danger was real, Kara decided, that she hadn't *imagined* she'd been assaulted.

"You must know something about the Worthingtons," Kara said frantically, taking a chance with Tessa because she believed she had no choice. "I'm frightened and I have no one to help me. You've lived here all your life. Please tell me what's going on in Homeplace. Help me."

Tessa looked down at her hands. She knew that strange things were going on. They always had. But what could she tell this woman? What help could she offer? She couldn't even help herself or her mother. Yet.

"Get away from there, Mrs. Worthington," she said, her voice a sharp whisper. "Take your child and go away."

Kara rushed over and grasped Tessa's shoulders, trying to make the younger woman look at her. "Why? Please tell me."

Tessa stiffened and backed away. "The Worthingtons will be here any minute. You'd better get ready."

"Get ready?" Kara repeated inanely. Get ready? What was she going to get ready for? She'd been assaulted. She needed help, not to "get ready" for her husband's arrival.

Or did she? The color draining from her face, she studied the girl as a fresh wave of fear washed over her. Tessa had warned her to leave, and in doing so, had only increased her fright, not lessened it. But Kara knew she would get no more information from Tessa.

In fact, she wasn't so sure she'd been wise to pressure the young woman. She was beginning to feel sick to her stomach. Her thoughts turned to her young son, left alone at Homeplace. No—worse. *Not* alone. Left there with the Worthingtons.

Too weak to stand on her own two feet, Kara sat back down on the chair while her anxiety spiraled to new heights.

In minutes John, Melvin, William, Lorraine, and Priscilla all were at Tessa's door. John burst in first without knocking, scaring both women so badly that they gasped in unison.

"Kara, what happened to you?" he asked.

Unreasonably relieved, Kara told herself that her husband's concern was genuine. He *was* worried about her! It gave her courage and hope. John's compassionate expression causing her to forget Tessa's warning, Kara let herself break down completely, sobbing in his arms, suddenly ashamed of her stormy exit from Homeplace.

"Oh, John," she exclaimed, her voice thick with tears, "I got lost. Somebody—a man—grabbed me outside Tessa's cabin. Thank God Tessa heard me screaming and I was able to escape . . ." As she talked, she felt John tensing up.

She drew back and looked at him. *He* didn't believe her! She could tell! She looked at the others. There were various expressions of disbelief and disgust on their faces.

"It's true!" she exclaimed angrily, starting in with the entire story again, as if she could make them believe by repeating it.

John silenced her. "When did you tear your stockings? Where did you get the river mud on your shoe? And where's your other shoe? You say the man attacked you outside Tessa's cabin? How did you know where it was? And this—man—did he do this to your clothes and hair?" His eyes said he doubted it.

The barrage of questions hit Kara like stones. What more could she say to convince him? She had sustained most of the visible lacerations before she was attacked, but *she was attacked all the same!*

There was a hard rap on the door. "Police!" a loud voice announced.

John glanced sharply at Tessa. "Did you call them?"

When she didn't respond, Kara did. "No. She called *you*. *I* called the police. The quicker someone pursues the attacker, the better chance he'll get caught. My God, you all should know that!"

They did know that, she realized. It was simply that they didn't believe anything had happened to her except that she'd let her temper get the best of her, and had invented an interesting story to cover her embarrassment.

"I'll handle this," Lorraine said.

"No, I will," John insisted.

Predictably, both of them went to the door to talk to the

police. Kara held her breath as she heard the whispered words: marital spat, frightened, overreacted, lost.

Finally, after taking off the one muddied shoe she still wore, she strode to the door herself. "I'm the one who called you," she told the two policemen. "I'm the one who was assaulted. *I'm* the one you need to talk to!"

They glanced at her; one frowned, the other looked at Lorraine.

"John."

Kara knew what it meant when Lorraine issued one of her son's names in that voice. John stepped back inside, taking Kara with him, and shut the door, leaving Lorraine with the policemen.

Kara didn't believe it. She *couldn't* believe it! "John, for God's sake, if you won't believe me, at least let the police investigate. It could have been the river murderer. It could have been Dee Dee's killer. Maybe she didn't drown herself after all! I swear to you that I was attacked, no matter how disheveled I got before I reached Tessa's cabin."

John looked away. Was Mother right about Kara after all? Did she go to these lengths to embarrass him? He'd seen Dee Dee commit this kind of behavior. *He* would not be another William!

Any fool could see where Kara had been walking, that the briars and brambles along the river had torn her nylons and dress, and the mud on her shoe was from the bank.

There was no thick vegetation around Tessa's house. It had all been cleared away years ago. Only a few shade trees had been left standing. And why had Kara come here anyway, when the main house was a mile away? Had she come here before?

Everyone turned in Lorraine's direction when she entered the crowded living room and slammed the door. "Let's go home! We've had enough of a circus here to last a lifetime."

Kara fought back bitter tears. No one believed her, and she didn't know how she could possibly convince them. Not the family. Not the police. Not even John. No one would listen.

BLOODY WATERS

Left with no choice, she followed the other family members to the two cars parked in front of Tessa's cabin. Kara had seen the road before, but she hadn't known where it went. She knew that Tessa came over to help at the house, though she hadn't known how far the young woman had walked.

Getting in the backseat of John's car, behind him and Lorraine, Kara felt like she'd shriveled up inside. She'd been subjected to many things in her life, and she'd even been accused of a thing or two she hadn't done; however, she'd never experienced a living nightmare like the one she was going through now. She *had been* attacked! She wasn't making it up.

Huddled into a small, defeated shape, she watched as Melvin, Priscilla, and William got in the other car and left.

Her only consoling thought was that she had escaped physical harm. She had survived. Apparently nothing less than a brutal beating or death would have convinced the others, but she knew she'd escaped serious harm only with Tessa's help, whether even Tessa believed her or not.

And, yes, there was one other consoling thought. Tomorrow morning she and Ricky would leave Homeplace forever. The decision had been made for her by the attack and the family's response. She had reached the limits of her tolerance. She didn't belong here. No one in her right mind would stay.

She'd had enough. Even without Tessa's scary warning. John's doubt had been the breaking point. He gave her no choice except to leave him. And, more importantly, Homeplace.

When they went into the house, no one said anything. Badly battered internally, Kara went to her baby's room, gratefully found him sleeping soundly, then went to the bathroom at the end of the hall. After she'd stripped off her clothes, she climbed into a tub of warm water and lay there, numb, oblivious to the stinging of the long, thin scratches on her arms and legs, and the barbs of the briars embedded like tiny fishhooks in one hand.

She gasped when the door opened. John came in, carrying a robe. Kara was too deeply distressed by his behavior to even speak to him.

"Kara, look at me," John ordered.

"Go away," she murmured. "I don't want to talk about it anymore. You don't believe me. There's no point. I can't stay here. It's over. We're over. Please leave."

Reaching out, he lifted her chin, forcing her to look at him. "With all we've already suffered this week, why did you pull this stunt tonight?"

Kara's fingers closed down on John's hand with strength born of anger and disillusionment. It took her a moment to find the words to tell him she'd been broken beyond repair in the short time she'd been back with him.

"I walked out of the house because I didn't want to explode in front of the family, John. I know you can't understand that. You and your family have no respect for anyone else's life. I believe your mother had no right to tell you or anyone else that I wasn't pregnant. You don't care. You don't care what she says or does. You think she's always right, don't you? That she can do no wrong."

John scrutinized his wife. Kara hadn't been what he thought she was. Still, he had married her, and he would *stay* married to her, no matter what it took to straighten her out. He wouldn't tolerate a Dee Dee as William had. And he wouldn't indulge the fact that Mother forbade divorce: He would remain married because he'd chosen this woman, rightly or wrongly.

"Did it embarass you that much because you hadn't conceived my child?" he asked with deceptive softness. "Is that what this little scene is all about?"

Kara stared at him. Was he serious? Was he asking out of kindness, or was he being sarcastic? She didn't know this man she'd married, this man she slept with each night and called husband. Maybe he was merely being his egotistical self. After all, she knew she could conceive a child. Could *he?*

"That wasn't the issue, John," she said, too weary to continue arguing with him. "You don't understand. And you don't believe—*or care*—that I was physically assaulted tonight. My God, John! I could have been killed! Don't you understand? Don't you realize that this maniac could at this very moment be harming someone else because I managed to escape?"

She reached out with a wet hand. Though she hadn't meant to cry, tears filled her eyes. "I swear on my parents' grave that I was attacked, John. I didn't make it up to get attention, or to get even with you, or whatever else you and your family believe."

John looked into Kara's eyes. Even now, sitting in the tub, her naked body scratched and scraped, he wanted her. She thrilled him as no other woman ever had. Not even Claudia Lindheart.

But he didn't believe her. Not for a moment. He'd not only seen Dee Dee put on this same kind of show to get even with William and Mother, he'd also witnessed more than one woman accusing a man of rape or assault out of vengeance.

"Kara, the river killer doesn't attack women," he said evenly. "He's a homosexual killer. He's not interested in women."

"Maybe this wasn't the same—"

"Don't start," he interrupted. "No one killed Dee Dee. She committed suicide. She probably jumped into the river where the eddy is. It's a dangerous place and she knew about it. That's where my father died."

Kara saw the futility of continuing—the conversation and the marriage. She believed that she loved John Worthington, but she had loved Richard, too. She would get over John in time, and the sooner she left here, the better.

For her and for the Worthingtons.

"I'm returning to California on the first plane I can get," she said raggedly. "I think it's best."

John seemed genuinely shocked. For a moment he gazed at her, as much in disbelief as he'd appeared to be when she'd said she'd been attacked. Then he shook his head.

Kara nodded. "I am leaving, John."

John shook his head again. "We're married, Kara. You're not going anywhere."

She looked away from him. "I want a divorce."

"No."

Incredulous, she turned to look at him. "I don't think you understand, John—"

"No, once again, I'm afraid it's *you*, Kara, who doesn't understand. We talked this out. No Worthington has ever gotten a divorce. No Worthington ever will."

His jaw muscle began to twitch. "I let you trot back to California once, leaving me here, a fool newly married without a wife. You're not running off again. It's not an option. You're staying. I won't allow you to carry on like Dee Dee did, bringing shame and humiliation on Homeplace and the Worthingtons. And you are a Worthington now."

"You're crazy!" she cried. "I won't stay married to you under these conditions. I was assaulted tonight, and you don't believe me! No one here does. Oh, John, don't you understand? This was a mistake! *We're* a mistake. I don't belong here. I'm not happy here. I will return to California with my child."

John glared at her. "No!"

Kara could feel herself getting hysterical. John couldn't keep her a prisoner here! He couldn't *make* her stay married to him! He *was* crazy! All the Worthingtons were! Suddenly she was afraid again, more afraid than she'd been while being attacked by the stranger!

She sank deeper into the water, as if it could protect her, as if it could hide her from the horror.

"Here," John said, holding his hand out. "These will help you sleep."

She saw that he held two of the tranquilizers that had been prescribed for her. "I don't want those," she said.

"You *need* them," he stated. "I'll get you a glass of water."

Kara started to refuse again, then it occurred to her that he might try to *force* her to take the medication. She didn't know what to expect of him anymore, but her instinct for survival warned her to be cautious, to be wary.

She had only herself to depend on here in this madhouse. She had to pull herself together for Ricky's and her sake. She took the pills, and when she saw that John was watching her in the mirror as he filled a glass with water from the sink faucet, she slipped them in her mouth under her tongue. She managed to hold them there while she drank the water.

Satisfied, John stood up. "I want you to make an appointment with Ellis tomorrow, Kara. You keep advocating therapy for troubled people. Maybe it'll be beneficial to you. I believe you've said it was in the past."

Kara didn't comment. When he shut the door, she spit the pills out. They had dissolved partly, but she hoped not enough to have much impact. From now on she intended to be alert in Homeplace. This entire family might be twisted, evil even, but they couldn't keep her here against her will.

A sudden memory of Dee Dee not being able to drive loomed in Kara's mind. Surely John would see that this wasn't what he wanted. He wouldn't hold her to her marital vows under the circumstances. *Would he?*

A vision of Ellis Davidson rose in her mind. If she hadn't had the pills in her mouth, she would have told John she didn't need a psychiatrist. What she needed was a divorce.

But perhaps she'd been fortunate that she hadn't been able to answer. Maybe she did need to see Ellis. Intuitively, she trusted him. She believed he could help her. If he would. If his loyalty to John didn't prevent it.

It was the only chance she had—a chance she must take.

14

Kara wasn't surprised to find that breakfast was conducted as usual the next day, as though nothing out of the ordinary had occurred the previous night. But what was to be expected where mayhem and madness were routine?

The talk turned to the funerals the family would attend the coming week—both Dee Dee's and Toby's—as casually as if they were discussing a social outing. Only William and Kara refrained from comment.

"Well, we were fortunate that Toby washed up before Dee Dee did," Melvin said. "The media tied the two together and played it up big as the first female murder by the river killer."

Kara's fork clattered to her plate. "I thought you said Dee Dee committed suicide, John!" she blurted, not realizing until she said it that she didn't want to engage in this kind of conversation in front of William, that she didn't want to be as callous as the Worthingtons.

Melvin shrugged before John could answer. "Who can be sure until the autopsy? Anyway, it doesn't look good for a Worthington to do herself in—even a sorry one."

"Doesn't look good for whom?" Kara asked angrily. "Do you only worry about your career, Melvin? Doesn't human life mean anything to you? Who will take the blame

BLOODY WATERS

for the murder if Dee Dee did commit suicide? Some innocent man?"

Melvin guffawed. "What difference does it make? Somebody's killing people. If Dee Dee's death is added in, it'll serve him—or her—right to get time for it, or better yet, to fry. The damned system is too liberal, and everybody knows it."

"Which brings us back to the topic of Asterson being innocent," John interjected.

"Oh, bull!" Melvin said. "We've got ourselves two killers, and you know it, Johnny-boy!"

"And another potential victim that nobody bothered to count," Kara said, outraged because no one would listen to her. "If you even *think* that Dee Dee may have been murdered, why doesn't anyone believe what really happened to *me* last night?"

"If you're so worried about killers, Kara," Lorraine said tightly, "why did you wander all over the riverbank and grounds last night alone? Tell me, if you will please. Weren't you intentionally putting yourself in jeopardy, knowing that Toby had been murdered and Dee Dee had vanished?"

Her eyes glowed wickedly as she challenged Kara.

"At that moment I guess I preferred to take my chances with murderers rather than stay here," Kara retorted, even though it wasn't the truth. She'd recklessly fled the dinner table without giving any thought to the danger beyond the mansion; the danger within had been her concern.

"Then *if* you were attacked," Lorraine said sharply, "as you claim, don't you rather think you asked for it?"

"I did not!" Kara cried, standing up and once more throwing her napkin down on the table. "Nobody asks to be assaulted! You people are all crazy! I swear I believe it's true!"

John grasped her hand. "Did you take your tranquilizers this morning?"

"I most certainly didn't, and I don't intend to," Kara said sharply, pulling free of him. "Excuse me," she said, "I'm no longer hungry."

195

She started around the table to pick up Ricky; before she could, Lorraine stood up.

"You may not be hungry, but the boy is. Leave him."

Ignoring her, Kara lifted the child from his high chair.

"No!" Ricky protested. "I wanna eat!"

"Not now," Kara said, trying to quiet him.

"I wanna eat now, Mommy," he insisted, as she stalked out of the room with him.

John stood up, too, giving some silent signal to his mother, who for once apparently obeyed.

The minute Kara reached John's room, she put her weeping child down and began laying her clothes out on the bed. She would leave here today if she had to walk!

John and Thelma entered the room; before Kara could stop him, John handed Ricky over to Thelma. When Kara reached for him, John put a hand on her arm.

"Just calm down a minute and listen to me," he said. "We need to talk."

"We needed to talk last night," she flung at him, watching as Thelma slipped out the door with Ricky and closed it behind them.

John exhaled wearily. "Maybe so. Maybe we're all so upset over what's happened recently that none of us is acting rationally." He tried to embrace her, but Kara evaded his arms.

"It's too late, John," she said. "It's over. I want to leave."

"Without giving us a real chance?" he murmured seductively.

She shook her head. "God knows I've tried. You destroyed my faith in you last night when you didn't believe me, when you didn't care enough to find out if I'd been molested."

"I am under great strain, Kara," he said. "Dee Dee's death was a shock. I truly thought she'd just run off."

"And that was fine, wasn't it?" Kara exclaimed indignantly. "If a woman's just a runaway wife, none of you Worthingtons gives a damn, do you? Leave them alone and they'll come home, dragging their tails behind them? Is that it? Is that the philosophy here?"

"Kara, Kara," he said wearily, "don't you know the strain we've all been under?"

"And what about *me?*" she asked. "Don't you think I've been under strain, too?" She looked at him accusingly. "John, you didn't even look for me last night. At least Dee Dee received that much attention. William was concerned enough to look for her."

John sighed. "You're not a dingbat like Dee Dee. I felt that you wanted to be alone, that you needed time to yourself at that particular moment. I did look for you when you didn't return."

His brown eyes searched her face. "Of course I was concerned. If I hadn't been, I wouldn't have nearly killed Mother and me getting to Tessa's cabin."

Kara could feel herself weakening. She didn't know whether to believe this mercurial man or not. He *had* seemed worried when he burst into the house.

"Do you love me, Kara?" he asked quietly.

When she looked away, John lifted her chin, forcing her to meet his eyes. "Kara?"

She could feel her own eyes filling with tears. God help her, she was afraid she did love him, but she would not relent. Deep inside, her sense of self-preservation signaled the need to flee this place, this man, while there was still time.

Last night he'd told her she'd never get a divorce, and she'd believed he was serious. But why? Because no Worthington could get a divorce by some decree handed down by Lorraine, because he did care about his wife, *or* was there some other reason?

"Do you love me, John?" Kara asked tremulously, naked fear in her eyes. She was visibly shaking.

John's steady gaze met hers. She wasn't exactly the woman he'd thought she was, but then that was probably true of anyone once the newness wore off. Kara was still the most exciting woman he'd ever met. He'd married her, and he wanted her. That was close enough to love for him.

"Yes."

"Then if you love me," she whispered, "move us out of

Homeplace today, this morning, right now. It's the only way we're going to save our marriage."

"Our house isn't finished," he reminded her.

She held his gaze. "I saw that last night. It hasn't been started. Why, John? Did you know that only the foundation is down? Why has no one worked on the house?"

John knew why: Lorraine had forbidden the builders to set foot on her land, but he hadn't expected Kara to discover that construction had ceased.

"Some kind of dispute between the workers and the boss," he said. "I've threatened to fire them all and hire another crew."

"Why didn't you tell me?" she asked.

He shrugged. "You've been unhappy. I didn't want to add to your distress. I know how much you're looking forward to moving into the house."

"John, I don't care where we move as long as it's away from Homeplace," she said fervently. "We can rent until the house is built. Please move us out of here!"

"Kara, I simply have to spend every spare moment on Asterson's defense," he said. "These other deaths have taken time away from his case. Maybe that's part of our problem. You feel neglected. As soon as I can wrap up this case and the house is completed, things will be different."

Although in her heart Kara wanted to believe him, she couldn't. She was reminded that he was the same man who'd been so cruel and insensitive to her last night.

"Make the appointment with Ellis, and let him help you through this time until I can wrap up Asterson's case," John murmured. "If you do love me, give us another chance."

Kara carefully considered what he said. Deep inside, she sensed that the marriage was doomed, yet she knew that John was making a concession by asking her to see Ellis, knowing how Lorraine hated psychiatrists in general and Ellis in particular.

And if, as she truly believed, the marriage was over, she believed that John was serious about making divorce difficult for her. She thought again that Ellis could make a valuable and much-needed ally, if it came to that.

"All right, John," she agreed.

He pulled her into his arms. "That's my girl," he murmured, his hands moving familiarly over her body.

Kara found herself oddly shy when the chauffeur dropped her off at Ellis's office, which was on the lower floor of an old Victorian house. The top floor was his living quarters.

After a receptionist announced her arrival, Ellis gave Kara a tour of the office and his apartment, as if she were a friend, rather than a patient. She was acutely aware of Ellis as she walked beside him. He had a quiet strength that contrasted sharply with his tall, well-defined body and dashing good looks. His skin was tanned, making his blond hair look even fairer and his eyes a dazzling green.

She tried to tell herself that she was simply desperate for a friendly face, for someone who cared about her, who might understand what she was going through. But it was more than that. It was also, she realized, a physical attraction.

Seeing Ellis again, being here with him alone, she recalled how interested she had been from the first day she met him. She felt a strange kind of connection to him, a bonding that made her want to let her guard down, to talk openly, to turn to him with all her disturbing thoughts.

She struggled to suppress the urge. The last thing she needed was more trouble in the situation she was already in. Ellis was a neutral party at this stage, a psychiatrist, someone who might be her saving grace if things worsened between her and John and the rest of the Worthingtons.

"My grandparents owned this house," Ellis explained, pointing out an old couple in a picture hung on the wall. "The house is over a hundred years old."

Kara couldn't think of anything to say. She could feel herself blushing. None of the the idle chitchat that passed for conversation surfaced. She could only think of how many times she'd seen Ellis in her mind. Maybe she'd built him up as something he wasn't, imagined an attraction that wasn't really there because she presently found her marriage so difficult and disillusioning.

"Is something wrong?" he asked perceptively. "Am I making you uncomfortable showing you around? I only meant to help you relax. Maybe I've made a mistake. I know we need to talk. I knew that the day Toby was found. Right from the first day I met you, Kara, I've wanted to be your friend."

He shook his head. "I'm sorry. I'm getting way ahead of myself. It's just that I know the Worthingtons, and I couldn't help wondering if you knew what you were getting into when you married John."

He held up his hand before she could speak. "Again, I'm sorry. I'm way out of line. I don't know what's gotten into me. Let's start over. Come down to the office, and *you* talk to *me*."

Kara put her hand on his arm. "Wait, Ellis, please. You're not making me uncomfortable. No, that's not true," she corrected. "You *are* making me uncomfortable, but not because of—of your openness. I do need to talk to you desperately about the Worthingtons—all of them, John included. I *didn't* know what I was getting into. I'm worried. *You* know something is strange about them, don't you, Ellis?" she asked anxiously.

She needed to know for her own salvation that someone else had witnessed how peculiar the family was. Either they were all crazy, she realized, or *she* was!

Ellis sighed. "I'm not going to beat around the bush with you, Kara. I've suspected something wasn't quite right with at least one of the family members for as long as I've known them, and my suspicions had been substantiated when I formally studied psychiatry. In fact, being around John's family—" He waved his hand. "This is so unprofessional of me. I'm in an awkward position here. I know you need my help, but I shouldn't be saying these things. I barely know you, no matter how well I feel that I do."

"Ellis, I would never repeat anything you've said about them," she hastened to assure him.

"I don't think you would," he said. "However, the

point is, I'm out of line." He motioned to her. "Come downstairs."

Kara followed him, unsure whether to be disappointed or not. While it was true that she didn't know him, either— they'd spoken so few times—she felt the same way he did, as if she knew him well.

The notion nearly immobilized her. She'd thought something similiar about John. She'd believed immediately that they had some connection that precluded the usual courtship period. And that was precisely why she was in this awful predicament.

But she and Ellis weren't like she and John. She felt strangely close to Ellis in a way she couldn't explain. Maybe she was grasping at straws. What she needed to do was see him solely as a psychiatrist who might be able to help her.

She was relieved at least in knowing that she alone didn't think the Worthingtons had emotional problems. This man, a trained doctor, had observed them firsthand, too.

"Now," he said, sounding distant and professional when Kara had taken the chair across from his desk, "let's start at the beginning. What brings you to me, Kara?"

She wanted to beg him not to be formal with her, to help her feel at ease, free to tell him all that was troubling her. But perhaps she had no right.

"I'm not happy being married to John," she confessed. "I never imagined that I would be marrying his entire family: Lorraine, Melvin, Priscilla, William"—she hesitated— "poor Dee Dee, while she was alive, Bucky, and even Lorrie."

Her troubled blue eyes met Ellis's green ones. She didn't know how much she should say to him, but it was now or never, she feared. "I think the entire family is emotionally disturbed to one degree or another, Ellis. Honest to God, I do. There are—are things going on at that house that aren't—quite kosher."

She glanced down at her hands, afraid to be too bold and afraid not to. When she looked up again, Ellis was frowning. She drew in a deep breath and plunged on, wondering if she was inviting more trouble for herself.

"Bucky hints at secrets. Tessa more or less warned me to take my son and leave Homeplace."

She searched Ellis's face for some kind of understanding, some recognition that he knew what she was talking about. She couldn't tell what he might be thinking, but she was in this now.

"I'm surprised that John agreed to my talking with you. He told me that the split between you and Lorraine occurred because you suggested that some member of the family needed, as John called it—couch time."

Ellis picked up a pipe and packed it with pungent tobacco. "Do you mind if I smoke?" he asked.

Kara shook her head. She could see that she'd revealed more than Ellis had expected her to. He was pensive as he lit the pipe and gazed at Kara through the light stream of gray smoke.

"This family is a mess," he finally said frankly. "Lorraine's mother was, I suspect, schizophrenic. Because her family had money, her condition was hidden behind polite terms like her 'delicate' condition and her 'fragile' health. People said she heard voices, and she spoke aloud to them from the time she was a teenager. My grandparents knew her well and often talked about crazy Louise Stokes."

Kara found her heart beating faster. She wasn't afraid of mental illness; having been exposed all her life to artists, she was well aware of depressions, manic episodes, and other mood disorders suffered by susceptible temperaments. But she also knew a little about schizophrenia. And what she knew was that it was thought to be inherited.

She immediately recalled the times Lorraine had gone off into trances, seemingly lost within herself, or the times she'd talked to God, or someone else Kara couldn't see. *All* the family members, except Priscilla—a part of the clan by marriage only—had a penchant for that, including John.

Kara felt an unnamed panic rising inside her. Were the Worthingtons mentally ill? And what did that mean for her?

"If it eases your mind," Ellis said gently, "I'm going to

tell you, if you haven't already guessed, that Lorraine was the family member I was talking about. I'm going to trust you to keep that to yourself, Kara."

"I will, I promise, Ellis," she said solemnly. "However, it doesn't ease my mind at all. I've already guessed that Lorraine is nearly over the edge, but then, I find her sons well out of what I consider the normal range."

"The normal range?" Ellis repeated. "I'm sure you know normal is relative."

Ellis was obviously being cautious, in spite of confiding his feelings about Lorraine. Kara, though disappointed, reminded herself to be equally careful. She knew she was prone to speak incautiously. She came here in the capacity of patient, yet both of them knew she was here because of family connections—Ellis and John's friendship.

"Although I've certainly never considered myself naive," Kara said carefully, "I'm the first to admit that I rushed headlong into marriage with a man I knew nothing about. I thought I knew John. It's only taken a few weeks of this—this nightmare—to prove me wrong."

"What nightmare?" he asked tactfully. "Tell me about it, Kara."

She sighed. She felt as if they were losing whatever closeness she felt they had, and she was wary. Even though Ellis had confided his thoughts about Lorraine, maybe it was a different situation when it came to John and the brothers. For all she knew, John had already talked to Ellis.

Briefly, she glanced away, unable to meet his eyes. "You say that you barely know me. Well, I barely know you." She looked at him evenly. "How do I know I can trust you not to repeat what I say to your friend, my husband, John?"

Ellis nodded understandingly. "You can trust me, Kara. I'm not at liberty legally or ethically to repeat what we discuss with anyone. I'm careful to be very brief on my notes should they ever be subpoenaed for court cases."

"Subpoenaed for court cases?" she murmured. "Why would that happen?" Instinctively, she felt that she'd walked into a trap somehow, but she wasn't sure how.

Even though she *did* trust Ellis, something was wrong here. Anything that had to do with court or attorneys triggered her fear of the Worthingtons.

Or was she going mad? Maybe it was she, all along, who'd lost her mind since moving here. She kept thinking people were trying to warn her about something: Bucky about his mother, and even John about Lorraine, Dee Dee about life at the mansion, Thelma about the river, Tessa about Homeplace—and now Ellis. About—about what or whom—*John?*

"John said you told a tale of being attacked by the river killer, Kara."

"It was no tale, Ellis!" she cried, furious because no one seemed to believe her. "I swear it happened! A man—someone—grabbed me! Nobody believes me because John and I had quarreled and I'd gone out on the riverbank alone."

Ellis studied her face. "Do you want to talk about it?"

"Why?" she retorted defensively, brushing at her long blond hair, drawing his gaze to it. "Do you think I'm lying, too?"

"No," he said convincingly. "I don't, and I suggest that you be extra vigilant from now on. I thought it might ease your own mind to talk about the attack."

Ellis *was* trying to warn her about John, Kara thought wildly. "Nothing will ease my mind until I leave Homeplace," she blurted, knowing it was true. "It seems to me, no matter what John says, that he's not willing to move away from the mansion."

"He told me you want a divorce," Ellis said, surprising Kara.

"I did say that," she admitted, "and he asked me to come see you, and to think it over before I ended our marriage." She lowered her gaze, long lashes shadowing her cheeks. "He's repeatedly insisted that I take tranquilizers to help me adjust here."

Pretending to be preoccupied with his pipe, Ellis tapped the ashes out. "I don't know how much to say," he finally murmured. "I can give you a mild sedative if you want, but that's not going to solve your problems. I do think it best to tell you that you shouldn't threaten John with a divorce unless you mean it."

"The family doctor has already prescribed tranquilizers, but I don't want to take them," she said, "and I wasn't *threatening* a divorce!" She held her hands out in a helpless gesture. "So many things—*horrible* things—have happened since I came here that I can't think of why I'd want to stay."

Ellis studied her for a long moment, so long that Kara wanted to demand to know what he was thinking. Before she could, he murmured, "John wants you to stay, Kara."

She sighed tiredly. "Sometimes I think he does, and sometimes I think he doesn't."

Ellis leaned closer, putting his elbows on his desk. "Kara, John intends to see that you never leave Homeplace."

Kara stared at him. "He can't forbid me, if I decide that's what I want!" she declared.

Ellis's green eyes were pensive, his expression troubled. "I truly don't know what to say to you about John—how to be fair. As you know, we've been friends since grade school. John was always loyal to me, despite his mother's objections, and I've tried to return his loyalty. John is, I believe, as 'normal' as can be expected, being reared as he was."

He settled back in his chair, hesitating as if he wanted to put some distance between them. Kara held her breath, waiting for him to continue.

"I'm in a very awkward position here," he murmured uncomfortably. "I feel guilty talking about John to you, but I also feel that I need to say these things." He hesitated again. "John has his aberrations—we all do—but John's most predominant one is a boyish fixation on sex, probably because of Lorraine's Victorian attitude and her religious mandates, drilled into all her sons since childhood."

His eyes met hers, and Kara could see a small blush on his tanned cheeks. "For John, you're a"—Ellis looked away briefly—"you're a sexual fantasy come to life. You're a—symbol—something he's wanted for a long time. He has no intention of letting you go."

Kara was taken aback even though she had had hints, glimpses of John's preoccupation with sex, of his obsession with it as though it were a forbidden pleasure he was indulging in—a sin he savored. She didn't need—or want—to ask Ellis if he'd gotten his information about her firsthand. She was sure he had. John certainly did see her as a trophy!

When she could speak rationally again, she insisted, "He can't force me to stay just because he wants me to. Let's be reasonable, for God's sake! This is the nineties!"

"It's also a small southern town in the Commonwealth of Virginia," Ellis said firmly. "We don't have irreconcilable differences as a reason for divorce. One can get a divorce, eventually, with cause, but it can be involved and messy if contested—especially if contested by a Worthington." His steady green gaze met hers. "I don't need to tell you that in a family of lawyers—especially lawyers named Worthington—you're definitely at a disadvantage."

She pondered the information unnecessarily. He *hadn't* needed to tell her. She'd already seen how easily the police dismissed her allegations of the attack because John and Lorraine discounted them. She'd seen how Dee Dee's disappearance had been handled. *And she was afraid*. But being afraid wouldn't help her.

"Then I won't bother with a divorce. I'll just pack up and get out," she vowed, speaking as much to herself as to Ellis. "Why put myself and my baby in further danger?"

"I don't think leaving's going to be that easy," Ellis said.

"What do you mean?" Her attention was caught by the seriousness of his tone. She shuddered. In the back of her mind, she had several ideas about what he might mean, and none of them were pleasant.

Ellis toyed with his pipe. "Kara, you're dealing with very determined people when you deal with the Worthingtons. Determined, powerful, system-entrenched people who are used to having their way. Go slowly and don't do anything radical. Think before you act. Do you understand that wanting to leave Homeplace isn't the same as storming away from the dinner table in a fit of temper?''

She wasn't sure she did understand, or maybe the problem was that she understood all too well. She felt the blood drain from her face. She didn't want to end up like Dee Dee, in any sense of the word. She suspected that, even with Ellis's help, should he be willing, she was facing a worse nightmare than she'd already experienced.

15

Kara didn't know if she felt better or worse after the session with Ellis. She did know she was more positive than ever that she had to get away. She told the chauffeur to take her to a travel agency, and when he said he couldn't do that, she found that her words about Dee Dee being a virtual prisoner at Homeplace coming back to haunt her.

But she was not the easy prey Dee Dee had been. She'd made a mistake in marrying into the Worthington family, but mistakes could be corrected, or at least left behind.

Deciding to follow Ellis's advice as much as possible, she told herself she could wait another week, she could get through the funerals with the family and buy time by seeming to go along with John's wishes. All the while she would formulate the best plan to leave.

John Worthington couldn't keep her here by force! She was fully in control of her faculties; she would take her son and leave Homeplace at the first viable opportunity.

Somehow the week passed. The funerals were more of the nightmare, and for once, Homeplace was full of people. It seemed strange to Kara to see the locals come and go, bringing food and offering solace to the Worthingtons, for she was still struck by the fact that only John had a real friend—Ellis.

Kara had made another appointment with Ellis for Friday, and she was surprised when John told her Lorraine canceled it.

"Canceled it?" she repeated stupidly, as she stopped dressing that morning and turned to him. "Why?"

She had been determined that she would either get to a travel agency somehow, perhaps during the time she was to have the session with Ellis, or she would use his phone to get Chelsea or Lanie to make travel arrangements from California. Somehow, if she could get a ticket, she would deal with the problem of getting to the airport.

As she stood in her panties and bra, John reached out for her. "Come here, Kara," he murmured.

Fighting to control her temper, Kara went to him. "Why did Lorraine cancel the appointment, John? And why did you allow it?"

He pulled her into his arms and began to nuzzle her neck. Kara drew back. They hadn't had sex since she'd made up her mind to divorce him, and she didn't intend to participate now.

John's eyes glittered angrily as he jerked her up against him.

"Please stop it, John!" she cried, startled by the force he used. "I want to talk, not have sex."

"You're my wife," he said in a low, hard voice. "I have a legal right to have sex with you, and I will exercise that right."

"You don't have a right to *force* me," she said, her voice as angry as his.

John whirled her around, threw her down on the bed, and fell on top of her. He was wearing only his robe; he was fully erect.

"Don't, John!" Kara demanded. "Get off me!"

To her shock, John put his hand over her mouth. Kara had the same sensation and the same fear she'd had when the attacker grabbed her outside Tessa's house. She struggled furiously, but John managed to rip off the bra and panties she wore, then clasp both her wrists in one hand above her head.

To Kara's horror and humiliation, he pressed her hips into the mattress with his body weight and used his knee to pry her thighs apart. Kara was powerless to move, though she kept struggling to free herself from his vice-like grip.

"You get this straight once and for all," John seethed. "You're my wife, like it or not. And if you choose not to enjoy your participation in this marriage, you'll not deny me mine. It's your choice, Kara."

"You bastard!" Kara cried.

"I'll let you think about it," he declared as he released her and tightened the belt on his robe. "And just remember that after last week, no one will believe anything you say. You've been the subject of speculation and suspicion since I married you, and you gave the townspeople what they wanted by crying wolf. Do you really think anyone will think *I* could rape you?"

"Why, John?" she whispered as she got up and covered herself. "Why do you want me to stay?" Her eyes sadly searched his. "Was it you who pulled me into the trees last week?" she asked fearfully, the thought dawning on her, crashing through her head like a wave.

John smirked. "You're joking, of course. I don't have to grab you in the woods! Didn't I just prove that?"

Kara shook her head, unable to comprehend that this was the man she'd thought she loved. "Why are you doing this to me?"

He shrugged. "I think we've already been through this. I married you. You're a Worthington. And you'll be one until the day you die."

Kara tried not to show her fear at his announcement. In her shock she forgot her resolve to be discreet, to play their game until the right opportunity presented itself for her escape.

"I want a divorce, John, but I'll leave, whether we divorce or not. You can't keep me here against my will. I don't care *who* you are!"

His brown eyes glowed. "Don't you get it? I want you to want to stay." He looked down at his robe belt as he pulled it a little tighter. "But if you need a better reason to stay, I'll give you a little incentive—for your own good, of course."

Kara stared at him wide-eyed. She no longer knew what to expect, what he might say.

"I've adopted Ricky, and, what with you being under a psychiatrist's care, and having been treated by one in the past, you will not be allowed to take *my* son, should you decide that you're determined to go yourself."

Her mouth gaping open, Kara tried to gather her wits about her enough to call him a liar. "You can't adopt him without his natural father's permission, or mine! Not even you, *Lawyer Worthington,* not even here. It's illegal!"

He smiled. "The boy's natural father didn't give a damn, as you well know, and you agreed wholeheartedly to it."

"I did not!" she shouted, her anxiety building. "You never even mentioned the fact to me."

He shrugged. "Funny how you could forget something that important, Kara. I guess it was at a time when you were so infatuated with me that you didn't know what you were doing."

"That's a lie. I don't believe you!" she cried. "You haven't *adopted* my child. You have no say-so whatever in his life. We haven't been to court. No judge has granted you permission to take part in my child's future."

"You're wrong, sweetheart," he said, his voice low. He walked over to the bureau and pulled out a set of papers. "Richard Noble Worthington, see?"

Kara stared in disbelief.

"Signed, witnessed, notarized," he said, indicating the seal on the last page.

"No," she said, shaking her head. "No, I won't let you get away with this. It's preposterous. I'm leaving and I'm going today—*with* my son!"

"Ah, Kara," John said, a hint of remorse in his voice, "Mother warned me about you, but I wouldn't listen. Everyone, it seems, would be wise to listen to Mother. She's always said that."

"You're mad!" Kara cried, struggling futilely to fight

back rising fear. "You're all mad! Your mother most of all."

He met her gaze. "None of *us* is going to a psychiatrist, nor have we been. Now, let me explain something to you: Mother has little use for you. In fact, she wants to have you committed to the mental institution. So far I've convinced her that isn't necessary, but she's set in her ways. Don't push her."

Kara couldn't seem to digest what John was saying. This wasn't a nightmare. It was a bad joke. They *couldn't* have her committed! Still, her fear ran right to the pit of her stomach. She recalled Bucky telling her not to push Lorraine.

"None of you would risk reputation or career to attempt to have me committed," she said as bravely and calmly as she could under the circumstances.

John shrugged. "Alas, the whole town has been apprised of your, ah, unusual behavior from the beginning, Kara, and known of Mother's disapproval of a wife who marries and vanishes, then returns and wants to vanish again. It seems that the murders in our picturesque little town have pushed you over the edge, as it were. Try to pull yourself together and conduct yourself like a proper wife, like a wife I still *want*—while you can."

He smiled slightly. "And by the way, sweetheart, I've taken my credit cards from your purse. And yours. Also, I didn't see any need for you to carry around money, so I took that, too. Now, if you'll excuse me, I need to wash up and get ready for work."

Kara sat on the edge of the bed, her mind reeling. This wasn't happening. This didn't happen to anyone in this day and age, did it? Fear struck her like a bolt of lightning. It did, of course. She'd read about such bizarre cases, but it couldn't be happening to *her!* This whole thing was preposterous!

Had Ellis been part and party to this? Had she unknowingly walked deeper into the trap by trusting him? And was she going to be a prisoner of the Worthingtons?

Not knowing what else to do at the moment, she dressed

and went to breakfast as if it were any other day. And, in truth, it seemed like any other day in Homeplace. Just another incident in the string of terrible incidents that had occurred here. Only now she was at the center of this one!

When breakfast was over, the brothers went to work, as if it were any other day. Even William, his wife now buried and gone, went on with the routine. If Lorraine knew what had transpired between John and her—and Kara suspected she did—she didn't act any differently.

But why should she? Everyone, no doubt, thought the issue of Kara's—insubordination—had effectively been laid to rest, as it were. But they were wrong. She'd die before she'd stay here against her will!

The thought made her feel weak inside. Was that what Dee Dee had said, too? And was that what had happened? Had Dee Dee walked into the river to escape the Worthingtons and Homeplace, the house she called a hellhole?

Kara looked at Ricky sitting beside Bucky, giggling with his uncle about something. She wondered how laughter could go on in Homeplace. She wondered how life could go on. And she wondered what she was going to do.

She would not take to drink like Dee Dee, and she would not walk into the river. The tragedy of the deaths of Dee Dee's babies washed over her. She was beginning to wonder if they'd died of natural causes. In this madhouse full of insane people, anything was possible.

Kara felt in great danger, and she feared for Ricky. She jumped when Bucky spoke.

"I've written a song," he said.

Kara looked around. No one else was at the table. Bucky was talking to her.

"Do you want to hear it?"

A small spark of hope surged in her heart. She wasn't totally alone. Bucky cared about her. Perhaps she should ally herself with him. If she could only get Bucky to take her to the airport, or anywhere away from Homeplace, she and Ricky could escape.

"Yes," she said, forcing a smile to her rigid features. "I'd like that very much, Bucky. Thank you."

When she went over to pick up Ricky, she saw that Bucky looked unhappy. The sense of hope she'd felt minutes ago dimmed. She didn't know why Bucky was looking at her son with such dissatisfaction, but she couldn't afford to upset him.

"Don't you want Ricky to hear the song?" she asked pleasantly.

Bucky shook his head. "It's just for you," he said. "I . . ." he lowered his voice. "I thought I'd show you something, too," he murmured. "Ricky might tell."

Kara could feel her panic building again, and she couldn't let that happen. "He can stay with Thelma," she said, although she was almost frantic now about letting her son out of her sight.

To Kara's relief, Bucky smiled. Bucky might be the only one she could count on. She was no longer sure about Ellis.

"Let's go walk," Ricky said happily.

Kara made herself wink at him. "Not this morning, sweetie."

Not ever again, she wanted to say. She realized how terrified she was of the river now, of her unknown assailant, of having something happen to her son, of being murdered herself.

"I want to go," Ricky insisted petulantly.

Kara exhaled wearily. "Later, Ricky. Right now, I want you to stay with Thelma. Mommy's going upstairs with Bucky. I'll be back in a few minutes."

Over Ricky's protests and tears, Kara took him into the kitchen where Thelma and Tessa were cleaning up. "Keep an eye on him for me, please, Thelma," Kara said, glancing at Tessa.

This was the first time since the night at the cabin that Kara had seen Tessa when she could talk to her. She wished that she and Tessa were alone, but even if Thelma wasn't here, Kara wasn't sure what she wanted to say. She couldn't deny that she resented Tessa for calling John instead of the police, no matter what the reasoning.

Deciding it was best not to say anything, she turned away

from the younger woman. "I'm going up to Bucky's room to hear a song he's written."

Thelma looked at Kara so strangely that she didn't know what to think. Was it a sin in this house to go to her brother-in-law's room? Or did Thelma, too, think that Kara was emotionally disturbed and read something more into the situation than just going to listen to a song?

"Is there something wrong with that?" she asked sharply.

Kara had to know if she was breeching some rule she didn't know about. She *needed* to win Bucky over, and to do that she had to spend time with him. She wasn't about to go down to the river, and there was no privacy anywhere in the house. His offer to sing to her in his room had seemed like a godsend mere moments ago. Now she wondered.

Thelma shrugged carelessly as though she hadn't reacted so oddly earlier. "It ain't my business what you do. Might not please his mama, though."

Another warning? Kara wondered. And so what if it was? She hadn't managed to do anything else to please Lorraine. Why should this be any different? She wanted to ask where her mother-in-law was, but she hadn't the nerve.

Kara shrugged and started to turn away when Tessa called, "Mrs. Worthington." Kara looked back. "I'm sorry about last week," the girl said. I—I wish you'd listen—"

Thelma glowered at her daughter. "Get the dishes finished and go back to your cabin. Don't be messing where you oughtn't. You hear me, girl?"

At that moment Bucky asked, "Are you coming, Kara?"

All three women looked at him, surprised. No one had heard Bucky enter the kitchen. His eyes brightened mischievously as he looked from one to the other.

Nodding, Kara murmured, "I'm ready."

Bucky smiled sweetly. "Me, too. Come on," he said, leading the way out of the kitchen.

He almost couldn't believe his good luck. He'd wanted to get Kara alone since they'd gone to Greensboro, but Dee Dee had drowned and messed up everything.

Well, he conceded, not only Dee Dee. He'd messed up, too, the night Kara went to Tessa's cabin. He hadn't really had any plan when she rushed away from the table, mad at John. He'd felt sorry for her because he knew how it was to be picked on in front of the whole family, and he'd wanted to comfort her.

He hadn't dared. He had to wait until dinner was over. Then he'd told Mother he was going riding, though he'd only driven his car to the bottom of the drive. He'd searched for Kara, but she wasn't at the river where he'd thought she'd be.

She was—well, there was no point in rehashing that. It only upset him. There was nothing he could do about it anyway. The family had been sure she was lying, and in a way, Bucky knew that she was. Nobody had tried to *hurt* Kara.

Oh, it was another one of those things that twisted him all around. He felt sorry for Kara because all the family had turned on her, but he didn't want them to turn on him, so he hadn't tried to defend her. She herself had admitted that the scratches and stuff had come from the brush and bramble along the river.

He really couldn't think about it anymore. He didn't want to ruin this time with Kara. And thinking about that night reminded him of the night with Marsha, how she had slapped him and called him an idiot.

"Bucky?"

He jerked spastically when Kara called his name.

"Are you all right?" she asked, frowning.

Standing dead still in the dining room, Bucky looked like he was off in some kind of trance. Kara couldn't help thinking about Ellis saying Lorraine was schizophrenic. Still, she'd have to take her chances on Bucky's stability. She had no choice. She had no friends here, no one else to turn to, and no way to get away, despite frantic thoughts such as stealing car keys or calling a cab. She knew she'd never pull it off.

"Yes, of course I'm all right," he murmured. "I was just—just wondering if you wanted me to share some of my secrets with you today. Remember when I told you about the secrets?"

Yes, she remembered, and sincerely suspected she was better off not knowing Bucky's secrets; still, it might be a way to ally herself with him.

"I'd love to hear your song and share your secrets, Bucky," she said with a smile. "You seem to be the only one in this house who cares how I feel."

She hadn't truly meant to add the last line. Maybe she was feeling sorry for herself after all, or maybe she was hoping Bucky would—whichever worked.

"I do care about you, Kara," he said gently. "I care about you very much. That's why I'm trying to make you feel better. I know John was mean to you this morning."

Kara felt her face redden. Did Bucky know John had threatened to force himself on her? No, she'd decided the last time she'd thought Bucky overheard them that he hadn't. He'd probably heard her yelling at John.

"It doesn't matter, Bucky," she murmured, looking away. "I'm sure I'll feel better when I hear you sing. I like your voice very much."

Bucky laughed softly. "I like *you* very much!"

Kara felt a chill when she followed him out of the dining room. She tried not to think about it as she made her way up the steps behind Bucky.

When they passed Lorraine's room, Kara thankfully saw that it was empty. Bucky opened the door to his room as if he were stepping into a palace, and Kara had to smile. He was so proud of his possessions that he couldn't seem to wait to show them to her.

The room was like a little boy's. There were trunks and bookcases and boxes holding all kinds of collectibles Bucky had apparently gathered over the years.

Kara didn't pay any attention to the fact that Bucky closed the door. After all, if he wanted to share secrets, he certainly didn't want anyone coming in.

"I'll sing the song in a minute," he said eagerly, seeing that she was looking at his favorite trunk. "Let me show you what's in here!"

He took the nearly invisible thin gold chain from around his neck. Kara had never noticed it before. There was a tiny pendant on it. No, it was a key, she saw. Bucky used it to unlock the trunk.

Kara stood there, staring in amazement as Bucky opened the large, ornate trunk. It was filled with *women's dresses!* Bucky seemed transformed as he gazed at them lovingly, then turned to Kara.

"Aren't they beautiful?" he asked. "Would you like to try one of them on?"

Kara remained motionless, not knowing what to say, what to do, as Bucky began to very carefully lift out several garments as though he'd forgotten he asked Kara a question. He seemed to get lost in himself more and more with each dress he removed.

"Some of them I wore in plays," he said musingly. "But not all of them."

Kara nodded, trying not to seem shocked, thinking she had to say something. "They are very lovely," she murmured.

So Bucky was a transvestite! That in itself shouldn't have shocked or surprised her, she thought. In fact, she might have even guessed it, but there in the trunk lay other garments—garments that did shock and surprise her.

There was a duplicate of each piece of sexy underwear John had bought for her. There was also a blond wig, much like her own hair.

And worse somehow—she wasn't quite sure why—there was a collection of little girls' dresses: dresses that clearly had been worn.

But by whom?

16

Bucky was mesmerized by the clothing. He continued to gingerly remove the dresses from the trunk, laying one carefully on the other, touching and stroking each tenderly, as if they were living things, until he came to the little girls' dresses.

Kara got the answer to her silent question.

"These are mine," Bucky said reminiscently. "Aren't they pretty? When I wore them, Mother loved me."

Kara stared at him, recoiling inside. The dresses weren't *baby* dresses. Some of them could have belonged to a schoolchild! Was Bucky the crazy one? Was he imagining he'd worn the dresses?

Bucky looked up at Kara from his position on the floor, where he was sitting by the trunk. She made herself stand still, instead of fleeing as fear dictated. There was nowhere to run.

"It's a secret, though, Kara," he said firmly. "A secret!" Kara hadn't been sure he remembered she was there. "Mother would come to my room late at night after my brothers were asleep and take me to the attic where the beautiful dresses were," he murmured.

His gaze strayed to the frilly white dress he held. "Then she would take all my clothes off and put lovely silk panties on me and one of the dresses. You see," he murmured,

"Mother doesn't really like boy babies. She didn't like Dee Dee's babies, but she loves Lorrie. And she loved me when I was a baby, and she put the beautiful dresses on me. She would take me on her lap and hold me and sing to me."

To Kara's dismay, he began to sing, "Pretty baby, pretty little baby. Pretty, pretty baby." He held the dress up to his lips and kissed it and rubbed his face against it.

Kara was mortified by the pathetic picture of Bucky and the dresses. She was repulsed. And she felt so very sorry for him. She couldn't stay. She didn't think he wanted her to, or that he was aware she was still there. For just a moment she reminded herself that he'd called her name seconds ago, but she was reasonably sure he was lost in his memories or imagination now.

Shaken, she quietly slipped from his room and closed the door. She glanced into Lorraine's room as she hurried past; she didn't see anybody. As she rushed down the steps, all she could think about was calling Ellis.

Somebody had to help her! She had to get away from here. Maybe she could get Ellis to come after her, or take a cab to his office and have him pay for it. Maybe she would even hitchhike. The danger could be no worse than being here.

. . . if anyone would pick her up. She wanted to make sure Ellis was in his office.

If she was pursued and caught, she knew she might not have another chance to escape. While she frantically dialed Ellis's number, she thought she heard a noise on the line. Maybe someone had lifted an extension phone in the house. Well, it didn't matter. It *couldn't* matter!

She had to do whatever she could now, this minute. She was more frightened than ever, for she was beginning to think awful thoughts about what had happened to the people who had been murdered—babies, young men on the river downstream from the mansion, maybe Dee Dee.

Ellis's receptionist answered the phone. "I've got to speak to the doctor right now!" Kara said urgently.

"I'm sorry, but the doctor is with a patient at the hospital," the girl said. "May I ask who's calling?"

"This is an emergency!" Kara cried. "I have to talk to him. When will he be back?"

"He should be back within the hour. May I ask the nature of the emergency? Perhaps you would like Dr. Neuman's number."

"No, no," Kara murmured. "I'll call back."

She hung up as if the phone had burned her. It was too risky to have Ellis call her here! She didn't know what to do. She wondered if she could go to Tessa, or if Thelma would listen to her and believe her, but she recalled the exchange between Thelma, Tessa, and her when she said she was going to Bucky's room.

Did Thelma know something, and if so, what was it? Oh, damn, she didn't know what to do, where to turn! She felt so desperate and so useless. She glanced at her watch. She would call Ellis back in a little while. Until then, she would have to bide her time. She went to the kitchen to pick up Ricky. She wanted him with her.

Upstairs in Lorrie's room, Lorraine smiled at the girl while they played a game of checkers; inwardly, the woman was seething. Bucky had taken Kara to his room! Lorraine couldn't believe it. She told him repeatedly that he must not spend time with the whore, and he'd disobeyed her. She'd been adamant when she caught him out on the sun porch with Kara that he must not be alone with her again.

She'd suspected him of walking with her on the riverbank, although he denied it. She'd tried to prevent the Greensboro trip, but it had happened too fast for her to effectively halt it.

Besides, she'd needed time to herself, time with both Bucky and the whore away from Homeplace to talk with John privately about all the evil in the house since his marriage. She'd needed to point out things that he, a mortal man, a man given to weakness of the flesh, had been ignoring in the harlot, perhaps in the hope they would change.

In fact, it was she who had suggested the visit to Ellis, just as she'd convinced him of the wisdom of adopting Ricky, although she loathed that boy carrying the Worthington name. There would be time to rectify that later. It had been the mother who'd become the more pressing problem.

Now the problem seemed even more urgent. What had Bucky said or done that caused Kara to phone Ellis with such hysteria in her voice? Surely he hadn't told her *their secret*. Bucky wouldn't do that.

Or would he? Had the whore pulled the wool over his eyes as she had John's? Had she plotted all along to seduce the sensitive, most unstable of William Buchannan Worthington's sons? His sinful seed had grown more dominant with each boy, it seemed. At least Melvin and William had married. They had not whored around. And despite William having boys, and Dee Dee's problems, Lorraine had managed to maintain a degree—with God's help—of influence in their lives.

Dee Dee, of course, had sinned in thought, word, and deed, and those sins had been washed clean, as it were. Sometimes it amazed Lorraine that the river took care of her problems so easily. It had with William. It had with Toby. It had with Dee Dee.

Now the remaining problem, the whore wreaking havoc in Homeplace had to be dealt with, and dealt with quickly. Had she already lain in sin with Bucky? And would John believe it if she had? She knew lust when she saw it, and she had seen it in Bucky's eyes that night on the sun porch as he stared at Kara in her sheer nightwear. And Bucky and Kara had hours alone in Greensboro to do only Jesus knew what.

"Grandmother!" Lorrie said imperiously, "it's your move!"

Lorraine looked down at the sweetest gift God had ever given her, at the female child she had longed for, and smiled. "I'm sorry, angel. I was lost in thought."

"I don't want to play any more," Lorrie said petulantly. "I want to go shopping like we always do."

Lorraine continued to smile. "Grandmother has chores to attend to. Now be Grandmother's good girl and occupy yourself. Next week I'll have a special surprise for you when we go shopping." Then, her mind on her youngest son, Lorraine went to Bucky's room.

Bucky knew the hallway so well after listening for years for his mother's footsteps that he heard her when she stepped on a particular board that creaked just before she got to his door.

In a moment of unparalleled panic, he started cramming his precious dresses back into the trunk, wincing at each wrinkle, each hastily shoved article, each crushed garment. He was barely able to slam the lid down and lock it with his key before Lorraine entered the room unannounced. He grabbed his bible, crammed the necklace in his pants pocket and lay down on the floor in front of the trunk.

"Mother!" he protested, red-faced, breathing hard, "I wish you would knock! I don't have any privacy here at all and I'm twenty-two years old!"

"Shut up, Buchannan," she hissed as she shut the door and marched over to him. "What was the whore doing in your room?"

"Nothing," Bucky said, but tears were already filling his eyes. He couldn't bear it when Mother spoke to him that way. He wanted to curl up and die when she acted as if she hated him. He couldn't hold up. It hurt too much.

"Tell me!" she ordered.

Tears started to spill down his cheeks. "I sang a song to her," he said.

He didn't want to lie to Mother, and he was trying his best not to. He knew how she felt about Kara. And he knew now he'd been weak. He'd invited the whore to his room. *And she'd told Mother!* Bucky had known Mother always spent this day with Lorrie shopping. She couldn't have possibly known Kara had been in his room if Kara hadn't told her.

Or Thelma. He wanted to think it had been Thelma, yet he didn't know what to think. Maybe it had been Tessa, but Tessa didn't usually talk to anyone—certainly not Mother. Unless . . . Oh, he didn't know what to think.

All he knew was that he was scared to death of Mother when she was like this. She used to turn him over on her lap and spank his naked rear when she was angry with him. Later, however, she began to slap his face with her open hand. Like Thelma did.

"Buchannan."

When Mother said his name like that, it was almost as awful as being slapped, because it had always been the prelude to punishment.

He brushed at his tears with a balled-up fist. He'd lost track of time. Had Kara had time or the chance to talk to Mother? And if she had, had she told about the secret? She'd promised that night on the sun porch that he could trust her. Then again on the way to Greensboro, she'd said they were friends and they could share anything. He'd shared his wonderful dresses with her.

Had she told?

Suddenly Lorraine spied the toe of a blue shoe—a woman's shoe, she was sure—peeking out from under Bucky's bed. The blood pounding in her head, she went to the bed, bent down and picked up the item. She didn't have to say a word. She merely held the shoe up as she approached Bucky.

It was Kara's shoe, the one she'd worn to the doctor's office the day she'd found out she wasn't pregnant, the one she'd lost in the woods outside Tessa's cabin. Clean, it hardly matched the muddied one the woman had limped around in at Tessa's cabin, but it was the mate all right.

Lorraine raised the shoe high above her head. Then she began to strike Bucky about the shoulders and back with it. Over and over again she brought the shoe down. Again and still again. Her heart hammered and her pulse raced and she continued to vent her fury on her son, clutching the shoe with all her strength and hitting Bucky violently.

Downstairs, Kara realized how dishonest or unaware— no, *dishonest* had to be the word—John had been when he told her that the rooms in the house were solid and soundproof. Although she hadn't heard Bucky's answer, Kara had heard Lorraine's voice quite clearly as she interrogated her son in that harsh, hateful voice.

Kara didn't know what to do. She suspected that Lorraine knew nothing about what was in the trunk, although she was amazed the woman had never looked.

But then maybe Bucky had given her no reason to treat him so harshly before. Kara suspected he'd been a model son, dominated by the matriarch Worthington, allowed his little eccentricities, as long as he kept them at home and didn't anger his mother. Now he *had* angered her!

Eventually Lorraine's tirade ceased, but then Bucky's groans began. Kara had had enough! Without considering the ramifications, she raced up the steps, Ricky in her arms. Bucky and Lorraine both whirled around when she burst into the room.

"Bucky didn't do anything, and *I* didn't do anything," Kara insisted breathlessly, glowering at the other woman, who quickly hid something behind her back. Kara imagined Lorraine was hiding whatever she'd used to cause Bucky misery. She didn't even want to think what it might be.

"If you want to restrict me to certain areas of the house," she said coldly, "then tell me the perimeters, but don't condemn Bucky for something neither one of us knew you'd consider out of line. He's my brother-in-law, for heaven's sake!"

"What do you know about him or Heaven?" Lorraine demanded. "How dare you charge in here while I'm with my son? How dare you have the audacity to—"

"I dare because I heard you all the way down in my room," Kara said. "And I dare because I'm sick of your threats and intimidations. Bucky has done nothing wrong—nothing except be born in this household. And I dare because I want you to know that you can't keep me here. I *will* be the first Worthington to get a divorce, so get ready for it."

Her ire spent, knowing she was stretching her luck, Kara turned and left as quickly as she'd entered. Her heart was hammering madly and her legs were weak. She didn't know what Lorraine would do now, but let her do her worst and get it over with!

The minute Kara was back in John's room, she called Ellis again. This time, thank God, she reached him.

"I have to talk with you, Ellis," she said. "It's imperative. I've got to get away from here. There's—There's new evidence of what we discussed, and I—I feel threatened."

"Calm down, Kara," he said gently. "Is that why you didn't keep your appointment today?"

For a moment Kara was speechless. Lorraine *hadn't* canceled the appointment. She'd simply told John she had, *or* had John lied?

"I was told it was canceled," she said.

There was silence on the other end of the line. Kara was afraid Ellis didn't believe her, and he just *had* to!

"John has taken away my credit cards and all my money. I have no way to leave here, and I have to get away, Ellis. Please believe me. Help me! I'm truly in fear for my life!"

There was an even longer pause. Kara was feeling frantic. She didn't hear a dial tone, but Ellis wasn't answering her! Dear God, he didn't believe her! What was she going to do now?

"Ellis, please!" she pleaded.

When he didn't speak again, she pushed the button on the phone. There was nothing. The line was dead. She didn't know how much Ellis had heard of what she'd said.

"Mommy," Ricky said, beginning to sound scared.

Kara tried to get herself under control. "It's okay, sweetie," she said reassuringly, then she saw that he was looking at the doorway.

Lorraine held the phone plug in her hand. *She'd* disconnected the phone! She let it slide from her fingers as she entered the room, Thelma at her side. Kara saw that the large woman had a glass in one hand and something else in her other.

Kara started backing away, instinctively fearing the worst, but she was powerless against the two women. The last thing she remembered was Ricky clinging to her leg, screaming as Lorraine and Thelma forced her down on the bed, Lorraine repeatedly slapping her. She felt the coolness of the liquid, spilling from her mouth as some of it followed behind the scraping of fingernails when a pill was shoved down her throat like one might force an ailing dog to take medication.

It was dark when she woke up. John was sitting on the side of the bed, offering her soup. She was sick to her stomach; she didn't think she could eat anything. She tried to talk to him, and found she couldn't. She felt drugged. When she closed her eyes, he held her head up and opened her mouth.

Or was she only dreaming it? Did John, too, give her a pill? She tried to turn away as she heard him say something about a tranquilizer, something about her opening her mouth to swallow. She tasted the thick richness of green pea soup before she slept again.

Bucky was so distraught that he didn't know what to do. Mother was being mean to Kara. She'd been shut up in her room all day. At least Mother was leaving him alone, but he felt guilty. Mother had left his room when Kara came up to defend him. He was so relieved when Mother stopped hitting him that he sank to the floor and stayed there for a long, long time.

It wasn't until later that he'd realized Mother had taken her wrath out on Kara. Kara hadn't even come to supper. Mother said she was sick. John took soup to her room after the others had finished eating. Bucky lay down on the floor with his ear to the floorboards, trying to hear what John was saying. He could only hear murmurs.

Distressed, agitated, Bucky went to his trunk and sat down near it, thinking how Kara had been in his room this morning. If only Mother hadn't been home! He'd asked Lorrie why they hadn't gone shopping, and she'd told him Grandmother had wanted to play checkers—*if* it was any of his business. Jesus, he hated that brat!

"I'm sorry," he murmured aloud for taking Jesus' name in vain. He didn't need any more bad luck. He didn't need to be punished for any more wrongdoing. He wished he'd put the shoe in the trunk, but he'd barely gotten his dresses back in time to save himself. He *knew* how mother felt about some of the dresses, even though she let him keep them in the trunk.

But she didn't know anything about the *other* dresses. That was his secret. And now Kara's. Or at least he thought it was Kara's and his.

Yes, it must be their secret. Otherwise, Mother would have surely punished him for that.

He didn't know what to do. He missed Kara. He loved Kara. He knew he did. He'd been unwise to bring her to his room without making sure Mother wasn't in the house.

He touched his trunk again. Then he closed his door. When he had unlocked the trunk, he took out the dress Kara had agreed was pretty. Maybe if he put it on, he would feel close to Kara. He would put the wig on, too. He carefully lifted it out and laid it aside, then he took time to straighten the other dresses before he closed the trunk again.

He was mad at Mother for punishing Kara. He knew he wasn't supposed to get mad at her. He was supposed to respect and love her. But she'd made Kara sick. He was sure of it. As he put on the dress, the thoughts began to come into his head, the voices that had began to argue more and more with him and with each other.

It was hard for him to know what was right. He wanted to hunt for a verse in his bible, but he couldn't think which one it was. It had something to do with smoting somebody or something. He couldn't remember. The voices were confusing him. He couldn't think straight.

Maybe if he went out on the river, it would clear his mind. The rest of the family was sitting on the sun porch talking loudly and argumentatively about something. He'd wanted to check on Kara, so he'd just slipped away. They hadn't missed him. People rarely did.

At the cabin, Tessa turned the small television on and stared at the screen. She knew she should study for her classes; however, she couldn't seem to buckle down. She was scheduled to graduate when summer classes ended.

She needed to prepare for the state exam, but she felt so guilty about Kara that she couldn't concentrate.

How she wished she hadn't been unfortunate enough to have the woman turn up at her door! She'd endured here for so long. She was so close to getting away from all this madness herself, so close to making life easy at last for her long-suffering mother.

However, Kara *had* turned up at the cabin, and the woman was in danger. Tessa knew it, but then they were *all* in danger on this piece of ground that was like a small mental institute, shut off from the rest of the world, and well it should be.

For a long time she'd wondered how her own parentage would affect her future, and it scared her. That was one of the primary reasons she'd become interested in nursing, that and the fact that she had to find a way to get her mother and herself away from here.

She knew now that she would be okay, if she and Mama could escape. They were so close. So very close. Mama was right. Tessa knew she couldn't let Kara threaten that. Still, her mind held on to the subject of the Worthingtons like a dog with a bone. Conscience was an all-consuming thing when it took hold.

Restless, Tessa flipped the TV off again. That was when she thought she heard the noise. It was probably just the wind in the trees; still she'd been so high-strung since the incident with Kara that she didn't dare ignore anything she considered a foreign sound.

She went to the front door and opened it just a little bit. She gasped when she was shoved backward. Holding up her hands, she tried to ward off the blow of the high-heel shoe, but it landed with deadly precision against her right temple. Her last thoughts were of Mama as she slumped to the floor.

When Kara awakened the next morning, her head felt as if it was splitting wide open. She opened her eyes and lay still, feeling like she'd throw up if she moved. John was still sleeping. She had a desperate urge to go to the bathroom and to check on her child, yet she felt as if she couldn't move. She tried to sit up on the edge of the bed, but her head was spinning.

John rolled over and perched on his elbows. "Feel better?" he asked.

She tried to focus; it was very difficult. "Your mother gave me a pill," she said, her voice raspy, her throat raw. She couldn't think what she wanted to tell him.

"I know," he said. "You weren't well. She told me she gave you one of the tranquilizers the doctor prescribed for you."

"No," she said. She was sure that hadn't been what Lorraine and Thelma had forced down her throat. It had been something else. Something harmful. A doctor wouldn't have given her anything like that, would he?

"No, what?" he asked.

Kara gazed at him blankly, trying to think. She tried again to get up, but her legs were quivering. John slid out of his side of the bed and came around to help her. She was forced to accept his assistance to the bathroom. She started throwing up the minute she closed the door. The handiest thing was the sink. She clutched it for dear life, and when she'd stopped retching, she gazed at herself in the mirror.

She had a sudden impression of Dee Dee. She looked like she'd been drinking. Her face was puffy, and despite all the sleep she'd had, her eyes were bloodshot.

Dear God in Heaven, was this what had happened to Dee Dee? Had Lorraine drugged her? And how long had it been going on?

"Kara?" John's voice penetrated her spinning thoughts. "Kara, are you okay?"

"Yes," she managed to murmur. She felt disoriented; she knew she had to get something in her stomach, something to offset the effects of the pills she had been given. She had to make herself go to breakfast.

In a fog, she washed her face and did her best to make herself presentable. Staggering like a drunk, she made her way out of the bathroom with only the greatest of effort. She knew she had to keep moving or she was lost. She managed to reach the closet, and, hanging on to the door, she dragged the handiest dress out.

"Kara, come back and lie down," John said sternly. "What are you doing?"

She drew in several steadying breaths, but they didn't help. She was nauseous when she faced him. Her vision was blurred, and the only reason she wasn't regurgitating was because there was nothing in her to dredge up.

"I'm going to breakfast," she said, feeling that her smile was lopsided, yet unable to do anything about it.

"You're not well enough," he insisted. "Get back in bed. I'll have Thelma bring you a tray."

No!" she said, too quickly, too vehemently. She struggled to overcome her panic. She wanted out of this room. She wanted to see her son. She wanted to eat what the others ate. It was critical to appear as normal as possible.

"Take it easy," John said. He patted a place on the bed. "Sit down before you fall down."

Dress in hand, Kara did as he told her, only as a precautionary measure. She thought she might fall down, and then she would not be allowed to go to breakfast. It took all her concentration, all her focus to smile at him.

"I'm much better today, John. It must have been one of those twenty-four-hour bugs. I'm starving. Isn't it time for breakfast?"

John glanced at the clock. Kara turned her unfocused eyes in the same direction. "Not quite," he said. "Lie back down. I'll take a shower and shave, then we'll see how you feel."

"All right," she said determinedly, knowing she'd slurred her words before.

A vision of poor tormented Dee Dee surged into her mind and her pulse began to race. She waited until John had slid off his side of the bed and gone to the bathroom. Then she forced herself to her feet again, making one slow movement at a time.

She pulled the dress on over the gown someone had put on her. Thankfully, it was a short, skimpy gown; she didn't have the strength to take it off. Then she stepped into a pair of sandals by holding onto the closet door again.

She felt so woozy, so sick, that all she wanted to do was lie down on the bed and clutch her heaving stomach. Mind over matter, she kept telling herself. Mind over matter.

In Ricky's room next door she found the bed empty. Fighting back roiling nausea and rising hysteria, she stumbled down the hall to the kitchen. She heard movements and followed the sound. Thelma was taking a pan of homemade biscuits out of the oven.

The older woman whirled around, almost dropping the hot tin when Ricky squealed at the sight of his mother and went rushing toward her. Kara quickly braced herself against a chair to keep the small child from bowling her over. She was barely supporting herself as it was.

"Hi, sweetie," she said, allowing him to hug her trembling legs as if nothing in the world was wrong. She quickly ruffled his blond hair.

"Mommy's sick?" he asked.

"Mommy's much better," she said, spacing her words. She looked at Thelma. It was difficult to read the masklike face or the expression in the old woman's eyes. "Good morning, Thelma," she said with as much enthusiasm as she could muster. "I am absolutely famished, and the bread looks so good. May I have a biscuit now?"

Thelma seemed leery, and a little surprised. She hesitated, and Kara tried to keep a positive thought. She had to get something in her stomach.

"I feel like I haven't eaten for days," she said. "I remember the delicious taste of green pea soup last night, but there wasn't nearly enough of it."

Looking confused, Thelma set the tin of biscuits on the top of the stove. Then she buttered one, poured a cup of coffee, and placed them on the round kitchen table. Kara stared, confused herself, not sure if Thelma was playing some kind of cruel joke on her or was acquiescing to her request. Kara first thought Thelma was going to sit down and eat, then she realized that the woman meant the coffee and bread for her.

Grateful, Kara gently pushed her child aside and worked her way to the place where the food was. She was trying to appear normal, though she felt like she might collapse at any second. Finally, seeing spots before her eyes, her head reeling, bile at the back of her throat, she seated herself. The smell of the coffee made her want to retch. She quickly got the biscuit and began to break off little pieces, the hot butter making them easier to swallow.

"I want some, Mommy," Ricky said, trying to climb up in her lap.

Kara was torn by her need to appear well and her child. "Go over and ask Thelma very nicely if you can have a biscuit," she told him, trying to look pleasant as she glanced at the woman.

Thelma still hadn't said anything. Kara didn't know what to say, what to think. She did know that Thelma had been a party to brutally forcing her to take those pills.

"He's done ate," Thelma said bluntly.

Even the small amounts of bread Kara had eaten were helping stabilize her. She was feeling less like she might heave any moment.

"He just wants what I have, Thelma," Kara said, smiling a little. "Would you mind if I fix him a biscuit? Honestly, I'm too hungry to share. I don't ever recall being so sick. All I remember is sleeping. I don't even know how I got in bed."

Thelma stared at her. Kara was very careful not to look angry or guilty about the lie she was telling. She was praying Thelma would believe her and would butter a biscuit for Ricky. Kara still didn't think she could stand; she knew the child wouldn't eat his bread. She intended to. She wanted to have something in her stomach before breakfast was served. She needed solid food and was afraid she might not get it when the rest of the family came down.

Thelma turned back around and Kara exhaled gratefully as the woman buttered another biscuit. "Here, Ricky," she said neutrally to the boy.

Kara prayed she was making some progress with Thelma. Now that she saw Thelma as another potential danger, she had to be very cautious. As she expected, Ricky took the biscuit, climbed up in the chair beside hers, and began to toy with the two halves of the bread. Kara finished her own and ate half of his.

Suddenly Melvin burst into the room, causing Kara to gasp. He only glanced at her, then told Thelma, "Give me one of those biscuits and some coffee. They found another one, and I want to get over there."

A wave of nausea engulfed Kara and she fought it back, trying to keep her equilibrium. She didn't need to ask another *what*. Someone else was dead.

17

"Another what?" Thelma asked.

"Murder victim."

"Oh, this has got to stop," Thelma murmured. "Lord, when is it going to end?"

Melvin shook his head. "Not until we get the son of a bitch."

"Who was it this time?" Thelma asked.

Melvin shrugged. "I don't know. The police called me because it happened on our property."

Kara watched as he grabbed a biscuit, poured himself a cup of coffee, then dashed away.

Kara fought the wave of nausea that suddenly surged inside her. She closed her eyes briefly, then waited for the onslaught of the other Worthingtons. She knew they couldn't be far behind, since Melvin had sounded the alarm.

John came in next. "Oh, there you are," he said offhandedly, glancing at Kara, then going over to Thelma, who was hurriedly buttering biscuits and pouring coffee. John was gone in a flash, and William appeared next. Always the most reluctant—understandably, Kara told herself—he lingered long enough to put jam on his bread, eat it, and drink his coffee in the kitchen; then he, too, was gone.

Lorraine, dressed as always, arrived soon after William

left. She paused only briefly in the doorway of the room, her surprise at seeing Kara hardly registering on her face.

Kara forced a smile at the woman she had come to hate as she'd never hated another human being on the face of the earth.

"Good morning, and thank you for taking care of me yesterday," she said, making a supreme effort to sound sincere. "I don't know what happened. I told John it must have been one of those twenty-four-hour bugs. Thank God, it seems to have gone."

Lorraine frowned slightly; making no pretense of civility, she nodded. "Perhaps."

"Where's Tessa?" she asked Thelma.

"She didn't come yet," Thelma said. "Sweet Jesus!" she suddenly cried loudly, grasping the edge of the counter. "Sweet Jesus in Heaven!" Her eyes wide and pained, she ran from the room.

Kara stared after her, trying to make some sense of it all. Tessa hadn't shown up. Melvin said the murder happened on Homeplace property.

"Oh, no!" she cried. "Not Tessa!"

Lorraine stared at her. "What?"

Kara shook her head. It couldn't be Tessa. Why would anyone kill her?

"What did you say?" Lorraine demanded.

Kara looked at her. "Melvin said another murder took place on Homeplace property. Tessa hasn't come this morning to help with breakfast, and she's never late . . ."

Her words trailed off as Lorraine's hawk eyes raked over her. Then the older woman left.

Bucky was the next to come into the kitchen. Kara was grateful to see him, though she didn't quite know why. Maybe just because he seemed delighted to see her.

"Good morning, Kara," he said excitedly. "Are you feeling better? I was worried about you."

"Thank you, Bucky," she said, managing a smile for him, despite the remembrance of how he'd looked when she'd last seen him, cowering before his mother, his dresses apparently safely hidden in the trunk.

"Where is everybody?" he asked. "Why aren't the others in the dining room?"

Kara focused on the cold, dark coffee in her cup. "There was another murder victim found this morning, Bucky, on Homeplace grounds. Tessa didn't show up for work. Everybody has gone to investigate."

"Even Priscilla? Are we in the house alone?" Bucky asked, causing Kara to stare at him without realizing it.

He looked away and so did she, aware that she must have looked at him oddly. She made herself smile. "I don't think she's gotten up yet."

Kara couldn't explain the awful way she was feeling inside. She was still physically sick, but this was something different, something terrible going on in her mind.

"Are the biscuits hot?" Bucky asked.

Kara told herself to pretend that there was nothing abnormal about him not commenting on the murder. After all, they upset him as much as they did her. But she had that bad feeling inside.

"I think they're warm enough to melt the butter," she said. She slid out of her chair. She was still weak, though she was considerably improved from when she'd gotten out of bed earlier. "I'm going to get Ricky cleaned up before this place turns into a madhouse," she said, taking him by the hand and coaxing him from the chair.

"Stay with me, Kara," Bucky said, looking back over his shoulder.

Caught in a moment of indecision, Kara wondered what to do. She wanted to call Ellis, yet if she angered Bucky, that might not be possible.

"What's going on? Where's Melvin?" Priscilla asked, entering the room on white heels, looking like a puzzled pretty little girl, all dressed for the day in a layered white dress. "He got a phone call and hurried out of the bedroom. I thought he was having breakfast," she said.

"There are only biscuits to eat," Kara noted, glancing at Bucky.

"Biscuits?" Priscilla asked, her expression quizzical. "Why? Where's Thelma this morning?"

"There was another murder—" Kara began.

"Oh, no!" Priscilla interrupted her irritably. "Not another one to contend with!"

Kara made her way out of the kitchen, concentrating on each movement and praying to God that Priscilla would keep Bucky occupied long enough for her to get to the phone. Bracing herself against the wall, she summoned all her strength and hurried to John's room to dial Ellis's office.

When she heard an answering machine pick up, she felt like breaking into tears. Frustrated and frantic, each action muddled by the medication she'd been given, she pulled herself together enough to write down the emergency number. It was for Dr. Neuman!

Fighting to think rationally, Kara called information, hoping against hope that Ellis was listed; gratefully, he was. She hastily scribbled down the number, then dialed it.

Another answering machine! Struggling against the futility of her situation, she held onto the phone long enough to leave a message, telling Ellis that there was something terribly wrong at the house and that she had to see him, no matter who refused his admittance. She begged him to come as soon as he could.

Finally it dawned on her that now was her chance to escape! She hadn't had her wits about her enough to think of it before. There was a second set of keys to Lorraine's car somewhere. The part-time chauffeur wasn't allowed to keep them with him. Lorraine's own keys were probably in her purse, as were Priscilla's, now that Kara considered it. It seemed less risky to search for Lorraine's than Priscilla's, with Priscilla right there in the house.

Her heart pounding, Kara left Ricky in his room and started up the steps. Desperate, she tried her best to hurry, but her brain worked like it was in low gear, giving commands to her body as if in slow motion. She was halfway up the stairs when she heard the other family members returning. Distraught at the delay and what it had cost her, she turned around, dizzy with the sudden movement, resigning herself to hear about the latest murder. She certainly couldn't be caught going up to the second floor, where she clearly had no business.

"Kara!" John called her name so oddly that her breath hung in her throat.

"Here, John," she said, pretending to be coming from his room.

"Come into the kitchen," he ordered sharply.

Tense, her inner turmoil and physical instability growing worse at the thought of whatever awaited her, Kara stiffly made her way back to the kitchen. Priscilla and Bucky were still sitting at the table. Melvin, William, and Lorraine were standing around it.

Kara felt herself being swallowed up by some unnamed fear that swelled inside her. She stared at the others. They stared back.

"Sit down," John said coldly.

Kara was too panicked not to obey.

"Where were you last night while we ate dinner?" he demanded.

A surge of adrenaline spiraling through her at the possible ramifications of the question sharpened Kara's mental faculties. She looked at John, amazed. "Are you serious? Where was *I?*"

"Just answer me, dammit!" he yelled, his brown eyes suddenly blazing, his nostrils flaring as if he smelled something foul. "Where were you?"

"You know where I was," she said, her voice implying that she didn't believe he was even asking the question. Her head felt like it was going to split wide open. She rubbed her temples as she answered him.

"I was *sleeping*. You woke me up to give me a pill and some soup, and I went back to sleep."

He turned away from her and ran his hands through his wavy black hair. Kara looked at the others, who continued to watch her as if she were a foreign creature they'd never seen before. The silence settled in heavily in the room. Kara was sure she could hear her own heart pounding.

"John," she said, her fear doubling, "you know I was sleeping. What is it? Why are you asking me?"

He spun back around and glowered at her. "Were you sleeping? *Or were you murdering Tessa while we all sat on the sun porch, feeling sorry for you?*"

Kara blanched. Her stomach somersaulted. The question was so outrageous, so heinous, so absurd, that she didn't think she could hang on to sanity any longer. This was the final indignity, the last straw, the ultimate insult. She—a murderess? And her own husband was asking her that!

She felt herself slipping away. Mind over matter, she repeated frantically. She had only herself to depend on in this hideous nightmare. Mind over matter. But it was so hard. She was sure she was going to lose consciousness. She'd endured too much madness already. John couldn't be asking—no—*saying* that *she* had killed Tessa!

She felt his fingers grip her shoulders. "Don't pull that fainting crap on me. Where were you?" He shook her savagely.

The violence of his actions caused Kara's head to clear a bit. Kara forced herself to concentrate. "I was asleep in your bed. You know I was!"

"What were you doing at Tessa's house last week, Kara?" he demanded, as if this were the inquisition and he was the inquisitor.

She blinked back tears, trying to make some sense of what was happening. She could see that John was perfectly serious. And she had no doubt that the others had already tried and sentenced her. *For murder! Tessa's murder!*

"I told you," she said urgently, as if she could make him believe her, even though she knew he'd never believed her initial account of why she was there. "I'd lost my way. I stumbled upon the cabin when I saw the lights."

"And did you *stumble* upon the cabin last night, *strike Tessa with your high-heel shoe, and throw her off the hill into the river?*" he literally yelled at her, leaning so close to her face that she could feel his heated breath. "Did you?"

Ricky came running from his room, screaming and crying. No one seemed to notice. Kara pulled him into her arms and began rocking back and forth. She didn't know which one of them needed the other the most—she or Ricky.

"My high-heel shoe?" she breathed in disbelief. "You think I killed Tessa with a high-heel shoe and threw her into the river? You *are* mad, John!"

"Am I," he demanded, "or are *you?*" He got right in her face again. "It was *your* shoe, Kara."

She ran her hands through her blond hair, attempting to think coherently, to make some sense of the accusation. "What high-heel shoe?" she asked at last. "What shoe am I supposed to have used, John? I do have several pairs."

John's eyes held a strange gleam. "The *single* shoe you had on when you *stumbled* into Tessa's cabin that night."

Kara's pulse began to throb fiercely at her temples, even though the claim of her involvement in Tessa's death was becoming more ludicrous by the minute.

"Do you really think that I would be stupid enough to kill Tessa with that shoe and leave it?" she asked. "That's ridiculous. I threw the muddied shoe away because I'd lost the match in the woods. I didn't even have that shoe yesterday."

"You didn't have it *after* you threw it away. You thought it was gone forever, didn't you? You thought you'd thrown it into the river, too, and no one would ever see it. Nor would you have to use a shoe that *did* have a mate. Unfortunately, my dear wife, you didn't throw the shoe as far as the woman. It lodged in the mud of the bank."

Kara listened as his words beat at her brain in slow motion; she was hearing what he said, but having great difficulty digesting it. Surely this was a terrible, terrible dream. She wasn't sitting here listening to her husband accusing her of killing Tessa—Tessa—dear God, she didn't even know the woman's last name, but now hardly seemed the time to ask.

Kara battled to draw on nonexistent strength. This was too horrendous an ordeal to undergo, and yet what other choice had she? She had learned already at Tessa's cabin that she couldn't defend herself to these people—her *family*—

"Think, John," she murmured. "Please think how preposterous it is to believe I murdered Tessa. I hardly knew the girl."

"No?" he challenged. "Then pray tell why you turned up at her cabin, of all places?"

Kara shook her head. "I told you over and over again," she said, losing what little control she was hanging on to. "I was attacked. I went to her for help."

"And what else?" he demanded. "What did you and Tessa talk about, Kara? What did you discuss with her in the kitchen?"

Her face turning red, Kara recalled Tessa's warning at the cabin that she should take Ricky and leave Homeplace, and how the girl had tried to talk to her in the kitchen when Thelma forbade it. But how could she tell John that?

She glanced at the others, Lorraine in particular, then exhaled wearily, desperation closing over her like a shroud. This was all too crazy, too sick to indulge, but she couldn't just say to hell with it and walk out. These people—her husband—was serious.

"John, please listen to me. I didn't know Tessa. I had no reason to kill her. She helped me when I was attacked."

"No, she didn't help you. She called me," he interjected. "Remember? Is that why you killed her?"

"No, no, no," Kara muttered, close to tears and knowing how useless they would be. "Please!" she cried loudly. "Please listen! Even if I had any reason to kill Tessa, I couldn't have. Your mother gave me a pill yesterday."

Kara glanced at Lorraine, then proceeded cautiously, knowing better than to explain that Lorraine and Thelma had shoved the pill down her throat against her will. Nor did she think it wise to remind John that he himself had given her a tranquilizer.

She pleadingly met his eyes, begging him to stop this tragic farce of an interrogation. "I never left the bed. You know that, John. I was too medicated to walk to Tessa's, kill her, and throw her in the river, for God's sake, even if I'd had any reason on earth to do that!"

Spent, she slumped over Ricky and stared blindly at his

blond head. How could John think she'd murdered anyone? How could he?

She could feel the tears building again, and she fought mightily not to sob hysterically. Her nose began to run. Unconsciously, she wiped the wetness on the back of her hand like a small child.

For one brief, hopeful moment, she thought that John had heard what she'd said. But the hope was soon shattered.

"Did you tell Thelma that you didn't even recall yesterday?" John asked, moving back from her, still glaring at her.

Kara licked her dry lips. "John, be serious. Don't keep asking these ridiculous questions. We're not in a court of law. I'm your wife. You can't think I killed anyone!"

She glanced around. "For God's sake, you all know I was here—sick. I didn't have the strength to leave the room, much less slip off, murder somebody, and sneak back!"

"Don't call on God in this house, harlot!" Lorraine muttered viciously. "You can't pull the wool over His eyes! Ever since you came here, evil has reigned in this house. No women were murdered until you slithered into Homeplace like a sly snake. Tell me, Kara, where were you when Dee Dee vanished? You were gone from the table, too, weren't you?"

Kara blanched as she clutched Ricky so tightly that he renewed his weeping.

"You're insane!" she charged recklessly. "All of you. You're mad. I didn't *kill* anyone."

At the newest outburst, Ricky sobbed loudly, but Kara couldn't calm herself, much less him.

"You were seen last night, Kara," John said. "Two fishermen in a boat saw you on the hill framed in the moonlight, in a white dress, your blond hair glowing."

Kara's hand flew to her mouth. She felt sure she was going to vomit any minute. She had a vision of Bucky's trunk, the beige dress that would look white at night, the blond wig. Inadvertently, her eyes went to his. He looked terrified.

Kara didn't want to betray him. God in Heaven knew she didn't, but she had to protect herself. She believed Bucky was the murderer of Dee Dee's babies, of the young men on the river, of Tessa, and of Dee Dee, too, if she had indeed been murdered. She looked away from his stricken eyes. She was horrified at the revelation.

"It wasn't me," she said over the convulsive cries of the child in her arms. "It might have been Bucky. Go see for yourself. He has a trunk full of women's clothes in his room. He has little girls' dresses. He has a blond wig. He even has lingerie like mine."

"You lying whore!" Lorraine said, storming across the room to strike Kara savagely across the side of the face before she could protect herself. "Daughter of Satan! Get out of my house!"

She began to pull on Kara while Ricky clung to his mother for dear life and Kara fought to be free of the older woman's clawlike hands. Finally Melvin and John separated them, mercifully urging Lorraine to accompany them and Bucky to his room.

"You stay with Kara, William!" Melvin commanded coldly.

Backed-up tears poured from Kara's eyes when Bucky looked at her as if she'd cut his heart out. Dear God, what choice had she had? He was sick and she was being blamed for a *murder!* She was surprised that the police hadn't come to arrest her already!

Although there was absolutely nothing she could do to ease her agony, Kara finally managed to quiet Ricky. Soothing him, holding him tightly, she ached for someone to hang onto herself, someone big and capable, someone to rescue her, but she had only herself to depend on. Her fate—maybe her very life—lay in the hands of madmen!

For a brief moment she longed for one of the tranquilizers the doctor had prescribed; however, she was afraid to move, and more afraid to take the medication even if she could get to it. A lot of commotion echoed from upstairs, then Kara heard the thunder of footsteps on the stairs.

John was the first to enter the kitchen. "You *are* a lying whore!" he said, shocking Kara with the vehemence of his newest accusation. Kara had foolishly assumed that John and the others would find all the evidence in Bucky's room. She hadn't even contemplated what would happen if they didn't. She hadn't imagined she had any reason to fear.

"Bucky doesn't have anything in those trunks but costumes he wore in plays," John said. "He showed them to you yesterday, didn't he? And you're seizing the opportunity to use him as a scapegoat. Why, Kara? For the love of God, why have you come here and done this? What kind of woman are you?"

"I didn't kill anyone!" she screamed, appalled that *anyone* could think it, much less the man she'd married with such hope in her heart. "John, listen to me! *I didn't kill anyone!* The killings began before I came. You can't think I'm the murderer!"

She started sobbing so hard that she couldn't continue. Was there no one to help her? To believe her? She turned to Bucky.

"Please," she begged hoarsely. "Tell them."

His sad eyes met hers briefly before he glanced at Lorraine.

"Please, Bucky, tell the truth. You said God hates a liar," Kara said desperately. If she could get Bucky into his religious mode, perhaps he would admit to her worse suspicions, or at the very least, tell the truth. "Tell them that you showed me the dresses—women's and girls'."

"I didn't show you all those things you said," he mumbled.

Bucky knew he wasn't lying. He *hadn't* shown them to her. He hadn't even known she'd seen the wig and the lingerie. He hadn't thought about them. He'd become so lost in his love of the dresses that he'd forgotten the other pretty things.

And now Kara had betrayed him. She'd told his secret. There was no telling what Mother would do. He trembled at the very thought. He was so scared that he was sick to his stomach.

He wanted to go to his room and lie down on his bed. He had loved Kara more than he'd ever loved anyone, and she'd betrayed that love. She'd played him for a fool. She'd made a promise, then broken it. She'd told their secret.

He had thought he could trust her, but she'd tricked him, although he wasn't quite sure how. The dresses had vanished from the trunk, and only Kara had known about them. Had she been the one to steal his beloved dresses, and how had she gotten into the trunk? He wore the key around his neck. He reached up to feel it. *It wasn't there!*

Then he recalled that when he'd been marched up the steps by Mother and the brothers, he hadn't had to unlock the trunk. It had already been unlocked!

This was all so puzzling. He needed to be in the quiet of his room with his bible, where God could tell him what he was supposed to do next. He couldn't stand it anymore. He was going to cry, and he didn't want anyone to see. Yet even as he walked away, he heard Mother's footsteps behind him. Footsteps he knew as well as his own. He began to quake.

Melvin, William, and John were holding a hurried conference right in front of Kara, discussing the possibilities that she was indeed the killer. She was going crazy in her mind. She tried to hang on to shreds of sanity, but she was weakened by more than the horrors of what she was hearing.

The effects of the pills lingered in her body, giving everything a hazy quality as reality waxed and waned. Perhaps it was for the best, she assured herself. If she were in full control of her faculties, she didn't think she could sit here and suffer through this without lashing out so severely at the brothers that they might have *reason* to lock her away.

Melvin was trying to convince John that he had brought Tessa's killer to town himself when he'd married Kara, when he'd told her about the other killings.

"Asterson is still the boy responsible for those," Melvin insisted. Then he turned to Kara. "But *there's* your other killer."

Grateful for any support, Kara saw with no small measure of relief that John was having difficulty accepting her as a killer, even though Melvin was explaining that Kara could have spit out her pills when no one was looking, easily dismissing her best alibi. It seemed ironic to her that she had indeed spit out the two tranquilizers John had tried to make her take the night of the attack at Tessa's cabin. She hadn't had that opportunity the other times.

As the brothers debated the issue as if she were any common criminal they were discussing, Kara was quietly going mad. With everything in her, she struggled to remain controlled on the outside, but inside she wondered how this nightmare would end. She thought of the phone call she'd made to Ellis, and for a moment she even doubted she'd done that. Maybe that had happened only in the desperation of her mind. And so what if she had left a message as she thought she had? Would Ellis get it? And would he act on it? What if he didn't?

Would these men—her husband and her brothers-in-law—have her committed to a mental institute, or worse, turned over as a murder suspect? The thought was too appalling to deal with. What would become of her child, left here in this madhouse? What would become of her, for she truly feared that she would be put away for a long, long time if Melvin convinced John she was a killer.

Her son had sobbed himself to sleep, but Kara still rocked in the chair slightly. Somehow the rhythmic motion calmed her. If she didn't move, she would literally bolt from this room, from this house, and go shrieking down the driveway of Homeplace.

And what would that accomplish, but to assure her of a terrible fate? Pulling the last vestiges of her emotional and physical energy together, she made herself speak to John in a rational voice.

"John, you know I'm not a murderess. You know I had nothing to do with Tessa's death. You—"

"Shut up!" Melvin said sharply. "You had your chance, now shut up before I shut you up. You're not blaming Bucky for this."

"You all know Bucky has emotional problems!" Kara burst out, unable to stop herself.

Melvin sneered. "Sure we do, according to you, at least. Then, according to your expert opinion, we *all* are crazy. Well, I'll tell you what, none of us was seen at the scene of the murder."

"I wasn't, either!" Kara all but yelled. "Why are you doing this, Melvin? Have you no sense of decency? Have you no conscience? Will you sacrifice anything or anyone to further your career? Isn't that what this is all about? Your political ambitions? Somebody will have a feather in his cap when these murders are solved, no matter how. And you want that somebody to be you. Well, not at the expense of my life, damn you!"

Adrenaline was suddenly surging through her, driving her on recklessly. "I will not be sacrificed for your ambitions!" she screamed uncontrollably. "I'm not crazy, and I haven't murdered anyone!"

"You are and you did," Melvin said simply, evenly. "Now shut the fuck up!"

Her energy exhausted as rapidly as it had come, Kara felt faint. John hadn't said a word—for her or against her. Melvin was the stronger brother. She knew that. Oh, God in Heaven, what was she going to do?

Her attention was diverted to Lorraine's harsh voice coming from the upper floor of the house. She couldn't make out what was being said, and she couldn't concentrate for fear of missing the discussion between the brothers. God, what a dreadful, dreadful nightmare! Surely any moment now she would wake up and find out that it was only that.

Abruptly Melvin left and John returned to Kara. Her mind actually turned within itself as he, fueled by his brother's reasoning, started in again, questioning her as if they were already in a courtroom and he was the prosecuting attorney. It seemed that the matter was more than critical, for indeed John was worried it would end up in a courtroom. And which was best for the family? A crazy wife or a murderous one?

His anxious demeanor indicated it was quite a disagreeable position to be in. The dilemma was really Kara's, but she'd gone beyond seeing it as one.

"Tell me why, Kara," John ordered for the umpteenth time, running his hands through his hair in frustration. "Are you mentally ill? Or are you deranged? Were you angry with Tessa because she didn't support your story that you were grabbed outside her cottage, or was it more than that? Tell me."

Kara no longer even bothered to answer. The mere fact that she was here being questioned as a murder suspect by the man she'd married had become so odious to her that she seemed to be standing outside herself, listening to the heated questioning. It was simply too absurd that she was the one at Homeplace being accused of murder. Her mind had shut off. She wasn't even aware when John gave up and left the room.

18

"Why?" Lorraine demanded of Bucky. "Why did you keep the dresses? I discarded them. I told you never to mention them."

"They were mine," Bucky sobbed. "They were mine. You loved me when I wore them. *I* loved *them*."

Lorraine's eyes glittered with fire and fury. "I put them outside in a box to be given to the poor when you were seven years old, Bucky. Have you had them here in this trunk all those years?"

He nodded, then, trembling, yet needing to know, he asked, "Did you take them from the trunk, Mother?"

He felt the sting of her hand before he ever saw it. "You idiot!" she cried. "Of course I took them. What if someone else had found them? What if one of your brothers had seen them? Now that I know you lie and deceive me, I don't know what to think! What if I hadn't found the key lying on the floor where you must have dropped it?"

The key, Bucky thought wildly. Mother had found it. Had it fallen from his pocket? He didn't know. His head hurt. He couldn't think anymore!

Mother was so highly agitated that Bucky tried to hide inside his mind to flee her wrath. It was a bad place to go. The voices were there arguing abusively; there was nowhere he could escape.

"What else have you done?"

He didn't know if Mother was asking, or the voices. But the voices knew everything he had done. He had only obeyed them. However, he had obeyed Mother, too. He put his hands over his ears. He was going mad from all the noise. He couldn't abide it when they all talked at once and Mother joined in, too.

He wanted to run away from them, but past experience had taught him that they went with him until he had obeyed.

"Buchannan!"

His name said in that way could only come from Mother. It wasn't from the collective voices. It wasn't from God or Jesus. Bucky met her eyes. He couldn't tell if he saw pity or disgust.

"What else have you done?" Lorraine demanded.

She had already accepted the fact that Bucky was the weakest of William Buchannan Worthington's seed, but how weak was weak? She had to know. It was her duty as a woman of God. It was her duty as the mother of this child.

Bucky averted his gaze. "Nothing," he murmured. "Nothing I wasn't supposed to do, Mother!"

The slaps came again in quick succession. Tears overflowed Bucky's eyes and slipped down his cheeks.

"What were you supposed to do?"

"God's will, Mother," Bucky answered in a tiny little voice. "Only God's will." He began to quote bible verses that outlined acts of immorality and how God wanted his people to punish the evildoers.

Lorraine gazed at him open-mouthed. She had been shocked before, but for the moment she was speechless with despair. She had tried so hard to instill righteousness in her sons. Had this one, like John, missed some of the lessons? She began to feel the shock of the connection of the verses he quoted.

Suddenly she fell down to her knees. "God in Heaven," she began.

Bucky fell down to his, too, murmuring the same words Lorraine did.

When John and Melvin entered the room, John snapped, "For Christ's sake, Mother, this really isn't the time to pray!"

Lorraine immediately stood up and spun around. "God will punish you for that, John. If you'd prayed more and whored less, we wouldn't be in this mess."

"Sit down," Melvin said, "and let's try to figure out what to do. We are in this mess! *All* of us. What do we do now, is the question."

Lorraine believed she'd already received the answer. Everything had been going along all right until the whore came. Bucky had mentioned some of the same bible verses Lorraine herself relied on in time of need. They had inspired her.

Kara felt as if she'd been a prisoner in the chair for hours. To her surprise, Thelma returned to the kitchen at some point and started cooking breakfast as if the morning hadn't already long ago passed, as if Tessa hadn't been found murdered in her cabin. Working furiously, making a lot of noise and moving faster than Kara had ever seen her move, she didn't say a word or acknowledge Kara's presence.

Kara stared at her, and tried her best to determine what was real here and what was unreal. Was Thelma aware that she had been accused of killing Tessa? Was that why Thelma didn't even look at her? And why was she back here working when her only child was lying dead in the morgue?

At some point the family came back downstairs. Kara was no longer amazed to see life going on around her. The most peculiar behavior seemed normal at Homeplace. Priscilla and Lorrie pulled their chairs up to the kitchen table, as if they usually ate here instead of in the dining room. Ignoring Kara, the brothers ate breakfast and they left.

Kara sat in the chair, immobile, her sleeping child crushed against her breast in arms which were numbed by his weight. If only she could think. If only she knew what to do.

And then, before she could do anything, any possible choice was removed from her. She instinctively fought to hang on to Ricky. The battle was futile. Startled awake, screaming and sobbing, he was pulled from his mother.

Then Kara felt the pills in her mouth again. Although she tried valiantly to avoid them, they were forced down her throat. The darkness came quickly; then she didn't have the option to think at all.

When she was awakened, the darkness was still there. It was inside and outside. Drugged, she felt sick when she realized she was moving. She heaved when she was thrown over someone's shoulder. She struggled to think, to fight, but there was no stamina for even the most basic thoughts, much less physical response.

Nothing seemed real, and briefly she dared to hope that she was dreaming. But this was no dream. It was a night terror like none she'd ever known. She soon felt the softness of the riverbank beneath her. The night air seemed to revive her a little, and she forced her mind to remember the command: mind over matter. Mind over matter. It was so hard; she was lured again and again toward the comforting oblivion of the blackness, yet she knew her survival depended on staying in the here and now. She forced herself to open her eyes, to try to understand what was happening around her.

She couldn't seem to make any sense of what was going on. Thelma and Lorraine were bickering as Kara lay on her side in the leaves and debris on the riverbank. She could hear the swiftly flowing water, rushing to God knew where, carrying God knew what.

Her vision was too blurred to be useful, so she concentrated all her efforts on hearing the argument between the two women.

"You killed my chile," Thelma hissed in a low ominous voice that caused Kara to shiver.

Who was Thelma talking to? Was it to her? What were

Lorraine and Thelma going to do with her? Bile rose in her throat as she thought of the river claiming so many bodies. Was hers going to be added to the number? Pure, unadulterated terror revived her to some degree, although she knew she was still helpless to physically resist.

Suddenly Lorraine spat savagely, "You stupid fool. I didn't!"

"You did! I know you did," Thelma retorted with equal venom. "You killed my chile just like you killed William's grandsons, Dee Dee's babies, only you killed Tessa out of jealousy, because William gave me the girl baby you wanted."

"Tessa's death has distorted your reason," Lorraine hissed. "Think before you continue to speak, or you'll find yourself accused of murder. You know I couldn't let William's evil seed live in male children to perpetuate his sins. Nobody knows Dee Dee's boys didn't die from crib death but you. Remember that! You're as guilty as I am. You're an accessory, not to mention the part you played in William's death."

"Don't threaten me no more," Thelma said. "I ain't got nothing to live for without my girl. She was all I had in life, and now you've taken that."

"You imbecile!" Lorraine snapped. "Need I remind you that Tessa was the product of rape? Don't forget that *I* was the one who came to your rescue when William attacked you."

"I didn't forget. I couldn't forget. You was the one who killed him with the poker, too. It won't me."

"But you helped me get rid of him, didn't you? Right here near this spot. Just as you helped me get rid of Dee Dee. Now, stop acting the fool. This—woman—has brought sin and shame to Homeplace. She's evil—she and her bastard. She will carry the blame for all the murders, and no one need be the wiser."

"God will be the wiser," Thelma said.

"God helps those who help themselves," Lorraine retorted self-righteously. "*She* deserves to die. It will be another suicide, just like Dee Dee's death. No one knew positively that Dee Dee didn't jump in the river, and they won't know this one didn't. Then it will all be over. There'll be no need for further killings."

Thelma fell silent for a moment, and Kara tried to stifle her ragged breathing. *God, Lorraine had killed Dee Dee, Dee Dee's babies, and her own husband, too!*

And now she was intent on killing her newest daughter-in-law! She was going to die unless she could prevent it. But how? Oh, dear God, she couldn't seem to move!

"There was no need for my girl to die," Thelma said bitterly.

"Tessa was going to confide in Kara," Lorraine insisted. "Bucky overheard them talking. He told me. Tessa would have exposed us all, ruined all the Worthingtons with something we were justified in doing."

"Bucky didn't hear no such thing," Thelma muttered. "I was in the kitchen with Kara and Tessa when Bucky came in. Tessa won't gonna tell nothing. You killed my little girl because you always hated her—and to save your chile 'cause you're thinking, too, that Bucky killed them boys, ain't you?"

"That's not true," Lorraine countered indignantly.

"It is," Thelma insisted. "You're a killer and Bucky's a killer and one of you killed my baby."

"God told me to do it," Bucky whined unexpectedly, pitifully. "Raymond and Draper and Toby sinned," he whispered, even at that awful moment recalling the erotic sensations, the sucking lips that had created a ring of fire around him, a strange burning heat that held him captive. He'd wanted them *not* to do those things. He *knew* he had, but the Devil had been there with them on those occasions, and he'd been powerless. It was only later that he was able to rectify the sins.

"They were in violation of God's laws," he murmured. "They lay with mankind as with womankind. They committed an abomination against me, and I had to cut them from their people and wash them in the river. *God* told me to punish the evildoers," he insisted frantically.

There was silence for just a moment. Kara heard the

river muttering to itself as if it, too, were hearing the shocking evil Bucky was confessing. The sound of the water seemed to grow louder and louder, roaring in Kara's ears until she couldn't hear anything else. She had suspected that Bucky was the killer, and she had suspected that both Bucky and Lorraine were schizophrenic, but to have it confirmed made her blood run cold.

She wanted, needed, to flee, to drag herself from this awful place and shut her ears and eyes to the madness of it all, but she couldn't move her numbed limbs.

"Sweet Jesus in Heaven, he *was* the one!" Thelma finally said. The confession must have stunned her, too, even though she'd said she thought it. "Bucky did do it! I told you he was sneaking off, up to no good down on the river, and you said it won't him!"

"I—I didn't know until yesterday," Lorraine said stiffly.

"And did God tell you to punish my chile, you crazy boy? Did he?" Thelma demanded of Bucky. "That loving girl who never hurt no one?"

Kara opened her eyes in alarm. Thelma was moving toward Bucky, stepping over Kara's body to get to him. She was terrified. She didn't know what the big woman was going to do.

Suddenly Lorraine stepped in between them. "I'll handle Bucky myself," she said firmly, as if she could halt Thelma in her tracks. "He did wrong, but by no will of his own. He felt he was doing God's work. I knew that when we prayed earlier. He won't do it again."

"I know he won't do it again," Thelma said. "When he killed my little girl, he killed the wrong person. I put up with all this—this sickness and sin myself to save my baby, and now she's gone—killed right when she had a new life."

"I didn't kill Tessa," Bucky cried. "Don't hurt me, Thelma!"

Again, all the world seemed to stop. Kara heard the savage beating of her own heart. She wondered if the others heard it. She was afraid she was going to start shuddering at any minute and reveal that she was awake.

"You *did* do it!" Thelma gasped, but there was uncertainty in her voice. "You did it 'cause you attacked Kara outside Tessa's cabin and Tessa knew it, didn't she?"

"I didn't attack Kara!" Bucky protested. "I didn't! I only wanted to talk to her, to comfort her, but she started fighting me when I tried. I—I got confused. Things started running around in my head, and I was scared, but I didn't *attack* her. I never did that."

Thelma's breathing was harsh and loud. "Then my girl did see you and you used the shoe Kara lost in the woods to kill Tessa, didn't you? Didn't you, boy? Don't lie to me!"

"No! No!" Bucky whined pitifully. "I went back and got the shoe later—for—for myself. I didn't kill Tessa with it. God as my witness, I didn't! Mama," he pleaded like a lost little boy. "I didn't do it."

"He didn't kill Tessa. I did," Lorraine said in a voice stretched thin and taut. "There was nothing else to do, whether you believe it or not. Just as there's nothing to do now except to kill Kara. Then it will all be over."

There was a brief pause, then Lorraine added, "You must believe that I didn't want Tessa to die. I didn't let her stay on Homeplace property all this time just to kill her now when she was about to leave. It's all Kara's fault. If she hadn't come here stirring up Bucky, stirring up Dee Dee, stirring up Tessa, none of this would be necessary."

"Her fault?" Thelma repeated. "She's as innocent as my poor baby, and you know it."

"She's not!" Lorraine hissed. "She's vile and sinful. Except for her, the killings would have ended with those boys who fouled Bucky and deserved to die, just as William deserved to die for the evil he did. If John, Dee Dee, and Tessa hadn't been tainted by the whore, the killings would have stopped with William, his evil seed and those boys, but *she* came here prying and snooping and causing problems. What if Tessa had finished school, gone away, and then felt free to tell tales she didn't understand herself, tales like Dee Dee told?"

"She wouldn't of," Thelma said, her voice as tight as Lorraine's. "She knew who her daddy was, and she didn't want to be tied to none of you. She just wanted to go away and live like a decent person, away from the dirtiness and shame here."

"Who do you think you're talking to?" Lorraine exclaimed. "Who do you think you are? Out of Christian charity my family took you in and gave you a home, allowed you to live in our midst, shared what we had with you. I gave your—your daughter a home. She repaid me by trying to harm us all by talking to Kara. Now, enough of this idle talk. Do as you've been told so we can all get on with our lives!"

Kara tensed. Her pulsed raced. Dear God, was her life over? She couldn't let it happen. She had to do something. Her panic made her more alert and she did her best to summon strength.

"Whatever you gave, Lorraine Worthington, you took away many times over. Now I ain't got no life left, and there ain't going to be no more killings," Thelma said, so softly that Kara strained to hear her. "The only evil in this town is right here on this riverbank, and I'll be the one to do God's work now."

Terrified beyond rational thought, Kara tried to discern what was happening when a sudden flurry of activity occurred. She thought Thelma was grabbing for Bucky, but the high scream that pierced the air sounded like a woman's. The shriek caused adrenaline to pump in Kara, making some movement possible. She struggled to sit up in time to see Bucky jump into the river where Thelma had thrown his mother.

Through the drug- and fear-induced haze, Kara made out two figures in the water. She fought against the blackness that threatened to overcome her. Her terror knew no bounds. She had a vision of her entire life passing before her. Was she next?

Abruptly, there were people surrounding her, talking in agitated voices, but it was the anguished cry of Bucky calling, "Mama, Mama," in a little boy's voice that filled Kara's mind.

Soon she was being lifted from the ground by male arms,

warm, comforting arms, and still she couldn't pull her gaze away from the river. She could see more clearly now.

They were below the mansion where the rocks jutted out into the water, sheltered by twisted trees and twining vines, the place where the eddy was, the place she had been warned away from.

She recognized Ellis's soothing voice, but she couldn't raise her head to look at him. She was trying to determine if what she saw in the pale moonlight was real. The eerie sight mesmerized her.

Caught in the eddy, clutching each other, Lorraine and Bucky were spinning around and around in a golden dance of death, being sucked down by the undercurrent, then surfacing, only to disappear again.

Kara saw something else: a floating tree, stripped of its branches, swept into the vicious merry-go-round with mother and son. Suddenly Bucky and Lorraine were no longer visible. The barren tree lurched free of the whirlpool and drifted away. The swiftly running river moved on, once more carrying its dead debris to some unknown destination.

"Kara." Ellis was calling her name. He sounded farther and farther away as she slipped into a black void.

When Kara awakened, she screamed out her fear. She had been put in the mental hospital! It had all been a drug-induced dream, and the Worthingtons had made her the sacrificial lamb! She screamed again and again.

A nurse came running into the room. "What's wrong?"

Kara couldn't stop screaming. She saw Ellis enter the room.

"Kara, you're all right."

"Oh, Ellis, help me!" she cried. "I didn't do it. I'm not crazy and I didn't kill anyone. Please. I don't belong here."

"Look," Ellis said gently, indicating the room. "It's only a hospital room. Of course you didn't kill anyone. You haven't been committed. You're here because you've suffered a terrible shock and I wanted to look after you. Everything's going to be all right, I promise."

Kara put her hands to her chest and tried to calm her

pounding heart. Was it true? Was everything going to be all right?

Ellis smiled gently at her. "It's over, Kara. The police have a statement from Thelma that solves twenty-two years of murder and absolves you from anything but being a victim who was the catalyst to end the Worthington murders."

Kara sucked in her breath, trying to digest what he was saying, trying to believe that she was free at last, free of the nightmare, free of the Worthingtons. In a horrible rush, the scene from the riverbank came back to her.

"Ricky?" she whispered urgently. "Where's my baby?"

"He's safe in my house," Ellis said.

"John?" she murmured.

"You can see him if you wish, but I don't know if it's a good idea at this time."

"I don't want to see him," Kara said quickly. "Bucky's dead, isn't he? It wasn't a dream—Bucky and Lorraine in the river?"

Ellis nodded. "It's a long sordid story, Kara. Go back to sleep, and when you've rested some, we'll discuss it."

"I have to know now," she whispered. "I can't go back to sleep with all this horror swirling around in my mind. It all seems so unreal to me. I heard Thelma and Lorraine talking—and Bucky. If what I heard was true . . ." Her words trailed off. If what she heard was true, it was still the most awful nightmare she could ever imagine.

"Are you sure you're up to it?" Ellis asked.

"I have to know," Kara murmured. "I have to know so that I can close my eyes without terror."

Ellis sighed. "It is awful, and you no doubt heard the truth. When Lorraine found out she was pregnant with Bucky, she also found out that William was cheating on her. She vowed she would revenge herself in the eyes of God, for she had unknowingly lain with a fornicator and become unclean herself. She was, as we discussed, schizophrenic, as was poor Bucky, and probably the other brothers to a lesser degree."

"Oh, dear God," Kara whispered.

"William's adultery was what finally drove Lorraine over

the edge. She turned to the bible and drew her own conclusions about how to absolve herself from William's sin and her guilt in being part of it."

Ellis sighed. "Unfortunately, everyone wound up paying. William, taking his anger out on his indignant wife, attacked Thelma after Bucky was born, to demonstrate to Lorraine that the household help was better than his own wife in bed. Lorraine, hearing the rape happening, grabbed a poker and killed him in the act. Then she somehow persuaded Thelma to help her bury William and concocted the story about him drowning in the eddy."

"But I saw Lorraine and Bucky spinning around in the whirlpool, didn't I?" Kara asked, the image so vivid that she couldn't dismiss it.

"Oh, the whirlpool's there all right, but Lorraine didn't want William to get off that easy. She buried him near the eddy, where she'd still have access to him."

"Oh, my God!" Kara cried.

"Then, so that Bucky could know his father and the evil he'd done, Lorraine apparently frequently walked with the child at night to William's grave and talked to him."

"Oh, poor Bucky," Kara said, her grief for that unfortunate soul intensified.

"That wasn't enough for Lorraine, who grew more deranged as time went on. She was determined to stop William's seed at the source. She wouldn't kill her own sons, but when Dee Dee had two male children, she smothered them with pillows, and no one knew it wasn't crib death. That is, no one except Thelma, and Dee Dee, who apparently was convinced her children had been murdered. She tried to tell anyone who would listen, but no one would believe her."

"That poor tormented woman," Kara murmured, so easily calling to mind the vision of Dee Dee leaning over Ricky's bed.

"When Dee Dee became a problem, Lorraine enlisted Thelma's aid in drugging the pathetic woman by threatening to have William dug up and Thelma charged with his murder," Ellis explained. "Tessa, born of the rape, was walking proof. Thelma was afraid, for herself and the child she loved, so she went along with Lorraine."

"Dear God!" Kara exclaimed. "Couldn't she go to someone, get someone to believe her, to help her?"

"Could you?" Ellis asked simply. "Could Dee Dee?"

Kara shook her head. She might be dead today were it not for Tessa's death—and for Ellis.

"When Thelma suspected that Bucky was the river killer and that he'd also killed Tessa, it was too much. She decided to put an end to the Worthington dynasty herself. She pretended to go along with Lorraine's plans to throw you into the eddy, making it look like a suicide because you were facing murder charges, but Lorraine was the one she threw in when Lorraine confessed that she had killed Tessa."

"How did you know?" Kara asked. "I mean why were you there? I remember you helping me up."

"I'd tried for days to reach you, to see you. I became frantic when John stonewalled me and wouldn't even discuss the situation. Some very powerful people were in the Worthington pocket, which made it difficult for me to intercede. Thank God, I convinced two detectives I know to help me. We were on the property when it happened, but we were farther down the river. We reached you too late to prevent more tragedy."

"What will happen to Thelma?" Kara asked.

"Nothing substantial, I'm sure," Ellis said. "John and Melvin will do anything to keep this as low-key as possible, to prevent a nationwide scandal."

"But how, with all that's happened?" Kara asked.

Ellis shrugged. "The Worthingtons own a part of all the local media, and, as lawyers, they have influence within the court system. Thelma won't say anything more. And while there are probably plenty of people who would love to know the sordid details, and there are personnel involved who might want the truth told, in the long run I suspect Melvin, William, and John can alter this sorry story adequately enough to save face."

"How?" Kara pressed.

"I don't really know, but I imagine Bucky may be sacrificed. After all, the town had already ostracized him anyway, but Lorraine's part and passing will no doubt be handled with all the delicacy possible. And after enough time's past, who knows? Some of them may even believe the sanitized version is actually what happened."

"Poor Bucky," Kara murmured. "It's not fair."

Ellis searched her troubled face. "What purpose will it serve now to further destroy this family? Or to thrust Thelma into the spotlight? All these people are reeling from the shock and sadness already. They have enough emotional pain and suffering, especially William."

"But justice won't be served with a cover-up," Kara murmured.

"Ah, but it will, much more so than if these murders had ended any other way," Ellis said. "Both Lorraine and Bucky are dead. Asterson will be freed on new evidence, or some such technicality. And you're free to go. John's not the menace his mother was, Kara, and without her dictates, the brothers will all fare better."

Kara looked into his eyes. "Free to go?" she whispered.

He nodded. "John wouldn't dream of contesting a divorce now. Too public. You and Ricky can return to California, if that's what you want." His eyes searched hers. "Or do you still love John, Kara?"

She shook her head. "I'm not sure I ever did, Ellis," she said, staring at her trembling hands. "I had a dream." She smiled sadly. "Like too many people, I suppose. I was looking for a prince on a white horse to make my life a fairy tale. I thought I'd find that here in this town."

Ellis took both her hands in his and stilled their trembling. "There are still fairy tales and princes to believe in, Kara," he murmured. "I know how you feel about the town, but truly it's as beautiful as you first thought, and most of the citizens are fine, caring people. You met the wrong element by your association with the Worthingtons." His eyes were playful. "Except me, of course."

Kara smiled gently. "All except you," she agreed. He was a prince.

He seemed pensive for a moment, then he said he'd order lunch for Kara and a shot so she could rest easier.

Kara was sure she couldn't sleep, even with the medication, but once she'd eaten some soup and crackers, she drifted off before a nurse could fulfill Ellis's orders.

When she awoke that evening, Ellis was sitting beside her bed.

"Feeling better?" he asked.

Kara gave him a hesitant smile. She didn't know if she'd ever fully recover, but at least the worst seemed to be over. She nodded. "I think so."

"I think you should stay in the hospital a couple of days," he suggested. "You need the rest."

"I don't want to stay two days," Kara murmured. "I want to leave as soon as possible. By tomorrow morning at the latest."

"What will you do?" Ellis asked.

Kara shrugged. "I suppose I'll take Ricky to California and try to get my old job back."

"Do you think they need more psychiatrists in California?" Ellis asked, grinning.

Kara laughed lightly. "Maybe. But not as badly as here, I don't think." There was a trace of bitterness in her voice; she felt disappointment and sorrow—for herself and her shattered dreams, but most of all for the people whose lives had been destroyed by Lorraine Worthington.

Ellis seemed distracted. She began to fear the worst again. "Is there something you haven't told me?" she asked anxiously. "Is there more to this nightmare?"

"No," he quickly assured her. "I'm sorry if I've given you that impression. I was thinking of something quite different—something very selfish, I'm afraid."

"What?" she asked, watching his face.

"Something I wasn't prepared to discuss with you until you'd had at least a little time to improve, but I'm afraid not to proceed with you wanting to rush off tomorrow."

"What is it, Ellis?" Kara asked. Suddenly her heart was beating fast again.

"Nothing to distress you, I hope," he said, seeing the

agitated way she looked at him. "I was just wondering if I would be welcome at your door if I ever decided to relocate to California."

"Oh, Ellis!" Kara cried urgently. "Let me caution you not to move anywhere until you know what you're doing and who you're doing it with. Look at me." Her frantic words tapered off as quickly as they'd begun.

Ellis smiled. "I am looking at you. I've been looking at you since the first time John introduced us, and I like what I see. I try not to act impulsively," he said, "however, there comes a time for action, or one simply misses out. It was my misfortune that John met you first, but still my good luck that I met you at all," he murmured. "I've made no secret of my interest in you, Kara. Only you being the wife of my friend prevented anything more than that."

Kara gazed at him. She had thought of Ellis in a romantic way. She had liked him from the first day they met. She knew she could trust Ellis, but she would take her own advice and move very cautiously before she became involved with anyone else again.

"You would be welcome at my door," she said at last. "As a dear, loyal friend."

"Of course," he said. "Friends are wonderful to have."

Kara nodded. She knew that Ellis understood that she was afraid. He would take his time with her.

She gazed out at the river, visible even from the hospital room. It looked placid and pretty as it wound its way around the town.

Kara looked at Ellis and smiled, her spirits suddenly lifting. Despite the anguish she'd experienced, she found herself a little giddy at the thought that the dream of the handsome prince might come true yet. That there still could be happy endings.

FROM THE BESTSELLING AUTHOR OF MIDNIGHT WHISPERS

DARKEST HOUR
V.C. ANDREWS®

From the most popular author of original paperback fiction ever, comes V.C. Andrews' newest, most terrifying story ever. DARKEST HOUR is the sequel to the Cutler family saga and tells the truth about the lies, secrets, and tragedies that would affect the family for generations.

DARKEST HOUR

POCKET BOOKS

Available from Pocket Books June 1993

583-01